SAVAGE LIAR

Sinfully Savage: Book Two

KRISTEN LUCIANI

Savage Liar © 2021 by Kristen Luciani

This book is a work of fiction. Names, characters, places and incidents are the product of the author's imagination or are used fictitiously. Any resemblance to actual events, locales or persons, living or dead is purely coincidental.

Except for the original material written by the author, all songs, song titles, and lyrics mentioned in this novel are the property of the respective songwriters and copyright holders.

All rights reserved. The unauthorized reproduction or distribution of this copyrighted work is illegal. This book or any portion thereof may not be reproduced, scanned, distributed, or used in any manner whatsoever, via the Internet, electronic, or print, without the express written permission of the author, except for the use of brief quotations in a book review.

For more information, or information regarding subsidiary rights, please contact Kristen Luciani at kluciani@gmail.com.

Cover Design: Book Cover Kingdom

Editing: Allusion Graphics

Photo Credit: Rafa Catala

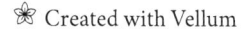

❋ Created with Vellum

Chapter One
JAELYN

THREE YEARS EARLIER

"Not guilty."

The words assault my ears and my heart, roaring over and over between my temples as the courtroom melee ensues. A collective, loud gasp follows the verdict, drowned out by a sea of shocked voices humming around me. Camera flashes snap left and right, temporarily blinding me as I jump up from the bench, craning my neck to see those two greasy bastards in their matching orange jumpsuits. They're the now-free men who shattered my world and now, thanks to the incompetence of the fucking asshole lawyer who was prosecuting my parents' case, get to walk away scot-free. I swallow down the scream bubbling in my chest, clenching my fists so tight, my fingernails might draw blood. Red floods my vision, my chest heaving as sharp breaths slice at my lungs.

My older brother Nate grabs my hand, standing up next to me and pulling me into his chest as tears sting my eyes. Every part of my body quivers and chatters, not from the cold but from the anger and regret that now clouds my life.

He tilts my chin up, staring into my eyes. His jaw twitches but his expression is impassive, as usual. It's very rare for him to freely give away his feelings, but the jaw twitch is his big tell. I know he's just as devastated as I am right now. He's just much better at hiding his emotions. Nobody but me ever knows what he's thinking.

Or plotting, for that matter.

But me?

I give it all away — my face, my body language, my voice. They tell all. There are never any questions about how I feel. I obviously suck at poker, and I let my emotions rage like wildfire.

Nate and I are the exact opposite in that regard.

But today I can see him falter. His carefully crafted exterior has a few hairline cracks that are rapidly spreading, threatening to expose what festers deep within his fortress.

Just for once, I'd like to see it crumble around him, exposing what I know is behind those walls.

Just for once, I want to see him shed his thick skin and grieve with me.

And by grieve, I, of course, mean kill.

Nate holds me tight against him as we sidestep spectators who are still marveling over the fact that the prosecutor couldn't get a conviction, and how one of the key pieces of evidence mysteriously went missing before the verdict was delivered.

Yeah, I wonder the same thing.

But when you go to battle with one of the biggest drug cartels in the world, be prepared to play the game according to their rules.

Everybody eventually bends.

Except my father, which is why we're standing here while all hope for justice dissipates into the air.

A knot in my stomach twists and tightens, my pulse throbbing against my neck as I catch a glimpse of the bailiff unlocking the handcuffs on the two men who destroyed my world. Brothers. Desi and Derek Bowman. Two mules for the Becerra Cartel out of Mexico. But they don't only run drugs. They also gun down anyone who doesn't share the same loyalty to the cartel that they do…basically, anyone who gets in their way of making a shit ton of money. I narrow my eyes at them. They're laughing, giving each other high fives and clapping their shady ass lawyer, Marlon Thomas, on the back.

He's the seediest of the seedy and expensive as hell. His only client is the Becerra Cartel and they keep him plenty busy from what I hear and read. If it wasn't for the deep pockets of the cartel and their partnership with the rival motorcycle club that the Bowman idiots belong to, they'd be behind bars before another second had the chance to slip on by.

I grip the top of the bench with both hands, stopping without warning, my heart beating out of control. White spots blast in front of my eyes and I sink back down onto the seat, my knees quaking. Nate sits next to me, cupping my chin in his large hand. "Jae, are you okay?"

I can hear his voice, but it's muffled, like it's coming through a thick fog. My knuckles turn white from the tight grip I have on the bench and blood rushes between my temples, the pounding intensifying as the Bowman brothers get closer and closer to the double doors of the courtroom.

Closer to freedom.

They get a second chance.

Unlike my parents.

Guilt hangs over my head like a dark, ominous cloud, hovering low like a menacing threat.

It should have been me.

Nate knows it too, although he'd never say the words.

The President of the Rebel Vipers motorcycle club can't afford to let others know what he's thinking.

Ever.

He says a few more things, but the only thing I hear are clanging cymbals echoing between my temples. Rod and Benny, Nate's closest friends and his Vice-President and Sergeant at Arms, are on my other side, murmuring words I can't make out because my ears are too occupied with other sounds…bloodcurdling screams, cries for help, and vows for revenge.

Revenge…against all of them!

I try to gulp down a deep breath, the spots now long flashes streaking across my vision. Flashes of white tinged with orange.

And yellow…the color of their teeth when their triumphant smiles pummel my heart from mere feet away as their lawyer leads them out of the courtroom.

The farther away they get, the faster my heart gallops, to the point where the white spots morph into darkness.

And the pits of my own personal hell swallow me whole.

My eyes flutter open and I bring one of my hands to the side of my head. "Ow," I moan, gingerly grazing my fingertips over a large and very painful lump. I wince as the sharp sting blasts through my skull. My stomach lurches as Nate speeds through a light. The sun sets over the horizon and I feel like I've lost hours.

Days.

Maybe a whole lifetime.

That's how long ago it feels since the fate of the Bowman brothers was decided, not by the letter of the law, but by the cartel.

"You wiped out in the courtroom, remember?" Benny volunteers. "Smacked your head pretty hard."

"Feels like someone slammed my head into a door about ten times," I grumble, expelling a shallow breath.

"With your big mouth, I'm actually surprised that hasn't happened to you yet," Rod quips from the front seat and I flip him off, settling against the leather. Muted white noise hums inside of my head, and fuzzy memories pop into my mind like bullets.

Seeing the Bowman brothers strut past our bench as free men.

Collapsing into the cold, hard floor of the courtroom.

Shock morphing into the most intense agony my soul has ever endured.

Torrents of tears and hysterics that followed.

"I gave you a Valium so you could calm down," Nate mutters from the driver's seat. "And you blacked out. I didn't expect you to sleep for this long."

The guys didn't take their motorcycles to the courthouse today. Nate wanted to be close to us, to keep an eye out…just in case. The cartel ordered a hit on my parents to send a message, but who knows if they forgot a post script? Nate figured we'd all be safer this way.

Together.

The rest of the club wanted to come, but Nate only allowed Benny and Rod to join us for the verdict. I stare at the back of my brother's head, his dark hair slicked back, his spine stiff as an iron rod. He clutches the steering wheel tight, his jaw even tighter. He didn't look as shocked as I felt when the verdict was delivered, and even now, it seems like he's on autopilot. A man on a mission…that mission is what scares me. Nate doesn't go off the deep end. He's level-headed, controlled, and calculating. He doesn't do crazy.

That's my department.

But right now, I can see his teeth are clenched, and if he was clutching someone's neck the same way he's gripping that steering wheel, their eyes would pop out of their skulls. Something is up with him and if I didn't know better, I'd think he was prepared for this.

It's almost as if he—

No. That's a crazy thought. He couldn't have known, right? Not after he convinced me over and over that justice would be served.

By whom, he didn't specify. I just assumed it'd be by the state. Maybe I should have probed him harder. But the reality is, I guess I clung so tight to what he said because I wanted to believe that they'd get what was coming to them, that they'd end up in gen pop with a bunch of derelicts, just like them, who'd slash their throats because their club has started more wars and shed more blood in south Florida than any other gangs and mafia families put together.

Needless to say, hate for their club runs deep.

But not as deep as their pockets because they run a plethora of drugs through their pipelines across the country. They don't like competition, and neither does the cartel.

And dirty money runs the fucking world, so...

Not guilty.

I squint, shifting in the backseat. "Where are we? And how long have I been out?"

"Headed toward the clubhouse," Nate says. "You've been asleep for seven hours."

"Jesus," I mutter. I guess grief really does take a toll on you. My brain just decided to give in to the blissful haze of nothingness. I wish I'd been able to stay for a little while longer.

"I think this is a bad idea," Rod grumbles under his breath.

"I didn't ask for your opinion, did I?" Nate snaps, hanging a sharp left. I grip the 'oh, shit' bar and hang on for my life as he zooms down the secluded dirt road that leads to the clubhouse.

"I really don't feel like going inside, Nate," I say. "I don't want to talk to anyone. I know they all mean well, but—"

"We're not going inside," he snips. "I'm dropping off Rod and Benny, who haven't seen us since we left the courthouse," he says in a warning tone, tossing a glance at Rod over his shoulder. Without warning, he skids to a stop half a mile back from the clubhouse. "Get out here," he orders the guys. "Your bikes are in the woods where we left 'em. Ride up to the clubhouse and stick to the plan."

I furrow my brow. "What plan? Nate, what the hell are you—?"

He turns to me, silencing me with a look that clearly says 'this isn't the time to run that big mouth.'

I get the message and snap my lips shut.

Rod and Benny exchange a look and Benny grabs me, hugging me tight. He's always been a good friend. God only knows, he's bailed me out of plenty of screw-ups in the past couple of years.

"Be good," he murmurs.

Tears spring to my eyes. It sounds suspiciously like a goodbye.

Oh no, not another one of those…

I don't know how much more I can take today!

I breathe in his familiar scent of worn leather, beer, and weed, squeezing him and burying my face in his cut until I feel Nate gently push me away from him. I blink back the tears, managing a quivering smile at Rod. "Bye," I mouth, knowing that if I try to speak, I will erupt into another round of hysterics. And judging by the serious expression on Nate's face, I know I don't have that luxury.

The guys scramble out of the car and disappear into the thick green foliage as Nate swings the car around and heads back down the dirt road.

"Nate," I say. "Tell me what's going on right now."

"Jae," he says, his voice thick. "What happens tonight marks the end of our life here. We leave and never look back, do you understand?"

My heart thuds hard in my chest, tiny hairs on the back of my neck standing at attention despite the balmy breeze flowing in through the car window. "Leave your club?" I say, my voice cracking. "You're the President! How can you just—?"

"I'm doing this for you, for us, and for the club." He slams his hand on the steering wheel. "Jae, the reason why Mom and Dad are dead is because of me, because I fucked up. I made moves that went against the cartel and against the Steel Reapers MC. I thought I was doing something good for the club, but it backfired. This is all on me," he hisses. "And the only way to make things right is to make sure that when we finally get our justice, they know exactly who served it."

"And then what? The cartel finds some other schmucks to come and off *you*?" My voice rises in panic. "How is that a good plan?"

Nate pulls over on the side of the dark road and turns to look at me in the backseat. "I knew this would happen the day the trial started. That evidence didn't just magically disappear, Jae. The cartel was never gonna lose this battle. Ever. And no, I can't singlehandedly take down a cartel, but I can sure as hell cut off their hands and their dicks. Send my own message."

"Then what?" I whisper.

"Then we disappear and start over somewhere far away from here. I leave the club behind, and they're protected because they had no involvement at all in what's about to happen."

"You'd give up the club? Just like that? You've been with these guys for years. They're your family."

He nods, his shoulders slumping a little bit. "They are. But so are you, and so were Mom and Dad. I can't help Mom and Dad anymore, but I can help you and the club." He lets out a sigh. "It's the only way. Rod will take over as President, and Benny will move up. They're the only two who know we're leaving, but I didn't give them details about why, and I didn't tell them where we're going. Better that nobody knows. I'm acting alone on this to keep heat off of everyone else. We'll be okay. I've cleared out all of the bank and investment accounts. We leave tonight."

I let his words settle into my conscious. Leave Miami and everything we've ever known behind? Forever? I mean, the club was almost as much my place as his. All of the people we'd known forever were part of it. It's our extended family, the only family we have left. And now we're supposed to just walk away? Into the unknown? "So you really did know," I muse.

"I had to be prepared," he says gruffly. "I couldn't wait until the verdict was delivered and then scramble to get our shit in order. I knew we need to act fast and to hit hard."

"How can you be sure they won't find us?" My voice trembles as the gravity of our situation settles on my head and heart like a lead brick.

"Look, the only thing you need to know is that I will always protect you, Jae. I made mistakes before, big ones. But I won't make them again. This is our only chance, the only way we survive what's going to happen next."

"And exactly what is that, Nate?" I ask, an icy coldness snaking through my insides. "What happens next?"

His eyes darken, lips stretched into a tight line. "We kill them all."

Chapter Two
SERGIO

PRESENT DAY

"Capacity is down by about twenty percent as of right now." Enrico, my top security guy, hands me a slip of paper with a bunch of numbers on it.

"Shit," I mutter, wishing like hell I hadn't been stuck in the entertainment sector of Operation: Make Vegas Our Bitch. My family recently partnered with a few others in an attempt to take over the gambling industry here in the States, and we're starting here in Nevada. But with all of the competition popping up all around our nightclubs, it's like trying to breathe life into a fucking corpse. Competition lurks in the shadows, just waiting for me to revive shit so they can snuff it out again.

I volunteered to come out here to Vegas, but it was a way for me to make my own name, away from Sicily and my past. It's not like I'm the underboss. That title is reserved for my oldest brother Matteo. I'm not the youngest, either, like Roman, who always gets the cush jobs because he's the baby. And thank fuck

I'm not my other brother Dante, who manages to set fire to everything in his path because he's such a ticking time bomb, always running into battle, usually without armor because he never thinks first.

But me? I get no special treatment. No favors. No latitude.

I'm just expected to deliver, no excuses, only results.

Nightlife in Vegas is hard to control, even for a group of families with deep pockets. We're competing with major drug cartels and motorcycle clubs out here, and they have tons of cash to throw at their businesses. They also run all kinds of shit through them — drugs, guns, contraband, women.

Nothing is off limits out here.

Hence the name Sin City.

And nobody seems to obey boundaries.

We've tried to keep things civil, but they see us as a threat to their livelihoods. I get that. Our mass invasion has the competition on edge, and they'd love nothing more than to exterminate us.

They're doing a damn good job of it, too, which is why I'm stuck in this role.

I'm supposed to be the savior, the guy with the master plan.

If I'm successful, I get a seat at the table.

If my idea tanks, I'll be running security right alongside Enrico.

A voice. It's all I want.

Well, that and a future that isn't dictated to me. I want to call my own damn shots for once. I figured I'd get my chance when I got out here. Running the Excelsior Hotel and Casino for the past year, the hottest new property on the Strip, has been great, but we're already solid on the hotel and restaurant businesses. And I'm not running the place alone. The Marcone family, also out of Sicily, has skin in the game.

I want something of my own.

And nightlife is the only area where we're slowly being choked to death.

Luckily, I have a plan that will loosen that noose.

I take a deep breath, staring out at the sea of faces gyrating on the dance floor here at Verve, my current nightmare. The numbers have been dropping steadily for the past month and there's only one way to stop the bleeding.

And that's to cut someone's jugular.

Metaphorically, of course.

Because the only way I can save my livelihood is to kill someone else's.

Unless he tries to screw with me.

Then, all metaphors go out the window.

"You really think your plan is gonna work?" Enrico asks.

I pull my eyes away from the dance floor and lift an eyebrow at him. "Nobody turns me down, Enrico. I always make offers that are impossible to refuse. This time next week, we'll be on our way to owning this city. Shit, we'll have more pull than the goddamn mayor."

A smile tugs at my lips. I haven't been out here long, but my footprint will be deep if I can make this deal.

And like I said, I always deliver.

Enrico claps me on the back and goes back to his position at the front of the club. I take a long gulp of the chilled scotch in my glass and swirl around the ice cubes, scouting the thin stream of patrons trickling in. My lips press together into a tight line because I know where the crowds are anxiously waiting on a mile-long line right now.

Fucking Nate Torres and his string of sex dens.

Soon, you'll be mine. All of you.

I take another sip, draining the glass, and as I lower it, my gaze connects with a group of women who just entered the club. Blonde, huge tits, short, tight dresses that barely cover their asses. They're giggling, clearly intoxicated as evidenced by the way they can barely walk a straight line in their ridiculously high heels.

I barely blink an eye as they pass because for Vegas, girls like that are a dime a dozen. Hot but old. Tired. As in, no challenge.

Stifling a yawn, I push away from my secluded spot against the wall and prepare for another lap around the place. I shake my head as I walk. This place should be so damn crowded that I have to shove past people. I don't even come close to grazing someone's shoulders, for fuck's sake.

The place is dying, just like the other clubs we own.

I let out a frustrated sigh, sweeping a hand through my hair as I lift the near-empty glass to my lips to suck down the last drops.

Just focus on the deal, Serge. And the future you're about to make for your—

Crash!

My body lurches forward, the glass flying out of my hand and shattering on the floor.

No danger to anyone since there's a big open space in front of me.

Cue the sarcasm.

I twist around, just in time to be knocked against a nearby wall by a massive guy who's pawing at me to keep his footing. I shove him away from me, straightening my jacket. "What the fuck is your problem, friend?" I growl at the guy, grabbing him by the shirt collar and flipping him around so that he's the one against the wall.

His eyes are glassy and he snickers, the stench of stale beer on his breath. "Fuck off, dude. Don't be such a tight-ass."

I slam him hard against the wall. "What did you just say to me?" I hiss.

"Look, it was-sn't me, okay?" he slurs. "It was her, that bitch behind you. S-she pushed me into you."

"Because you grabbed my ass!" an angry voice from behind me bellows. "Do I look like an animal at a fucking petting zoo?"

He leers at her over my shoulder as I bite back a smirk. "These girls-s. They run around barely dressed and expect guys-s to keep their hands to themselves-s, like they aren't begging for it."

I hear the girl gasp, and she pushes her way between us and gets right in his face. "Look, dick, if I want to walk around naked, I have the fucking right to without being fingered by your diseased digits!"

"Well, technically, you can't walk around naked because it's against the law," I say, just feeding the fire a little bit more. Not like she needs it. She's five foot nothing, so I have at least a foot on her. But what she lacks in size, she definitely makes up for in attitude. I glance down at her back since that's pretty much all I can see with her squeezed between us. Long, dark hair cascades down her spine, and as she shakes the guy pinned against the wall, I catch a hint of citrus wafting up to my nostrils.

Seems ironic that such a sweet scent is emanating off of a body this primed for slaughter.

She flips around, not letting go of her assailant, and my breath hitches.

Fuck.

Almond-shaped green eyes narrow to slits, practically disappearing under her thick eyelashes as her lips twist into a scowl. Demonic is probably the word I'd use for that expression, but damn, it gets me hot.

So hot that I want to take her to my office and bend her over the couch while I fuck that rage out of her. Judging by the way her nostrils flare, I can sense there's a lot of it, and I'm definitely up to the task.

"This is Vegas," she seethes. "If I want to pole dance nude in the middle of the Strip while snorting cocaine and guzzling vodka, I'm pretty sure the cops would leave me alone." Her lips curl upward. "Hell, they'd probably try to join my party."

"I can't imagine any living, breathing man who wouldn't." I smirk and she returns the smile, letting go of the guy and shoving him away. She flips her head around toward him. "Keep your fucking hands to yourself!" she snaps before turning back to me with a seductive smile that has my cock twitching because this girl is hot as fuck and nursing a raging inferno inside of that tight body.

I run my eyes over her curves, highlighted by the tight black fabric hugging them. She sticks her hands on her hips and tilts her head to the side. "See anything you like?"

"I like it all." I snicker. "Not that I'm gonna touch it because I've seen what you do to the dumbasses who dare."

"Some guys just forget that they need an invitation to the party. They don't understand that crashing it can be dangerous."

"So what were you gonna do to that guy if I hadn't gotten in the way?"

She lowers her gaze, staring up at me from under those long lashes. Then she slides closer to me, doing an exaggerated head tilt. Her eyes blaze, a rush of heat smoldering in my gut as the seconds pass. Finally, she parts her deep red lips. "I was going to sterilize him," she murmurs.

And fuck me, those words are the sexiest I've ever heard.

Meaning be damned.

"Would have been bad for business," I say. "I can't have a gorgeous, out-of-control woman storming the place, assaulting my customers. You'd scare everyone away." I rest one hand against the wall, blocking her in on one side.

"Oh, so you're afraid of me?" she asks in a teasing voice. "Am I really that much of a monster?"

"I'm not afraid of anything. I'd let you assault me anytime you'd like." I grin. "And I'll bet that the monster inside would definitely enjoy the experience."

"You sound pretty confident about that."

"What can I say? I know my talents."

"I'll bet plenty of women know them, too." She folds her arms over her chest, and I can't help but steal a glimpse of her tits. They're peeking out of the neckline of her dress, begging to come out and play.

An image of her riding my cock with those tits bouncing flashes in front of me, and I have to squeeze my eyes shut for a second to keep my cock from busting through my pants.

"Something wrong?" she asks.

"Very wrong," I say. That's a gross understatement if I ever heard one.

"You know what else would be wrong?" she asks in a breathy voice.

Uhh, if you dropped to your knees right now and sucked my cock?

That would be wrong — and oh so right — on so many levels.

But I'd be a willing participant in a hot second.

"What?"

"For you to keep staring at my boobs like you're trying to will them out of my dress." She quirks an eyebrow. "You're almost as bad as the other guy. At least he had the balls to grab one." With a quick wink, she slides away from the wall and struts toward the bar to re-join her group.

I turn my head, and thanks to my club being near-empty, I can see her hips swing gently with each step. She moves slowly, methodically, as if she knows—

With a quick flip of her head, she gives me a self-satisfied smile over her shoulder.

Yep.

That I'm watching.

And I am.

She's definitely got my attention.

Now I'm really curious to see what she's gonna do with it.

Chapter Three
JAELYN

I can feel his eyes on me with every step I take toward the bar.

Good. He's curious.

Or horny.

Either way, I can use those things to get into his head.

The one on his shoulders, that is.

Nate told me to be inconspicuous but really, what was I supposed to do when that disgusting beefcake put his hands on my junk?

It's not like I planned to send him flying into the reason why I'm here tonight.

As I peek over my shoulder to give Sergio Villani a final once-over, I instinctively lick my lips.

Good Lord, he's so much more delectable in person.

Not that I'm in the market for anything other than a little reconnaissance. I'm just here to kill a couple of birds with one stone.

One, to try and fit in with the dancers from our nightclub, The Sapphire Lounge.

And two, to dig into the man who's very intent on buying the success that he clearly can't generate himself, judging by the fact that I'm able to get a drink at eleven o'clock on a Saturday night without having to elbow a single person.

"Figure out his angle," Nate said before I left the club. "Get a read on him and watch out for any of his associates. I know the rumors, but I wanna see if anyone on our radar shows up there."

I studied the pictures Nate dropped on my desk for an hour.

Just call me Columbo.

I toss a casual glance back in Sergio's direction, eyeing his muscular form as he huddles together with a couple of other guys dressed from head to toe in black. They don't look familiar. Must be low men on the totem pole.

I know exactly who I'm looking for.

It's the same person who's looking for me and Nate.

The one we've managed to escape for the past three years.

But nothing lasts forever.

And that's why Nate sent me in here.

The Italians and the Russians are laying pipe all over this city, trying to grab whatever power they can. It only makes sense that the Mexicans would want to get in on the action so they can take advantage of new distribution lines for their drugs.

And once they show up on the scene, it won't be long before they find us…if they haven't already. That's what Nate is afraid of. What we did on the night of the verdict, ambushing the Bowman brothers to get our own justice, was devastating to the Becerra Cartel. And they're an unforgiving bunch of assholes.

Go big or go home.

A chill crawls down my spine.

Well, we can't go home. They made sure of that. We lost everything when we fled Miami three years ago, and there isn't enough money in the world that can replace what's long gone.

What the Becerra Cartel stole from us.

My throat tightens, and I grip my shot glass tight, coaxing the disturbing memories back into the recesses of my mind.

I can't fall prey to that kind of destructive emotion right now.

Emotion equates to weakness.

And weakness makes you vulnerable…to a lot of bad things.

Like death.

And if the Becerras are in with the Italians, it won't be quick and painless.

It will be the exact opposite.

"Jae," Ashleigh nudges me. "What are you staring at? You're, like, in a trance."

I give my head a quick shake and turn back to my assistant, the only girl at the club I'd actually call my friend. And even then, I keep her at arm's length because everyone can be bought.

I've learned that harsh lesson.

I scoff. "Can you believe that guy I pummeled before is still hanging around? I mean, how did they not kick him out?" With a roll of my eyes, I turn back to the girls, the dancers who aren't on schedule to perform at Sapphire, and force a fake bright smile. Nate says if I smile more, the girls won't be so intimidated by me.

But I prefer it that way.

I don't need to be their friend.

I'm better on my own, just like I have been since we left Miami.

A heavy weight settles over me.

Dammit! I don't want to think of Miami!

It haunts me enough when I sleep at night, more so now that the threat is looming again.

Nate's the one who heard about the Becerras working their way west toward Vegas. One of the guys in his inner circle caught wind of it from a neighboring motorcycle club.

Some might say we're stupid for not leaving Vegas before the threat becomes a reality.

We say we're not gonna let the Becerra Cartel strip another fucking thing from us.

And if this buyout meeting turns out to be a ruse for some grand-scale attack on our place, we'll be ready for it.

Getting that information may prove to be a little bit tricky, though.

I mean, how willing is this guy Sergio going to be to divulge business secrets to a girl whom he—?

I quickly flip around back to Ashleigh.

A girl whom he can't seem to stop looking at.

And said girl can't quite keep her eyes off of him, either.

Dammit, I didn't want to get caught staring. I was trying to be slick about my sidelong glances and I failed.

Epically.

I take the tiniest sip of vodka, nursing the clear liquor as I nod and smile at whatever bullshit gossip the girls are giggling about…which of the dancers frequently star in their own gang bangs, which one fucked a horse, which one used to be a dude.

I really couldn't care less what they do in their own time, as long as when they're in our club and on our stage, they make us fat wads of cash.

Money is really the only savior for us right now.

It gives us choices.

After the Bowman brothers' massacre, it was the only reason we were able to make such a clean getaway.

It's how we were able to build up this club and its sister clubs within only a few short years.

The more we have, the more opportunities we can grasp.

And that's why Nate is so intent on not selling. If these guys are clamoring for our business, that tells us there's way more money up for grabs. Why should we give up our claim to it and let the Italians pocket our hard-earned success?

We're not letting anyone chase us out of this city!

I tap my fingernails on the side of my glass.

I have a job to do tonight, and standing here listening to this drivel is getting me nowhere fast.

I sweep my eyes around the perimeter of the room, peering into the darkness. It seems that my target has slipped away.

Dammit.

I can't afford to miss a single detail.

What if I could get into his office?

Would there be some incriminating information in there?

Then I let out a snort.

Yeah, sure, Jae. I'm sure he'll have a Post-it stuck to his desk that says, "Friday, 10:00 P.M. - Shoot up The Sapphire Lounge with my new friends in the Becerra Cartel."

Maybe he has a reminder in his phone?

I give my head a quick shake.

This is ridiculous. I have to find him and figure out a way to get the details I need.

Because this place…I look around and a shiver runs through me since there's not nearly enough body heat being generated…is a joke that is rapidly on its way to becoming a faint memory.

And desperate situations unravel quickly.

I gulp down the rest of my shot and hand the glass to Ashleigh. "I'm going to the ladies' room," I say.

She nods, still captivated by stories of the illustrious lives of our Sapphire dancers. A smirk tugs at my lips as I watch her soaking in the sordid details with rapt attention. Ash has the look of a porn star, but the innocence of a virgin, and sometimes I wonder how she fell into this life in the first place.

I run a hand through my hair, slowing my pace as I pretend to search for the restroom. I'm really searching for Sergio. Maybe he's hunkered down in his office with an associate. He wouldn't do business out here in the open.

I creep down a short hallway, my brain rattling in my skull, vibrating from the pulsating electronica echoing through the vast space. Up ahead, I see a sign for the ladies' room, but I don't stop. And there are no other doorways in this hallway from what I can see. Where could he have gone?

I keep walking, looking, and listening until I strike gold…maybe.

An unmarked door.

I twist the knob and push it open.

Bingo!

There's a staircase leading to a second floor.

I take a deep breath and step inside the doorway, not knowing what the hell I'll find up there.

But I came here on a mission, and I'm not leaving until I complete it.

A lot hangs in the balance, and I'm not willing to take another loss.

The walls leading up are dark, matching the décor of the club. But there are faint lights shining down from the ceiling that guide my path. My heart races as I proceed up the steps, swallowing a gasp as my phone vibrates in my clutch bag. I fish it out and lean back against the wall, clicking to accept my brother's call.

"Hey, how's it going? You see anything interesting?"

"No," I whisper. "Not yet, but I might be on to something."

"Why are you whispering? And why don't I hear music?"

"I found a staircase," I say in the softest voice possible to avoid it echoing on the landing. "I think it might lead to an office, maybe his. It looks private and hidden, so I'm going to sneak up there to see if I can hear—"

"Jae!" Nate exclaims. "Are you fucking crazy? I told you to keep an eye on him, to see who he talks to, to watch him in the club! Don't fucking stalk him into a restricted area, for Christ's sake! We're trying to figure out who we're dealing with, not get you killed!!"

"Well, we obviously know who we're dealing with, Nate," I mutter. "I mean, the guy is practically oozing olive oil and marinara sauce. He's clearly connected. And I think there might be something going on here tonight. He was huddled with his guys, and then he disappeared." I let out a huff. "And thanks for the vote of confidence, by the way."

I take another step.

It's dark.

Desolate.

I hope that means nobody is lurking around up there, just waiting for the quivery voice at the bottom of the staircase to appear.

That would be very bad, especially since I only have a can of Mace in my bag.

And it's been a while since I used it, so hopefully, the nozzle isn't all crusted up.

"What if he left the place, Jae? Don't go up the goddamn stairs! Get the hell out of there before you get hurt, or worse!"

"Relax," I say. "And give me a little more credit. It's not like I'm little Miss Innocent. I am perfectly capable of taking care of myself, or did you forget that I'm pretty damn skilled with a knife?"

"And you have a knife on you right now?" he asks in a gruff voice.

"Well, no, but—"

"Exactly. Get the fuck back to your friends! I never should have told you to go to that club in the first place." Nate tries to control his voice. "Jae, please. This is dangerous. Don't go up there, okay? Please just listen to me."

I let out a sigh. "Fine," I say. "I'll go back to the girls. And we'll just wait until Sergio shows up at Sapphire for your meeting to see whether or not he's working with the Becerra Cartel. And if so, oh well. We'll just agree to be sufficiently fucked."

Nate snorts. "Relax. We'll come up with another plan. I never should have asked you to go there tonight. I need you here, anyway. This place is a madhouse, and without my right hand, it's murder."

"Ha," I say in a light voice. "Funny. You said the 'm' word. You don't know how close to accurate you might be."

"Smartass," he mumbles. "I'll see you later."

I click to end the call and lean back against the wall as I stuff the phone back into my bag, pull out my Mace, and take another tentative step upstairs.

To find Sergio's office.

Because there's no way I came this far to duck back without any answers.

I creep up the full flight of stairs and tiptoe down a corridor lined with modern-looking wall sconces lighting the way.

A few feet ahead, I come to a closed door with a bright light shining out from under it.

But there is nobody standing outside.

I furrow my brow.

That doesn't make sense. What the hell kind of mafioso doesn't have security staked outside of his office, you know, just in case?

It makes my job easier, but it's really kind of stupid on Sergio's part.

I press my ear to the door, struggling to hear something…anything…but it's all in some other language.

Italian.

One of the voices switches back to English, but it's one I don't recognize. It's not the sexy, growly, hungry voice of Sergio. This one is raspy and gritty.

"So you got the meeting scheduled. Good. Now, how about the cash?"

I recoil.

Meeting.

What meeting?

Oh, please tell me what meeting!

"Don't worry. I'll have it ready in time."

A shiver flutters over my skin.

Sergio.

"And what about the other guys? They're fucking persistent, boss. Like flies on shit."

Some rumbling follows, mumbling in Italian in a voice that sounds less than thrilled.

What other guys?

The voices drop and now I can only make out single words.

Barely.

And I don't like any of them.

Bad situation...that prick...fifty million...kill...bloodbath...

I swallow a screech of frustration and stomp my foot against the floor.

The beat drop is so damn heavy that the clanging between my temples drowns out the voices.

Heavy footsteps clunk along the floor behind me and I spin around, fully expecting to see some angry bouncer ready to pull me out of this restricted area and back up to the lounge. But when I flip around, my breath hitches.

It's not a bouncer.

It's a group of four men, short, dark-skinned, all wearing menacing smiles on their bearded faces.

"Are you here for the meeting, sweetheart?" one of them asks. "I didn't realize there would be entertainment."

My heart stills in my chest, and I twist around to see that there is no escape route behind me.

There's just another wall.

I wandered into a dead end.

And suddenly the words I overheard explode in my mind like bullets.

Ha, ironic.

Kill. Bloodbath.

Fuck!

"I was, ah, just looking for the restroom," I say, keeping my voice as steady as possible. I straighten up as much as possible and push past the first two, still holding my breath as I shove through the second string.

I almost let it out when one of them grabs my wrist and yanks me back so that my face is pressed against his stubbled cheek. "Up here?" he says, winking at one of the other guys. "I think she's lying, what do you say, *ese*?"

"I think she's looking for some action," the other guy replies with a leer. "Maybe we take her as a parting gift. I can think of some things we can do that'll get her blood pumping." He lets out a low-pitched chuckle. "And our cocks pumping."

I struggle against them, my piercing screams ricocheting off the walls as I kick, scratch, and punch with every ounce of strength in me.

Suddenly, the door flies open and Sergio appears. His eyebrows knit together, a furious expression on his face as he looks left and right before his gaze settles on me. "What the fuck is going on out here?" he growls. "And why is she up here?"

"We found this *puta* outside your door, Villani," one of the men says. "She one of your bitches?" He wrenches my arm behind me and I spit right in his eye, the fucker that he is.

I tug my arm, pushing off of his beefy chest, and Sergio puts up a hand.

"Let her go," he says in a threatening voice. "I'll take care of her, not you." His eyes flicker at me and I am plain speechless about what I've wandered into.

Holy Christ.

How exactly is he going to take care of me?

Sergio levels one of the guys with a look. "Where's your boss?" he snarls.

The guy shrugs. "He was busy," he says in a flip tone. "Said for me to come and get all the details."

Sergio nods, his eyes narrowing. "Well, you tell him that if he wants to work together, he can come and talk to me himself. I don't take meetings with his fucking peons, you understand? *Ese?*" He grabs my other arm and pulls me close so that I face-plant right in the center of his chest.

I can't help but breathe in his delicious scent. And dammit, I want to run my hand down the front of his starched shirt, tracing the outline of his defined pecs beneath it…

Oh holy hell, Jae!

You're in the middle of some impending rumble, and all you can do is think about this guy's chest?

I inhale once again, resting my face against the fabric for a split second, biting back a moan.

And the answer is yes.

That is the only thing clouding my mind and my better judgment in this second.

Ugh! I'm not that girl!

I try to pull myself away, but Sergio's grip on me is tight.

He wants to keep me right where I am.

I can't lie. My knees quiver the tiniest bit at that realization.

For whatever reason, he likes me pressed against him.

Typical guy.

I'll take it.

My eyes flicker over to the thugs who are slicing into me with death stares.

But I'm impervious, happy to say.

The meanest looking one turns his scowl up to Sergio. "This isn't finished."

"Actually," he replies. "It is. Take that message to your boss." His arm winds around my waist, pulling me even closer, something I didn't even think was possible.

"He won't be happy to hear that," the guy bites back.

"Well, then, maybe he'll remember how important it is to make time in your schedule for the person he needs something from. Because that's what this is. Not the other way around, you get that?"

I swallow hard as the guy's face gets more and more pinched with anger as Sergio spews those words.

Without another word, he turns and leads his pack of slimy asshats up the stairs and back into the club. Sergio pulls away from me and nods at his guys. "Make sure they leave, yeah?"

And just like that, we're alone.

Now, I'm no stranger to seedy business. Nate's motorcycle club was always dabbling in illegal dealings, and since I was around the clubhouse pretty often, I'd overhear some off-the-record conversations. Nothing crazy since the important stuff was left for church, but if you kept an ear to the ground, you'd hear enough to know that there were enemies out there.

Hell. That's how I found out about the Becerra Cartel scoping out a partnership with the motorcycle club in the first place. The girls would screw around with the guys and overhear things when they were buried between their legs, blowing them. Then, they'd gossip about what they heard.

I sensed danger back then and I can smell it now.

Let me just say that the air around us is damn pungent.

Sergio looks down at me, his expression grave. "Do you know who I am?"

I tilt my head back so that I can meet his eyes. "Well, you never told me your name, but—"

"Why'd you come up here?" His voice is gruff, almost accusatory.

I shrug. "You disappeared and I, um…" Heat coils in my belly as his eyes narrow. "I didn't think we were finished."

"And so you figured you'd just wander to the back of this club, find a hidden staircase, and come upstairs to see if I was around so we could…?" he stops abruptly, lifting an eyebrow at me.

"Uh…dance?" I barely squeak out. "I wanted to dance with you."

He backs me against the office door, his eyes dark. "I think you're full of shit."

My throat tightens as he locks my arms tightly in place so I can't do a damn thing except head-butt him.

"I don't think you're looking for a dance partner," he grunts. "So why don't you tell me what you really want?"

"I promise, I just wanted to dance!" I hear the way my voice pierces the air and I hate myself for it. But it really is hard to breathe right now, and for as turned on as I am by his alpha badass kitsch, I am a teeny bit scared of him snapping my arms out of their sockets.

"You think I'm some kind of fucking idiot?" he hisses, tightening his grip. "Because I can't think of a single reason why you'd be up here right now…" he pauses, his eyes narrowing to slits. "Unless you're a cop. Is that it? Are you here to investigate my operation, sweetheart? You looking to make a name for yourself down at the precinct to prove your worth to the clowns you work with? You got cause for being here right now? If so, you'd better fucking arrest me. If not, then get the fuck out of my club," he seethes.

"It doesn't seem like you want to let me go," I rasp, my body pinned in the most delicious way possible.

His lips curl into a sneer. "I never said you weren't hot as fuck. And I'm a guy pressed up against you. Can't blame me for taking advantage of the situation. Now, are you gonna read me my rights or not? I suspect the answer is no because this place is tighter and cleaner than a million virgins."

I shake my head. "I swear I'm not a cop," I whisper.

"And you really only wanted to dance?" He quirks an eyebrow. "My instincts are pretty fucking awesome and I'm not buying that shit."

I swallow past the lump in my throat. "Can you ease off me, please? I can't really breathe."

"You gonna pull a gun on me if I do?"

"I don't have a gun. I told you, I'm not—"

"A cop, yeah, I get it." He stares at me for a second, then pulls away.

I immediately wish he was blanketing me again. God, I'm twisted.

"You know what I'll do if I find out you're lying?" he hisses.

My mouth is drier than the Mojave right now, and it's not out of fear, but from sheer animal lust. I shake my head.

He smirks at me. "Nothing, because then you'd have something on me. See how that works? I don't know who you're used to working with, but I guarantee I'm not like anyone else."

Oh no, you most definitely are not. I bite down on my lower lip, trying hard to look as seductive as possible. "So, are we cool now? How about that dance?"

"As the owner, I don't typically intermingle with the guests."

"But you want to make an exception," I say, twisting a lock of hair around my finger, forcing my lips upward into a coy smile. "Right?" I sway next to him, brushing my chest against his. I almost expect him to recoil, but he stands perfectly still, still staring at me with curiosity.

"There are a lot of guys downstairs you can dance with," he murmurs.

"I know those guys," I say. "They're all cut from the same cloth and I wanted something different tonight." My breath hitches as goosebumps splay across my skin under his heated gaze.

"You got involved with my business." His face darkens. "I don't appreciate it when people interrupt my meetings."

"It didn't seem like your meeting was going to get very far, anyway," I purr, flipping my hair over my shoulder. At this point, I need to make him believe that it's him I want, not information, especially since he already has zero trust in me. And the way his eyes are stripping me bare right now, I seriously doubt he's thinking about that meeting anymore. And since I have no visual on the kingpin, I'm just as clueless as I was before about the whereabouts of the Becerra Cartel.

The thugs who were ready to attack me a few minutes ago weren't in any of the pictures Nate gave me to study. As far as I know, they could be part of any crew…any crew with a taste for blood, that is.

Things could have gone down a lot differently if Sergio hadn't come out of his office in time. But he's here now.

And we're alone, for better or worse.

I'm no closer to finding out his intentions for our nightclubs or who he's aligned with, but I'm damn near to the point of exploding from the rush of desire coursing through me.

"Should I have saved your life before?" he asks, brushing his fingertips over my bare shoulder. "Are you worth it?"

"You have no idea how much," I reply in a breathless voice. Oh my God, who am I? I'm not the girl who does the whole flirting thing. I don't get that fluttery feeling in my gut when a guy makes sexy innuendoes. I don't fall for the 'come hither' look.

But something about this guy, this alleged dangerous and calculating man, makes me quiver and quake like a teenage girl with a crush.

"You're gonna have to prove it to me," he growls, pushing me against the wall and sliding himself between my legs.

Oh Lord, yes.

Fuck dancing.

Let's just stand here…forever…

He runs a hand down the side of my neck, gently fisting the hair on the back of my head. And the tingles that follow?

They don't just swirl in my belly.

They command my entire body.

"So, dancing," he says, his lips crooking upward. "That's what you want to do?"

The lump in my throat is so large, it takes effort to nod my head.

He hovers over me, his lips close enough to mine that I can bite them. The seconds later, he pulls away and motions to the stairs. "After you."

Shock settles into my bones since dancing…fully clothed…was not really on the forefront of my mind.

And judging by the thickness pressed against my leg, it doesn't seem to be on his, either.

But dancing it is.

Any excuse to keep myself close to him.

You know, just in case anyone else shows up for a 'meeting' and I can link him to the Becerra Cartel.

I lace my fingers with his, flashing him a sly smile as I lead him to the staircase and slowly walk down the steps toward the main club floor.

Yeah, sure. I'm all about digging for information on the Becerra Cartel right now.

Digging into Sergio is more like it.

Once we're on the main floor, he takes the lead and snakes an arm around my waist, guiding me to a darkened area of the dance floor. "I don't like to be in the spotlight," he murmurs against my ear as he slides his hand onto the small of my back. Our movements are fluid, we're fused together, grinding and swaying to the sultry beats. I wrap my arms around him, trailing one hand down his muscular back as my own back arches. His cock hardens as I rub myself against him, shifting my hips against his, rocking to some tune playing in my head, not the crazy pulsating beat that has faded to the background.

Our hands grope, our bodies gyrate, and I can't remember a time when I've felt more alive and alert.

Good God, if this is how he moves with clothes on, imagine how he'd ride me while I'm face-down in his bed…

"Are you gonna tell me your name? Or are you just about the anonymous torture?" He mumbles against the side of my hair.

"Torture?" I tilt my head back, widening my eyes like I don't know exactly what he's insinuating.

"Your body. Your face," he says, cupping my chin. "You're fucking gorgeous from head to toe."

I allow myself a self-satisfied smile. Looks like his self-control is waning.

I bet I could get him to tell me anything right now.

Anything…

"Names can mess everything up," I say with a playful grin. "Don't you think? Makes everything so real. Besides, I haven't decided if *you're* worth it."

When his hand lightly grazes my ass, it's a warning for me to push it away, to knee him in the groin, to stomp on his foot.

But I ignore the flashing red lights and let it happen.

Until he drops it like he's just stuck it over an open flame. He steps back with a cocky grin on his face. "I guess it's good that I decided for you, then." He sweeps a hand through his thick, longish dark hair. "And if you're not a cop, you've got some other agenda that you're baiting me for. So why don't you take it to the bar, have a drink on me, and enjoy the rest of your night?"

My jaw drops as he saunters off of the dance floor, leaving me gaping after him.

Did that just happen? Did he seriously just blow me off after accusing me of having an agenda? Which I absolutely do have?

So I shouldn't be so shocked.

Sexual tension can only take you so far when you have self-control.

And Sergio clearly does.

A rush of cool air blasts me from an air-conditioning vent overhead, and I wrap my arms around myself.

Well, here I am, duped and freezing my ass off with nothing to keep me warm but my own damn arms, so yeah!

It fucking happened, and I have absolutely nothing of value right now. What a waste of a night!

"Jae!" Ash runs over, her blue eyes wide with concern. "Where have you been? You said you went to the ladies' room like, an hour ago!"

"It wasn't that long," I grumble, stalking off the dance floor without a glance backward.

"What were you doing?" she asks, hurrying after me.

"Nothing important," I snip, tucking my clutch bag under my arm and stomping across the floor of the lounge to where the other girls are standing.

"This place is so beat," Violet complains. "Let's go somewhere else."

"I'm actually really tired," I say, forcing a big yawn. "I'm going to go home."

Ashleigh's eyebrows knit. "Are you sure you're okay to drive?"

I nod. "One-hundred percent okay. You guys go and have fun. I'll see you tomorrow."

Ashleigh links her arm with mine as we walk out to the parking lot. "I'll go with you to your car so that you're not alone," she murmurs.

But I give her a little shove toward the rest of the group. "You know that Vi will leave your ass here if you're not in her car once she starts it. Just go. Have fun." I smirk. "Just not too much fun."

Ashleigh bites down on her lower lip, peering into the distance where I parked my car. "Why couldn't you just park it here where everyone else did?"

I roll my eyes. "I figured it would be packed and I didn't want my car buried."

She snickers. "Oh, well, that actually makes sense, you know, in theory."

"The reality is a much different thing." I smirk and give her a quick hug before pushing her toward the girls. "Now go!"

"Okay," she says with a bit of hesitation. "But call me as soon as you get home."

"Promise." I smile. It is kind of nice, I guess. Having a friend. Or as close as I can get to one, anyway, since every time I even think about getting close to someone, things go sideways.

My lips stretch into a tight line, fists balled at my sides.

Or they fucking disappear after blowing my ego to complete bits.

I turn back toward my car with a huff and hurry along the uneven pavement. Tall, thick grasses line the fenced-in area of the club and if it was busy, there would be wall-to-wall cars and I wouldn't have my heart lodged in my throat as I walk-jog.

But that's not the case, and it's a little eerie to be out here by myself, even with the Mace in my bag.

Speaking of which, maybe I should get it out, just in case.

I fumble inside of my bag, not stopping for even a split second, until my fingers close around it. A couple of quick sprays confirms that it is, indeed, useless. I toss it to the side and keep going just as I see a long, dark shadow move in my periphery. I pick up the pace, my heels clicking along the pavement as deep, shuddering breaths heat the back of my neck. I scream, quickly ducking to the right and pulling off my shoe. I spin around with the heel poised to impale who the hell ever dared tail me to my car.

Because, it seems that whatever the fuck else can go wrong tonight, will.

And I have to be ready.

A strong hand grasps the back of my neck, tugging my hair backward so that I stumble into a thick, hard body firmly rooted behind me. I yelp as I spin around, shooting out my arm and slamming my makeshift weapon straight into the guy's cheek.

He stumbles backward, giving me the chance to get the hell away from him. A loud roar erupts from his chest as he pulls the blood-soaked heel out of his flesh. I kick off my other shoe, my feet pounding the pavement as I head for my car ahead in the darkness. He grunts, low and menacing, his beady black eyes so dark, he looks like a demon. It's definitely the leader of the dipshit crew who was trying to meet with Sergio. I don't dare look back. I just run, ignoring the bits of gravel slicing at my soles. But damn, it's so dark. So dark and—

I scream, stubbing my toe into the side of a pipe sticking out of the road. I pause only for a second, but it was one second too long and he grabs me by the hair, yanking me backward.

"You thought you were gonna get away before, didn't you? Thought he was gonna protect you? But *putas* like you never think about anything besides sucking cock. Well, I've got a cock for ya. A nice fat one that you're gonna enjoy." He points a knife blade at my jugular, his other hand tugging my hair. "Drop to your knees, bitch, and open wide!"

My screeches shatter the air and I know there's a knife blade pointed at my neck, but there's no way I'm sucking anything! I let my body go limp against him, catching him off-guard enough that he has to either catch me or let me hit the ground.

Either way, I win.

And he chooses to let me fall, fucker that he is. I fall between his legs and flip around, driving both of my fists straight into his groin. I use every shred of power in me and he collapses to the ground, narrowly missing my head. I roll out from under him and leap to my feet as he writhes around on the ground, clutching himself. I take the opportunity to stomp on his cock once more before I kick him in the head and in the throat for good measure. He tries to grab for me, but I easily sidestep his fists.

Blood rushes between my temples as I back away from him, running toward my car. I move as fast as I can, turning back to make sure he hasn't miraculously rolled to his feet. "Help me!" I scream at the top of my lungs. "Someone, please!"

"What the hell is going on out here?"

I hear a deep, male voice along with scattered footsteps pounding along the pavement in my direction. I keep jogging, taking large gulps of oxygen, daring to look back for one split second.

I squint in the darkness.

Yes, it's definitely him.

Sergio Villani.

He slows down when he sees the guy still floundering on the ground, and then rushes past him until he reaches me. "What happened? Did that cocksucker come after you?"

"He grabbed me," I seethe. "Forced me to the ground with a knife to my throat."

"And he's the one laying on his back now." He grins at me. "Impressive."

I glare at the guy. "I did what I had to do. And I'd do it again! *Harder!*" I shriek.

He pulls away and looks at my feet. "Where are your shoes?"

"I kicked one off and stabbed him in the face with the other one."

"I won't lie. This whole Black Widow routine you've got going on is making me kinda hot." He smirks.

I roll my eyes.

"*¡Maldita puta! ¡te mataré!*" he screams at me as Sergio's guy shakes him and smacks him on the side of the head.

I glare at him, not really sure what he said, but it didn't sound good.

Sergio grabs him by the collar and shakes him, pulling him close so that they're practically nose to nose. My eyes fall on a marking on my assailant's collarbone, something I didn't see earlier because it was hidden by his shirt.

I clap a hand over my mouth, bile rising in my throat, the image branded in my memory forever. I'll never forget it…never forget what I saw that night.

It's how we found out who killed Mom and Dad, how we knew the Becerra Cartel tore apart our family and our lives.

My fingers twitch as I run them over the symbols sliced into the leather headrest of my parents' totaled car. I drag them over the blood splatters, leaving streaks of red in their wake. Tears run down my cheeks, dripping onto the leather, still warm from where my father's body lay hunched over the steering wheel. A sob erupts from my chest as I stare at the message that was left for Nate…for us.

305 BC.

Nate told me the numbers are the Miami area code. The BC was for Becerra Cartel.

They carved their message into the driver's seat to make sure we'd find it, to make sure it would haunt us forever.

For as long as I live, I will never be able to erase that image from my mind. I'll never be free from the guilt that plagues me every day. I'll never forget my last words to my father. I'll never forgive myself for what I did.

And three years later, I'm still searching for a way to eradicate that guilt, to avenge my parents' senseless death. They were innocent. They were good. They didn't deserve to die.

Sergio motions for one of his guys to come closer. "Marvin, take Javier inside and get him cleaned up. Then get him a drink. I'll be in later and we can have a little talk about how you're supposed to behave when you're looking to partner with someone."

"I need to get to a hospital," Javier moans, still hunched over. He spits at me as Marvin pushes him toward the back door of the club.

My hands tremble as I smooth down my hair. Javier works for the Becerra Cartel. Sergio is going to have a meeting with him to discuss a partnership. He's sending him inside to get cleaned up and to have a drink?!

I bite back the words that are on the tip of my tongue. I want to lash out at Sergio so badly but I can't. He's meeting with Nate in a week. I can't tip him off about who I am and why I'm here, even though I want to take a fist to his handsome face.

Swallow it down, Jae. Keep your shit together or you'll rain holy hell on everything!

If Nate was pissed about me staking out Sergio's office, he will probably skin me alive if I give him anything he can use against us. For all we know, Becerra is in on this buyout and they might be planning to make a move when we're distracted by offers and deals. Tipping off Sergio now means their first attack may come a lot sooner than anticipated.

And we're not about to give up the keys to our kingdom…not by a longshot.

"You're pale," Sergio says, peering at my arm. "Are you okay?"

"I'm fine," I say stiffly, but my heart is thumping out of control and I can't decide who's more to blame…Javier or Sergio.

"You don't look fine."

"Yeah well, excuse me for being a little shocked that you're not going to beat the hell out of him or anything," I huff. "Clean him up and get him a drink. What the hell is that? You really want to work with someone like that?"

He levels me with a stare. "It's business."

"It's bullshit," I hiss, stopping with that because even though I want to say so much more, I know I can't. I have a chance to get some information, real information that may actually help us, and I can't jeopardize it.

"Come inside. Let me get you a drink," he says, studying my face.

I swallow hard, the realization of what I just saw choking me almost as much as my throbbing pulse. Adrenaline floods my veins, and if I'd known about that ink when he was lying on the ground…holy crap, what I would have done to him! "I don't need a drink."

Oh yes, I fucking do!

He doesn't listen and moments later, we're back in his office, me still barefoot. He leads me inside before slamming the door closed.

"You didn't have any security guys outside your office before," I say, my voice thick. "I'd have figured the manager of a club like this would have been a little more careful, especially with guys like Javier skulking around."

"Why are you so interested in him, anyway?"

I shrug. "Just an observation."

He turns to stare at me before grabbing two shot glasses and a bottle of what looks like whiskey. "It wasn't my choice to leave myself exposed like that," he says in a dark voice, pouring the amber-colored liquid. "But it's been handled."

He hands me one of the glasses. I swallow it down fast and it singes the sides of my esophagus, scorching a path to my empty belly.

"Good?" he asks, lifting an eyebrow.

I nod. "Yes," I choke out, gritting my teeth as he works. "So you run a nightclub, not very well, by the way, since it's deader than a cemetery down there. And you work with some seriously nefarious people. Interesting life you lead."

He chuckles. "That's probably the tamest way I've ever heard it described."

"So it's worse?"

"Let's just say it's a lot more colorful."

"Colorful…like blood red being the primary hue?"

"You ask a lot of questions for someone who doesn't like to answer them."

He's right. I'm the queen of evasion. But it keeps me alive, so divert, divert, divert!

Sergio grins at me and puts the glass to his lips before tipping it back.

I don't want to smile at him. I want to hate him for what he's planning to do to us. I want to incinerate him for working with the cartel. And most of all, I want to gut him for all of the bullshit he fed my brother about a buyout. He wants money, yeah. But I bet it won't come from us. Sergio's pockets are going to be lined by the Becerra Cartel if he can make the deal with us.

Our enemy.

Sergio doesn't give a shit about me and Nate.

He only cares about building his own empire.

And he'll sell us out to anyone who can clear his path.

I think I need another shot...

Because even though I know all of those things, it doesn't stop the butterflies from fluttering around in my gut.

It doesn't stop the tingles from shooting up my arm as his fingertips graze mine when he refills my glass.

And it doesn't stop my heart from leaping into my throat when his heated gaze lands on me, hot, hungry, and oh so intense.

I take the second shot, letting the liquid heat my insides. "Thanks," I mutter. I need to get out of here now. I've already seen, heard, and felt enough.

Now I have to figure out what to do with all of it.

He puts down his glass and inches toward me. Blood rushes between my ears, drowning out every sensible thought running through my mind right now.

"I'm going to leave now," I say, not moving a muscle as he continues to creep closer and closer like a predator eyeing his prey.

"Okay," he says, closing the rest of the distance between us. He runs a hand down my spine, stopping just above my ass. He presses me into him, his other hand tangled in my hair.

Oh, Jesus. What is he doing? And why am I letting him do it?

He drags my head backward, exposing the column of my neck. He sweeps his tongue down the side, eliciting a gasp from my lips. Wetness pools between my legs as he pushes me against the locked office door, his hands on either side of me, holding me captive in an invisible cage of unbridled lust.

His lips hover over mine, his hot breath fluttering against my prickled skin. "Is this what you wanted when you came looking for me before?" he growls, one of his hands inching up my skirt. He cups my pussy, sliding my panties aside and sliding his fingers inside of me. "Did you want me to do this?"

I shake my head, too breathless to even respond.

"No?" he whispers. "Did you want something else?"

I nod. My throat is so tight right now that I can't even squeak out a reply. But fuck yes, I wanted more. And I hated myself for it!

Still do.

His lips curl into a smirk and he attacks my mouth in a frenzy. Our tongues tussle, snaking around one another like heated coils of carnal lust. I fist his thick, dark hair, capturing his lower lip between my teeth as his fingers work my clit. With his one free hand, he yanks down the top of my dress, clasping his lips over each of my taut nipples, paying equal attention to both.

My head falls back against the wall, rolling left and right as he feasts on my breasts.

This is crazy! And wrong on so many levels!

But yet I can't make him stop.

Nor can I stop myself.

His thick cock is rock hard against me and my legs instinctively fall open, my pussy begging me to start the party. I yank off his belt and pull open his pants, sliding them to his knees.

He grabs a condom packet from his pocket and rolls it on, positioning himself at my entrance. I lift my leg, locking it around his waist as the head of his dick grazes my opening.

Oh my God, what the hell am I doing right now?

I have to stop! I have to push him away! I have to get out of here right now!

I grab his shirt, pulling him close, smothering his mouth with my own as he plunges into me. My pulse hammers against my throat, my mind an explosion of flashing lights. Electricity crackles between us, sizzling every single nerve ending in its path as he drives into me, deeper, harder, and with increasing urgency.

He lifts my other leg, burying himself deep inside of me. I try to bite back the screams, but they pierce the otherwise still air. My pussy clenches him tight as I arch my back, forcing my hips upward to meet his thrusts. I bury my head in his neck as he plunders me, wrecking me in the same instant. I quiver against him as the orgasm charges through my body like wildfire that scorches everything in its path. I throw my head back, my legs still wrapped tight around his torso as he thrusts a couple of more times and collapses against me.

We clutch each other, entwined, breathless, and sated.

It's perfect.

And horrible.

I need to get the fuck away from him immediately, if not sooner!

I slide down the length of his body, averting my gaze as I fix my dress. I can feel the heat from my body explode into my cheeks as I comb my fingers through my hair. I wiggle my toes on the floor.

At least running away will be easier without five-inch heels hampering me.

I clear my throat. "Thanks," I murmur because what the hell else am I supposed to say?

"That's it? Just a 'thanks?'"

"Thanks, it was good."

"Ouch." He drops the condom into the trash, zips up his pants, and steps away from me. "Never heard that one before."

I try to bite back the smile, but despite myself and the completely messed up situation, I can't. "First time for everything?"

"I guess." He grins. "You got a name? I don't usually ask, but I don't know. You're…different."

I clear my throat. "Um, Jae."

"Jae as in…?"

"Jae," I say firmly. "Just Jae."

"Okay, 'Just Jae.'" He grins. "You look like you need another drink. Can I tempt you?"

I shake my head and swallow hard. "I'm fine, thanks. I have to go."

"You shouldn't be driving right now. You sucked down those two shots real fast."

"I shouldn't have done a lot of things," I say in a low voice, my eyes tangling with his. "But I'm making the smart decision and leaving before I do any more of them."

He places his hand over mine, the one I'm using to clutch the doorknob. "You didn't ask my name. Don't you wanna know who I am?"

My lips stretch into a tight line. "That's the problem. I already do. And it's why I need to go."

Chapter Four
JAELYN

Once I am outside of the club and away from the man who is equal parts devastatingly handsome and just plain devastating, I dart across the parking lot and run toward my car. Short, sharp gasps slip from my lips as tiny bits of gravel and sand slice at my bare feet once again. I clutch my one remaining shoe, ready to fling it at anyone who dares lay a finger on me in my mad dash.

But nobody shows up to scuffle with me a second time.

And good old Javier is probably getting nice and liquored up, courtesy of one Sergio Villani.

A deep flush heats my cheeks as I pull open the door to my Mercedes G wagon and slide into the driver's seat. My head collapses against the seat as I slam my fists on the steering wheel.

"Fuck!" I scream, the piercing sound shattering the otherwise still air.

I came here on a mission, almost getting myself completely maimed…or worse…in the process. I did my reconnaissance, confirmed that Sergio is working with the Becerra Cartel, and fucked the target!

What was I thinking?!

My chest heaves, my heart pumping furiously as I slam my foot on the gas and head back to the Sapphire Lounge. The streetlights blind me as I swerve in and out of lanes on the Strip, weaving around cars not going fast enough for my liking.

How could I give in to the temptation of forgoing my plans and throwing myself in the arms of the man who has just become one of our mortal enemies?

And if he's in bed with the organization who killed my parents, then he's as ruthless, calculating, and murderous as they are.

He, like the head of the Becerra Cartel, needs to suffer.

And I need to have my damn head examined for letting myself get sucked into his funnel cloud…his delicious, sensual, and very carnal fu—

"Stop thinking about him!" I let out a loud screech. That's all! I just have to forget what I did. It meant nothing. I was charged up on adrenaline and let lust consume my sensibilities.

Period!

I make a sharp left down the road leading to the club. It's dark, desolate, and not frequently traveled, which makes the club well protected. It also adds to the air of exclusivity, but let's be real. Security is a necessity, and being in the middle of the desert shields us from the very people we've been trying to evade.

Nate needs to stop this meeting from taking place!

I speed down the road and maneuver my car into my designated VIP parking spot. I slip on my emergency pair of heels before I get out and run inside, past the staggering hordes of people clamoring to get through the deep blue glass doors.

I don't bother searching the main floor because I know my brother.

Sure enough, I find him in his office, huddled over a group of security monitors.

"We…have…to…cancel," I rasp, clutching the back of a chair for balance since my impromptu jog has me completely out of breath and energy.

"Cancel what?" he asks.

"The meeting! With Villani!"

Nate jumps up from his chair and joins me on the couch where I've just collapsed against the luxe pebbled leather. "Jae, what the hell are you talking about? Tell me you didn't fucking stake out his office like I specifically told you not to!"

I take a few gulps of air and he shoves a shot of vodka into my hands. "Calm down and talk to me," he murmurs, sinking down next to me.

"O…kay," I say, my hands still shaking. "Don't be mad…"

Nate rolls his eyes and scrubs a hand down the front of his face. "Goddammit, Jae…"

"Look, I know it seems bad, but I did what I had to do."

"So you lied to me."

"Well, of course I did! I had to! I didn't go there to gossip with those twits and drink cosmopolitans all night long!"

Nate throws his hands into the air. "You're gonna give a me a heart attack one of these days, do you realize that?"

I manage a small smile. "Eh, I just keep you on your toes."

"Talk," he says in a stern voice.

"I met Sergio Villani," I say in a low voice. "And for the record, the guy is a complete dick. He's arrogant, and egotistical, and… and…" I let out a huff before the other more salacious words come spilling out of my mouth. "Just a total prick, completely full of himself. He walked around like he owned the place."

"Which he does," Nate affirms.

I let out a frustrated sigh. "Right. Anyway, when I went to his office, he was about to meet with a group of guys. Real dirty scumbag types. Things kind of went sideways, though. The meeting didn't happen."

"Why not?"

I shrug. "Something about their boss not being there in person. Sergio got a little bit pissed off at that and refused to talk to them."

"I don't get it. How does any of that tell you we need to cancel the meeting? We needed to find out his agenda…what he wants from us and who he's working wi—"

"He's working with the Becerra Cartel!" I sputter.

Nate's lips twist, his eyes blazing with pent-up fury at the mere mention of the name. "How do you know that, Jae?" he hisses, inching closer to me.

"Don't be mad," I whisper.

"Oh, fuck, I wish you'd stop saying that," he mutters, sweeping a hand through his hair.

"The guys he turned away got a little, uh, handsy with me. He stopped them, kicked them out of the club. But when I walked to my car, one of them grabbed me. Attacked me." I bite down on my lower lip, opting against reliving the disgusting experience. "Sergio and his guys came to my rescue. But as they were dragging him away, I saw it. The same symbol that was sliced into the headrest of Dad's car. It was them, Nate. They were there to discuss something, a partnership."

Nate's head falls into his hands and he mumbles to himself before he looks up at me. "Do you realize how stupid it was for you to go after him like that? How dangerous? What if they hadn't gotten to you in time? You could have been hurt, or worse."

"I know but—"

"No!" he thunders, putting his hands on my shoulders. "I've already lost so much, Jae. Things could have gone in a very different direction tonight. You got lucky, do you understand that? You escaped some potentially serious shit!"

"Yes, I get that! But Nate, I escaped. Just like you said." I shake my head. "Don't you understand you're the most important person in my life? I won't just sit back and let anyone bulldoze you or what you built! To me, you're worth the risk." I manage a quivery smile. "And I know you'd do the same for me." Tears spring to my eyes for the second time tonight. "And we're all we have now," I whisper, squeezing his hand.

"I should have never asked you to go there," he mumbles. "I'd have never forgiven myself if anything happened to you."

"Hey, we're together in this," I say, nestling my head against his chest. "I'd do anything for you."

"And I was stupid to think you'd actually follow instruction," he says with a smirk. "I mean, seriously, kid. You're about as subtle as a hand grenade."

"Yes. I can't argue with that." I smile. That's actually kind of an understatement, and we both know it.

Still, it makes me happy to know that no matter what, I'll do anything for him.

And I know he'd do the same for me.

"So what happens now?" I ask. "I mean, we definitely need to cancel, right?"

Nate lets out a deep sigh but doesn't respond.

I pull away from him, my eyes wide. "Wait, you're not considering keeping that meeting, are you? After what I found out?"

Nate frowns at me, his forehead pinched. "Jae, do I have to spell it out for you? If Villani is working with the Becerra Cartel, canceling the meeting isn't gonna save us. The reason you're here right now is because they didn't know who you were."

Well, yeah, that and the *other* thing.

"If they're here, if they're trying to get inside, there's no fortress strong enough to keep them out. We have to come up with another plan. Or…" He pauses, rubbing the back of his neck.

"Or what?" I say, my spine stiff as I feel the tension weaving through each vertebrae.

"Or we leave Vegas. For good."

"Well, there is no fucking way I'm going to run away again! They don't get to keep uprooting us from our lives, Nate! Running is for the weak!"

"Running kept us alive," he hisses at me.

"Yeah, well, now we have…you know, stuff," I sputter in frustration, throwing up my hands. "Like money. And a crew. And *money*!" I swallow hard, thoughts popping between my ears like bullets. "We can stand our ground. We can win this! But it has to be on our terms. If Becerra is moving in, let's cockblock the bastards! They're out for blood, so let's give it to them!" I will not leave. I will not run again. I will defend what we have left because it's everything to us. My pulse throbs against the side of my neck. There has to be something we can do, some way to keep control, some person we can manipulate!

"Oh, so you wanna take on the cartel?" Nate shakes his head and goes over to his desk. He pours himself a shot and gulps it down, narrowing his eyes at me once his glass is empty. "That's your big play?"

With a thumping heart, a slow smile lifts my lips. The fog lifts and I can finally see what we need to do and how we can do it. The wheels turn so fast, I can almost smell smoke billowing out of my ears, but holy shit, I have the answer. Now I just need to get Nate onboard. "Yes, take on the cartel! That's exactly what I want to do, but I don't want to do it alone." I take a deep breath, bracing myself for the accolades that better tumble from my brother's lips when he hears this stroke of brilliance. "Let's use our prospective partner Sergio Villani and his desire to control Vegas as part of our battle plan, brother."

"And how exactly do you expect that to work? All of a sudden, we just strip down and jump into bed with the families that are looking to snuff us out?"

Yeah, he doesn't need to know I kind of already did that…

"Well, you refuse to cancel the meeting. So let's be ready. First, we'll let him think we're not interested in selling, for any amount. Let him see how much he has to gain by grabbing hold of our business. Make him work for it. We put up a front, tell him there's no way we'd sell, that he'll never get what we've built. Guys like him love a challenge. Besides, based on what I saw tonight, they definitely need an injection of people and cash since that one club was pretty much on life support. We make it too tempting for him to walk away and then we agree to a partnership on *our* terms."

"Wait, so you're saying we need to sell?"

I look at Nate. "I'm saying that we need to consider taking on investors if we want to keep what we have. It's not an outright sell, but yeah, screw it. If we can partner with them before Becerra can, we get Villani's protection. That's what we really need if we want to keep ruling this city. So what if we give up a piece? We'll still own most of the pie."

"That's assuming they go along with the plan of not being in complete control."

"Some is better than none. And none is pretty much what they have right now, so…"

"And if the thugs in the cartel ride shotgun with him the night of the meeting? If we don't have a chance to execute your plan because we're busy getting executed ourselves?" Nate quirks a brow at me.

I shrug. "We've taken them out before. We can do it again. I'm not worried."

"You're kind of insane, you know that, right?"

"And you're kind of in love with my idea." I smirk at him. "Admit it! You like the plan!"

"It keeps us in the driver's seat."

I nod. "We set the terms when we finally have Villani begging us for a piece of the action. Our partnership will keep Becerra far away because they won't want to declare war on the Italians and risk getting skewered by their Russian allies unless they have a death wish."

Nate strokes the stubble on his chin. "It would preserve the club and our business—"

"And our lives."

"You're assuming we're not too late and that Becerra hasn't already convinced Villani to partner."

"I'm being optimistic. Keep your friends close and your enemies closer. If we can make it seem like we don't need Villani, he'll be back to convince us that we do. And he'll have no clue how right he will be."

"You really think this can work?"

"Positively." I don't mention the fact that it lets me put my powers of seduction to blissfully good use with Sergio Villani. Nate wouldn't appreciate that too much.

Make him want me.

Er, I mean, the clubs.

He'll be putty in my hands. Guys like him love a challenge. They always take the bait if they think they're the ones running the show.

When we send him away with his dick between his legs, he'll be back, guns blazing. His little family unit won't be happy to hear that he couldn't deliver. So he's going to do whatever he can to reverse his luck.

I'm positive of it.

As positive as I am about the butterflies dancing around in my belly when I remember the way his fingertips grazed my heated skin only a short time ago, and the tingling in my groin when the memory of his body pressed against me springs to mind.

Putty in my hands, hm?

Or did I mean that I'd be putty in *his*?

Chapter Five
SERGIO

"You cut off Javier's fucking hand!" My brother Matteo thunders, slamming his fist on my desk later that night. "Are you insane?"

I shrug.

Maybe.

No, scratch that.

Definitely.

"He got handsy with the wrong person."

"Who? The girl? How many times have I told you not to mix business with pleasure?"

"Enough so that I tune it out every time you say it?"

He stomps across my office and then stomps back to lash out some more. "I knew this was a bad idea. You trying to work a deal with the cartel?" He shakes his head. "It should have been me," he grumbles.

"So that's the big problem, isn't it?" I say, jumping out of my chair. "That I'm the one who handled the situation. That I was the one who got the chance to make the deal!"

"It was a stupid decision made by the syndicate families," he mutters. "And by Papa. Now look at the shit storm that's blown in here because of the way you handled things!"

"Listen," I say, standing in front of him. "Sure, maybe you'd have done things differently. Maybe you wouldn't have gotten so fired up when you found out that he attacked an innocent girl. You've always had more patience than me in dealing with the real derelicts."

He rolls his eyes. "I'm gonna assume that's some backhanded compliment."

I grin at him. "Yeah, sure, assume away. You know what they say about people who assume, right?"

He flips me off and keeps pacing. "You sent a message to Becerra, and that was after he offered you a piece of his distribution."

"If he was serious about working together, he should have gotten his fat ass here the other night instead of sending his dipshit crew in his place. But he didn't give a damn. He sent his own message by not showing up. And that message was 'hey, kid, get ready to eat shit pie and beg for seconds!'"

"Look, we're close to taking full control of this city, Sergio. You're about to hand Nate Torres a windfall for access to his pussy empire, and we could have had the chance to hook into another drug pipeline, the biggest one. Everything was in place until you fucked it up!"

"It's not like I killed the guy," I say, sweeping a hand through my hair.

"You made a statement," Matteo groans. "And now we all have to deal with the fallout."

"Look, I'm sure Becerra will make contact and we'll see what he has to say. As far as I'm concerned, we're even now. He disrespected me by not coming, I cut off his guy's hand. He's lucky I didn't cut off the whole damn arm."

"Yeah, and that would have made you even how?" Matteo's eyes darken. "Tell me about the girl. Why was she targeted?"

I avert my eyes, fumbling with a pen. "She was with me when he showed up here."

"Here at the club?"

"No, here in my office."

Matteo presses a hand to his forehead. "And why was she in your office, Jesus Christ?"

"Relax, she wasn't inside." Well, not until later, but I'll keep that quiet for now. He doesn't need any more ammunition against me. Knowing him, he's filing it all away for the next sit-down with the syndicate families. Besides, I wouldn't put it past him to stick this pen in my eye socket if he had all the sordid details of our little tryst, and I'm kind of attached to my eyeballs. "I guess he wanted to get back at me by going after her."

"And who is she?"

"Don't know."

"Are you fucking kidding me? How can you not know? She didn't have a name?"

"She didn't offer it."

"And you didn't ask?"

"Not my MO."

"Serge, you cannot screw up this meeting with Torres. If you don't deliver, you give up any shot at grabbing that seat, do you understand?"

"And since I'm sure you're rooting against me, challenge accepted."

Matteo lets out a little roar, I guess out of frustration. If I were him, I'd probably do the same thing. I'm fucking infuriating sometimes, I know it.

"I have to get back to New York at some point," he says. "I can't stay out here forever to make sure you don't fuck shit up beyond repair. I need to feel like I can trust you with our operations out here, and right now, I don't."

I can't blame him, not that I'd ever admit it. I let my anger rage and didn't think about the consequences. And yeah, I may have gotten a little crazy with that machete. I probably went overboard when I slammed it down on his wrist. Enrico read me the riot act when we were alone. But I couldn't get the brunette's tear-streaked face out of my mind. She'd been so sexy and self-assured in the club, white fucking hot.

But outside, after Javier attacked her, she seemed…I don't know. Broken? Shattered? Something just…flipped.

And the sex…fuck.

Incredible is an understatement.

I couldn't understand why she'd been so quick to walk away from that.

Before she left that night, she said she knew me, said she had to leave before making another bad decision.

It's ironic that I did exactly that because of her.

I'd be lying if I said I haven't lain awake at night thinking about my dick buried deep inside of her and those final words she'd spoken afterward, wondering if I'd have been able to make her stay if I tried a little harder.

Speaking of…

Who the hell was she?

And how can I find her again?

Because I'm damn curious to find out what bad decisions she was on the brink of making.

Chapter Six
SERGIO

"*This place is key to our expansion plan in Vegas, Sergio. Don't fuck up the meeting or I'll put you on a plane back to Sicily and you'll spend the rest of your life picking goddamn grapes!*"

It's been a week since my fallout with Javier, and Matteo's caustic words still ring out in my mind as I swing my Porsche Panamera around the circular driveway leading up to the Sapphire Lounge, Nate Torres's very exclusive night club. I've spent the majority of the ride in my own head, half-listening to my guys, Bruno and Enrico. I grit my teeth, squeezing the steering wheel tight as the tires squeal to a halt outside of the faceted, blue glass doors.

It really pisses me off when he pulls that 'I'm the big brother, I'm the boss of you' shit.

I don't care that he's next in line to take over the family businesses once my father retires. He doesn't get to fly into my territory, tell me how to do my fucking job, and then fly out after he collects his cash...cash I made for the family syndicate! Besides, I'm not the one he needs to worry about. He should be more afraid of how my youngest brother Roman will set fire to our Manhattan empire. Matteo put Roman temporarily in charge of New York operations while he and his wife Heaven are out here living it up in Sin City, and if I know Roman, he's stirring up plenty of shit for Matteo to wade through when he gets back.

I look to my right, catching the eye of my cousin Bruno. "Are we clear on how this meeting is gonna go down?"

Bruno nods, nodding toward Enrico sitting in the backseat. "We're ready."

I push open the door and step onto the pavement, sliding my key and a fifty-dollar bill into the valet's hand.

The valet nods and slides into the front seat, maneuvering it into an empty spot with all of the other high-roller cars — Maseratis, Lambos, Ferraris, and Bugattis.

There's a shit ton of money here tonight, and plenty more for us to steal.

We just need total control of this place.

And that's only the beginning.

Good God, the amount of cash we can funnel through this place and its sister clubs is staggering. And once I close the deal, I'm gonna be the one to run the whole operation. At least, that's my plan.

How can they deny me if I'm the one who lays claim to it?

The shit with the cartel will fizzle out, and they can go and screw themselves if they don't like my decision to opt out of their proposed partnership.

If I can get my hands on this goldmine, we won't need the Becerra Cartel.

They, like everyone else here in Sin City, will need *us*.

It's a very good position to be in.

I stare at the entrance of the Sapphire Lounge, my guys flanking me on each side. I take a deep breath. Dry desert air mixed with sex and wanton lust. It's an intoxicating scent, one that seems to hang low and heavy over the very long line of anxious patron hopefuls looping around the corner.

It's hard to believe that the guy running this place has transformed it into the hottest club in the city. It's nestled at the far end of the Vegas strip, a little off the beaten path and in a location that gives it an exclusive allure. It's all glamour with its sleek architecture, rich foliage, and nondescript signage.

You don't need a sign to tell you you're here.

The who's who of Vegas make it damn clear that you're in the ranks of the VIPs once you step through the signature double doors.

He who controls the Sapphire Lounge controls Las Vegas nightlife, especially with the sister lounges scattered around the city — Platinum, Ruby Red, and Emerald. This cluster of nightclubs makes more money in a given night than all of the others in Vegas put together for a whole week. Hottest bartenders and waitresses, sexiest dancers, tightest pussies.

There's nothing off limits at these places.

And that's why they ended up on our radar.

The future of our grand plan to command every last corner of Las Vegas lies just beyond those double doors.

I need to make this goddamn deal!

I walk right up to one of the security guys manning the door. "Sergio Villani, here to see Nate Torres."

He looks at me, and suddenly the typical bouncer dickhead expression disappears from his face. "Mr. Villani," he says. He pulls out his phone. "Mr. Torres mentioned you'd be joining us tonight. I'll let him know you're here."

I give him a swift nod and he ushers us into a roped-off area that's just beyond the main doors. It's a small lounge, empty with the exception of a bar.

"Hey," I say to the bouncer. "We're actually gonna take a walk around the main floor. He can find us out there."

The bouncer nods and points us in the direction of the main area. Once he disappears, I turn to Bruno and Enrico.

"I'm going to take a lap. I wanna check a few things out. Go grab a drink but keep your hands to yourself." The corners of my lips curl upward. "Show some self-control for once, yeah?"

Bruno snickers and he and Enrico head toward one of the bars, leaving me alone to take in the scene.

Pulsating music vibrates the floor under my feet, and on either side of me are darkened rooms brimming with bodies — drunk, high, and writhing against each other. But the room I'm in, the center room, doesn't have a dance floor. It looks as if it is made entirely of glass. All of the ceiling beams, the columns, the bar — everything has a glossy sheen that glows blue under the flashing ceiling lights. There are white leather couches lining the perimeter of the room that take on a purple hue under the blacklights. The space is packed with men and women who came for the erotic entertainment, the line for the bar at least ten people deep.

And they're all drooling at the people working behind the bar in the meantime.

The owner knows exactly how to reel in the bucks, I'll give him that.

I lean against a wall, crossing my legs at the ankle. Eight months ago, my family partnered with three other families to form a consortium, the Marcones, the Severinovs, and the Salesis, with the goal of commanding the major gambling hubs in the United States.

Las Vegas is our first major conquest.

And for as much control as we have over this town, we have nothing when it comes to nightlife. Hotels and restaurants, yeah, we're covered. But our nightlife is more like foreplay for the main event.

And we want the multiple orgasms, too.

It all starts with the Sapphire Lounge.

I glance over toward the stage. Glittering white lights shimmer down the back curtain, and two side stages are in full swing, dancers swinging around poles, climbing them in what look like eight-inch heels.

I'm about to turn away because if you've seen one great pair of tits, you've seen them all. And as an aficionado who doesn't go a night without them in my hands or in my mouth, I choose to scout out my target instead.

I'm sure he's doing the same thing right at this minute.

When Torres agreed to take the meeting, I figured he was hungry. From what I've heard, he doesn't ever take meetings and he never shows his face in the clubs. He's elusive as hell, which means to me that someone, or multiple someones, want him dead.

But that's his fucking problem.

Mine is proving my worth to our syndicate.

And that means I don't leave here without this guy's agreement to sell.

"You look like you could use a drink," a sultry voice murmurs against my ear. I take in a sharp breath, a rich, perfumed scent immediately infusing my senses. It smells so familiar…

A quick twist to my left puts me face to face with a raven-haired girl in her early twenties. My breath hitches as her porn-star body grazes my side and piercing green eyes stun me into silence.

It's…her.

Just Jae.

The one who's starred in all of my twisted, X-rated fantasies for the better part of the past week.

The one who said she knew who I was before disappearing from my club and my life.

I guess she didn't want me to know she worked for the competition, especially since said competition is kicking my club's ass.

When the cloud of lust and confusion lifts, my mouth finally decides to wake up. "Is that an offer? I was hoping I'd get another shot."

She cocks her head to the side, her long eyelashes fluttering over black-rimmed eyes. "I just take the orders. I don't fill them."

Hm. I can think of a lot of things I'd like to fill *her* with.

Again.

I grin. "So you work here, then? No wonder why you didn't bother mentioning that the other night."

"I do work here." A slow nod follows, a seductive smile lifting her lips. "Among other things."

"That sounds promising," I say, my voice husky. Matteo's warning rings out between my ears again, but I silence his annoying-as-fuck voice even though I know my focus is wavering. Red warning lights are flashing in my periphery, and it's time to get my shit in order and mentally prepare for the meeting. But dammit, this girl is making my brain short-circuit and I can't seem to stop the impending damage. I feel like a runaway train right now, and the end of the tracks is rapidly approaching. Still, it doesn't slow me down one bit. "What kinds of things?"

The girl closes the space between us, trailing her hand down the side of my jacket. She flips her hair so that it cascades down one bare, tanned shoulder, leaning in so close I can almost taste her cherry-red lips. And oh, God, I wanna take a bite… Her voice drops conspiratorially. "The kinds of things that keep entitled, thug assholes like you away from things that belong to *me*."

My jaw drops and I recoil just as I spot Bruno and Enrico approaching us through the crowd. "Who the fuck are you?" I hiss. "Since we never actually covered that the other night."

"Who I am doesn't matter. *Yet*," she says in a sweet voice, twisting around as two other men in dark suits head in my direction. "What matters is what I can do to you. And trust me, it won't be as painfully excruciating as you think." She grins, a dimple appearing in her left cheek. "It will be worse."

My cock is in such a twist over that total mind-fuck that I can barely squeeze out a response. It doesn't help that her perfect ass swinging from left to right is the sum total of my focus right now. And seconds later, she's sucked up into a crowd of people.

"What the hell was that all about?" Bruno hisses, keeping an eye on the suits and their menacing faces.

"Not sure," I grumble, squaring my shoulders as the suits stop in front of me. I rub the back of my neck. If the stress knot wasn't tight before, it's damn close to paralyzing me now. I don't know who that woman was, but she clearly knows me. And from the sounds of it, she's not my biggest fan.

Too bad. I really had high hopes about how I could change that opinion.

"Mr. Villani," one of the suits says in a deep voice. "Come with us."

The guys and I follow them to a private elevator which goes down, not up. Interesting. Maybe there's something metaphorical about sitting in the criminal underbelly of this salacious haven for the sex-depraved.

My ass will happily grace that throne.

Because that's the only way this chapter ends.

Regardless of what the sexy-as-fuck waitress on a power trip thinks.

We get off the elevator and my hand instinctively grazes the gun pressed against my back. I don't usually take meetings in dark, convoluted mazes with only one way in or out. And I sure as hell don't take meetings where I'm not the one in control.

So right now, I'm at a double disadvantage.

Matteo wouldn't be thrilled.

The suits finally stop in front of a door and knock three times before a voice tells them to come inside.

One of the guys pushes open the door and a tall, dark-haired man stands up from behind a long desk. I reach out to shake his hand but he only stares at it. I lift an eyebrow as he folds his arms over his chest.

"This isn't a social call," he grunts. "So let's not pretend it is."

What a dick. But since said dick has something I want, I let it go, fighting the urge to pound in his jaw for disrespecting me like that. He obviously doesn't know who he's dealing with.

But then again, neither do I. Nobody knows much about this guy, where he came from, and where he got the money to turn one club into a sex conglomerate. And to be honest, I don't really give a fuck about his past. I just want to secure my future, and I need his signature to do it.

"Fine," I say, my voice strained. "You know why I'm here. I want to buy you out. Sapphire, Emerald, Ruby Red, Platinum — everything. And I'm prepared to pay."

"I'm not for sale," he responds in a short voice.

My eyes widen. "When I contacted you, you said you'd be open to negotiations."

"I lied."

I clench my fists, rage bubbling in my chest. "Why did you take the fucking meeting if you had no intention to sell? Why waste my goddamn time?"

"Because I had to show you that for all of the 'influence' you think you have here in Vegas, you'll never get what's mine.

You'll never own this city, Villani. I've worked long and hard to build all of this, and your muscle doesn't mean shit to me. I'm not afraid of you or your..." He nods toward Bruno and Enrico, flashing a smirk that makes my fists tingle with destructive energy. "Associates."

"Do you realize how much of this city we control, Torres? We own the people who have the power to make decisions...do you get that? If you try to do any business in this county, we will shut your fucking ass down, do you understand?"

"So now you're threatening me?" he asks, his expression dark. "In my club? That's ballsy, Villani. You do remember that you and your dipshit pals here are just a little bit outnumbered."

"That's right."

My head jerks toward the open door when I hear the sultry female voice once again. Her expression matches that of Torres, and for as vicious as she wants me to think she is, I'd still bend her over a couch and fuck her senseless if given the chance.

"Jaelyn, I told you to stay out of this," Torres grunts through clenched teeth.

Her nostrils flare. "I'm just trying to make sure that these guys deliver a very clear message back to their mafioso buddies that they can't bully us!"

"And I said I'd handle it, didn't I?"

The girl, Jaelyn, narrows her clear eyes to slits. "Have you? Because they're still standing here!"

The dots are connecting fast and furious and I don't like the fucking picture at all!

I narrow my eyes at Jaelyn. "So the other night was just a little reconnaissance, huh? Well played. You'll find out really fast how this game ends now."

Torres rolls his eyes and looks back at me. "My sister is very loyal. Almost to a fault."

"That's the thing about family," I seethe. "They always have your back. No matter what, no matter where, no matter who. And I think you know exactly who I'm referring to when I say *family*, don't you?"

"Is that supposed to scare me, Villani?" Torres asks. "Because it only makes me want to bring you down harder."

"It's not supposed to scare you," I say. "It's just supposed to wake you up to reality. That is, *if* you survive long enough to wake up."

Torres walks out from behind the desk, about three inches taller than me when we're standing toe to toe. But I don't cower.

Ever.

This is our fucking town, and if he won't give up his piece of the pie nicely, I'll just have to use other methods to show him how painful a rejected offer can really be.

For *him*.

"If you think that dragging me down here so you can swing your dick around was a smart move, you're wrong," I growl. "I came here prepared to make a deal, a deal you led me to believe could happen for the right price."

"Don't blame me because you couldn't read between the lines," he seethes right back. "Italians, Russians…who the fuck else do you have in your little power circle? Not that it matters. I've battled with enough scumbags to know one thing. You find their weakness and expose it, like a nerve. Then they back down because they don't want anyone to know that there's a kink in their armor and that their armor is actually made of fucking paper."

Blood rushes between my ears as his venomous tone slices into the air between us. My gun is burning a hole in my pants right now. I wanna grab it and fire a shot right between his fucking beady ass eyes.

"See, that's the difference between us and the scumbags you've dealt with. We don't have any weaknesses. Just a whole lot of strength in the form of cash. Taking over your places would have saved us the trouble of building new, but because you decided to fuck us over, that's exactly what we'll do. Build bigger and better. And we're gonna squeeze the fucking life out of you, sucking every penny out of your little pussy palaces." I force a hateful smile. "And when we're done…when *you're* done…I'm gonna watch you run from this town with that dick in your hand because there won't be anyone left to swing it at." I glare at him, pushing my chest against him. "I will crush you and take everything you have. Then I'll really go to work on you. and if you're wondering, that's not a threat. It's a fucking promise!"

"You know what you can do with your fucking promises? You can shove them right up your—"

"Jae!" Torres says in a stern voice as his sister starts to lay into me. "Enough."

"Well, are you just going to let him talk to you like that?" Jaelyn shrieks, her hands on her hips. I can't stop my eyes from sliding to my left where she's standing, all five feet of her, in that borderline obscene black dress. She's got a lot of rage packed into that tight little body, and I have plenty of thoughts about how to drain it from her.

Torres looks at me, a smirk on his smug face. Fucking A, I wanna bust up that jaw of his. Shatter it. Demolish it, even!

"I am the host here, right? It's not polite to rough anyone up in my place." He leans close to me. "So I'm gonna give you a chance to tuck your own dick between your legs, turn around, and get the hell out of here. I hope your little crew takes the news better than you. When I send a message, no response is ever necessary. They're gonna realize soon enough who I am and what I can do." He pauses with a snicker. "Maybe they should have sent in their A Team this time. Maybe I'd have been a little more open to the 'offer' if it was delivered by a different messenger."

Anger percolates deep in my chest, a slow, rumbling explosion about to erupt out of me. Streaks of red flash before my eyes, and before I can stop it, I launch my fist, firing a shot to the side of his nose. He stumbles, barely, and I wish I could say that the sight of his blood makes me feel better about being duped.

It doesn't.

And even if I could pound the shit out of his face, it still wouldn't be enough. He cut deep with his words, and now I have to turn around and take this shit show back to my family.….my family who already had zero faith I could pull this off. I'd convinced them I could make the deal, to prove I could run the expansion project, to rub Matteo's nose in my conquest. I was supposed to lay claim to this goldmine, dammit!

Instead, I walked into a setup where Torres disrespected me, tore me down, and now, has the fucking balls to laugh at me.

I grit my teeth, my pulse thrumming as I pull out my gun and point it directly at his face. Bruno and Enrico pull out their guns, one on Torres, one on Jaelyn.

"Do you really think it's a smart idea to pull out your weapons? You do know you have to get out of here, right? And my guys have eyes on everything?" Torres taunts, sweeping a hand under his nose to catch the drizzle of blood.

Out of the corner of my eye, I see Jaelyn's eyes flash just as she swings her arm around, knocking Enrico's gun to the ground.

A loud crack explodes into the air, and I throw myself against her, pushing her to the floor as everyone else in the room ducks and weaves to escape the stray bullet that fired from Enrico's gun.

I stare down at Jaelyn, into her hate-filled eyes, feeling her heart race against my chest. She reaches up and grips my throat tight, cutting off my air as her legs squeeze against the sides of my torso. "Who needs guns?" she hisses through clenched teeth.

I pry her hands away from my neck, slamming her hands to the floor above her head. "So you like it rough, huh?" I growl. "I'll remember that for next time."

"Fuck you!" she says, fighting against me with a brutish energy that makes my cock thicken, despite the fact that I have her hulking brother hovering over me. I stand up, grabbing her by the arms and yanking her up along with me. Enrico's gun is back in his hand, back on her.

She looks at him, tilting her head to the side. "Are we really doing this again? Wanna know what I'll do to you the second time around? I won't just knock that gun out of your hand. I'll take it and shove it down your fucking throat!"

"Jae!" Torres thunders.

"*What?*" she screams, balling her hands into tight fists. "I am trying to defend our empire here, Nate! I mean, he threw a punch at you, for Christ's sake!"

He levels her with a stare. "Take them upstairs and make sure they get the fuck out of my club." He looks back at me. "We're finished. *Capice?*"

"We may be finished for now, but this ain't the end, Torres. *Comprende?*" I say in a mocking tone.

"You're just letting them go?" Jaelyn says, her cheeks flushed pink. "That's all? After they threatened us?"

Torres shrugs. "I have something they want. Something they need. I'm the one in control here." He looks at me. "Empty threats don't scare me. Nothing does, you get that, Villani?"

I nod. "That's because you're fucking stupid, Torres. It's just a question of finding the right nerve to expose, yeah? Isn't that what you said earlier?"

"Good luck with that," he says. "And thanks for coming by. Always nice to meet the competition before I crush it."

I tuck my gun into the back of my pants. "I'd be careful about where you swing your hammer, Torres. You don't wanna hit the wrong target. It might hit back and crack open your fucking skull."

I stalk out of the office with Bruno and Enrico in tow, headed for the elevator.

High heels click on the floor behind us as I stab the Up button and the doors slide open.

"Hey! He said for me to show you out!" Jaelyn pushes past the guys and plants herself right next to me. Anger hums through her, the negative, yet very carnal, energy crackling between us.

"We don't need an escort, sweetheart," I grumble, pulling out my phone and staring at the screen. Texts from Matteo wanting an update. I swallow down the expletives sitting on the tip of my tongue.

If I didn't know better, I'd think he set this whole thing up just to make me crash and burn.

Then again, that would clear the way for him to swoop in and save the day.

I grip the phone tight, a sharp breath expelling from my mouth.

I wouldn't put it past him. He's always gotta be the one to bring the big deals to the table. He'd never like the idea of me one-upping him. And this would have been a big win for us. A big win for *me*.

And that's why the negotiations have just begun.

Even if Torres doesn't know it yet.

I'm getting his business.

His kingdom will be *mine*.

"What's the matter, *sweetheart*? Are you trying to figure out how to spin this meeting so you don't look like a complete fuck-up in front of your family?" Jaelyn says with a self-satisfied smirk on her face.

I've never hit a woman before, never felt enough rage to actually take a hand to one, but this bitch has wiggled under my skin and I can't decide if I wanna ass-ram her or tear that tongue out of her mouth with my bare hands. "No, I'm actually trying to kill you with my mind right now," I sneer, shoving my phone back into my pocket. "And I need you to shut the hell up so I can concentrate."

"Well, don't try too hard," she coos. "I wouldn't want you to waste too many brain cells since it doesn't seem like you have many to spare."

The elevator dings once we get back up to the ground floor and the doors open. Jaelyn shoves Bruno and Enrico out, giggling as they stumble into the main club floor as she loops her arm around mine. She presses herself tight against me, locking my arm with her vise-like fingers. "Don't get excited," she murmurs. "I just want to be sure you stay on track and do not pass go. Because there's no get-out-of-jail-free card for you, Sergio. If you get thrown into the cage, you stay there."

I stop short as we pass a thick glass column with lights streaming through it, backing her against it. She lands against the glass with a tiny yelp, clearly shocked that I had the balls to turn the tables, in *her* place. I can feel Jaelyn's heart pick up speed as I shove my chest against hers, the pressure forcing her tits to creep upward, closer and closer to the low neckline of her dress. I lick my lips as I stare down at the luscious peaks, dragging my eyes toward her fiery gaze.

"Like what you see?" she asks in a breathy voice. "Because I'll fucking poke your eyes out with my fingernails if you stare at them for a second longer."

"Oh, so you don't like me looking at them? Is that why you've used every chance you can to shove them in my face?" I back away, a grimace twisting my lips. "You want me to touch instead?" I grip her hip with one hand, slowly sliding it up the side of her torso. Her body trembles beneath my fingertips, but she makes no moves to stop me. Her chest heaves, her legs falling open against my knee.

"Take your hand off of me," she snips, pushing her shoulder into my chest. But I have too firm a grip on her, and if I'm being honest, I'm finally starting to relax and enjoy my visit to the Sapphire Lounge. I'm not really in a rush to let her go.

And she doesn't seem to be fighting against me too hard, either.

"Jaelyn! There's a problem with one of the girls!" A high-pitched voice laced with panic pierces the carnal fog clouding us and I loosen my grip on her, backing away. Her full lips stretch into a tight line and in that second, I'm imagining all sorts of things I'd like those lips to do. X-rated images wallpaper my mind when a searing pain shoots up my calf as she drives her high-heel into the toe of my leather shoe.

A loud groan escapes through my clenched teeth and she pushes past me. "Gotta go!" she says in a cheerful voice with a small wave. "Fuck you very much for coming!" And just before she turns away, she flashes a sparkling white smile, the brightest and widest one I've seen all night.

So She-Devil *does* know how to do more with her mouth than just spew venom.

Nice.

Let the fantasizing continue.

My eyes drop to the tip of my shoe. She really dug in that heel. Thank fuck for quality Italian leather. I wince, putting weight on it as I turn toward Bruno and Enrico where they're waiting by the exit.

It isn't until we're outside that Bruno opens his mouth, but I hold up a hand to silence them. This is enemy territory and they're not going to get a single syllable out of us while we're still on their grounds. Whatever he has to say can just wait.

Once the valet pulls my car around, we all jump inside. I zoom around the circular driveway, peeling down the tree-lined private road headed back to the Strip, not even close to being far enough from the toxic Torres family.

Spying on me like that. As if they can beat us at this game!

Shit. I thought we were dysfunctional, but them?

They're goddamn nuts.

Especially the girl.

And while that may be fun in some scenarios, the one where I take my big fat rejection to the table doesn't rate.

I slam my hands down on the steering wheel over and over, letting out a roar of frustration...sexual and otherwise. "What a clusterfuck that was!" I bellow. "What the hell am I gonna tell Matteo? This is just what he wanted, you know. For me to crash and burn like that." I shake my head. "I didn't even get to the money part of the offer, for Christ's sake. They fucking baited me!"

"He was never gonna sell," Bruno grunts, turning up the air conditioner. Even at night, the Las Vegas heat is oppressive and my car feels like an oven even though it was only sitting outside for less than an hour. "Did you see the line outside when we left? And it's barely eleven o'clock. That place is packed like that on a weeknight, can you imagine how much cash they bring in on the weekends? You were never gonna get that pie. Not even a slice, Serge."

"Where the hell did he get the money to build up those clubs, anyway?" Enrico says. "He's been here for how long? A few years? Who's his investor? There has to be outside money, no?"

"There isn't much on him," I mutter as the trees whizz by. "He and his crazy bitch sister came to Vegas a few years ago. No word on where they came from or why they left. They don't have a huge organization, either. They keep a small circle, only the best and only who they absolutely need to keep things running smoothly. It's tight — and lethal enough to keep them in power."

"If they don't have backing, it shouldn't be hard to take them out," Bruno says. "We have three other families in our back pockets. It's not a war they'd wanna start."

"We're not going to war," I snip, taking a sharp left. "That's exactly what Matteo wants me to do, to lose my shit and blast them back to whatever rock they crawled out from under. But I'm not gonna do that. I'll find another way." I peer out the windshield into the darkness. My headlights only give me so much visibility. The only other lights illuminating the road right now are shining from the sky.

It all contributes to the exclusive and intriguing vibe.

Goddammit, I want that vibe! I will find a way to own that vibe!

A sudden lurch makes me yelp, and the car bounces and shudders as I let up on the gas.

"What was that?" Bruno asks. "Did you hit something?"

"What, like a cactus?" I say in a snide voice. "I can't see shit out here right now!"

A thin stream of smoke pours out from under the hood, and within seconds, billowing clouds immerse us.

I swing the car over to the side of the road and hop out. I reach out to pop the hood and the hot metal singes my fingers. I pull them back with a gasp. "Sonofabitch!" I shout at the sky. What in the hell else can go wrong tonight? We're on a desert road headed back to the city with barely any cell phone service. This area is famous for being a dead zone.

Sitting fucking ducks is all I can think right now.

"What are we supposed to do? Hoof it back to the city?" Bruno asks, throwing his hands in the air.

I pull out my phone and hold it into the air. No bars.

I fist the sides of my hair. It's rare I let anyone see me lose control, but my cousin and Enrico are my right-hand guys. If I'm gonna lose my shit, they're the only ones who'll ever witness it.

I pace around the car, hoping that I'll step into a space where I can communicate with someone…anyone…using this damn phone. I roll my eyes skyward. I really didn't want to have to deliver the news earlier than necessary to Matteo, but we can't exactly hoof it back to the hotel. I grit my teeth, dialing Matteo's number, walking around like a fool, hoping the call will connect.

And then, miracle of all miracles, it does.

It finally rings once, twice, three times…

"Are you serious?" I scream into the phone. "Where the hell are you?"

A screech of tires on the pavement jolts me and I jump, twisting to face the bright headlights flashing us.

"Hey, somebody is coming. Maybe they can help us—" Enrico starts to say, but the rest of his words are drowned out by a smattering of gunshots peppering the doors and windows of my car. I dive to the ground, Bruno landing right next to me.

"What the hell is going on?" Enrico yells, fumbling for his gun. I've already got mine in hand, firing off shots at the windows, hoping to pierce the skulls of whoever is inside driving that van.

A cold sensation snakes around my gut.

Whoever is inside.

Whoever, my ass!

I may not know who's inside of that van, but I sure as hell know who sent them.

Fucking Torres!

He didn't like me making a threat, so he decided to carry one of his own out in retaliation.

I stagger toward the side of my car, gunfire exploding into the otherwise still air. The van has slowed to a stop and the back window opens, unleashing a sea of bullets cracking and popping against metal and glass. Seconds pass, stretching into what feels like years as I duck and weave to escape the flying shards of glass.

I pop my head around the top right bumper, still ducking low to the ground as I fire one last bullet at the tires. A screeching sound is followed by a loss of control as the van skids left and right before peeling away on the dead tire.

I collapse against the side of the car, short, harsh pants expelling from my lips. Breathing feels like the slivers of glass are digging into my chest, slicing at my lungs, and I lay my head back on the roof.

"Guys," I rasp when I can draw in enough air to mutter the words.

But I'm greeted by silence.

"Guys!" I yell, twisting around to look for Bruno and Enrico. I don't see them so I run around to the back of the car where Enrico is sprawled out on the ground, blood gushing from a wound in his side. Bruno leans over him, pressing his jacket against it in an attempt to stop the bleeding.

"It's not working," he grunts. "If we don't get him the fuck out of here, he's gonna bleed out!"

A blaring ringtone erupts from my pocket and I grab my phone, stabbing the Accept button. "Matteo?" I yell.

"Why aren't you back from the meeting yet? Are you still negotiating, *your* way?" he snaps.

"Don't fucking start with me! That asshole tried to kill us!"

"Didn't I say you were out of your league with him?"

"Matteo," I say, my voice shaking. "The guy fucked with my car and then sent his guys after us after the meeting! They shot Enrico and he's gonna fucking die if we don't get him help! So find the Doc and get out here! We're on the road leading to the club." My eyes fall to Enrico's face which is getting whiter by the minute. "He's in bad shape," I mutter. "Hurry!"

Matteo mutters some colorful expletives and hangs up the phone without another word to me, but I'm sure there will be many more spewed at me later on when we get back to the hotel.

I stuff my phone back into my pocket and drop to my knees next to Bruno. I bring a hand to Enrico's face. His skin is cold and clammy, his lips as pale as his skin.

I slam my fist into the side of the car, pounding it against a bullet lodged into the bumper as a deafening roar erupts from my lungs.

"What are we gonna do now?" Bruno mumbles.

"First, we save Enrico," I say, clenching my fists tight. "And second? We show Torres exactly what retaliation feels like, Villani-style."

Chapter Seven
JAELYN

Electronic dance music blares from the speakers set up around the perimeter of the nightclub. The beats ricochet off of the walls, pulsating between my temples as I walk into the dressing room. Cassia and Velvet are at each other's throats again. The two biggest pains in the asses on our payroll also happen to be the two biggest stars on any given night. This place isn't big enough for both of them, and someone made a colossal screw-up when they put them both on the schedule for tonight. Everyone knows they're never supposed to perform on the same evening, but somehow, here they both are. And now both are threatening to walk out if the other doesn't give up her spot to be *the* star pussy.

All of the girls are getting ready for their dance numbers as I storm into the room, my fingertips digging hard into my flesh, my fists balled tight at my sides. I walk right up to Cassia, who, in her heels probably has about six inches on me. She opens her mouth to speak and I silence her with a death glare.

"Cassia," I say, struggling to keep my voice even. "Tell me something. Why do you work here?"

She furrows her brow, her lips curling into a smirk. "Because you guys pay the best of any club in Vegas and I make a shit ton in tips." She pauses, shooting a nasty look at Velvet. "And because you give me top billing whenever I dance."

I look at Velvet, my eyebrow lifted. "I assume the same goes for you?"

Velvet's spine stiffens and she sneaks a look at Cassia before meeting my fiery gaze. "Yeah, Jae, this place is the best."

"So," I bark. "Since you both seem to be happy with your current employment, are you really going to fuck it up for yourselves? Do you want to moonlight at the fucking Flamingo instead? Or are you going to deal with the fact that someone accidentally put you here on the same night and give the audience what they happily overpaid to see?"

Cassia and Velvet exchange a grudging look, both mumbling something I can barely register. But I don't really care. As long as they dance, I don't give a shit how they feel about each other. Or me, for that matter.

They aren't here because they love what they do. They're not here to make friends. They're here to do a job and to collect all of the green that comes with it.

I'm here to make sure they earn every red cent that goes into their hot little hands at the end of each night, so settling little bitch brawls before they rage is a pretty important part of my job description.

I stare at them both, stone-faced, for a long minute before they back away to get ready for their performances.

"Nice job," Ashleigh whispers.

I roll my eyes at her, biting down on my lip to keep from smiling. Everyone sees me as the big bad bitch manager and I always play the part. Trying to be friends is pointless. I just don't have it in me to care about anyone besides my brother. Besides, these bitches are crazier than I am. "Come with me," I say under my breath as I turn to leave the dressing room.

She follows close behind as I push open the door and pull it closed tight behind me. "Hey, so who were those guys with you before?" Ashleigh asks, her voice rising with interest. "You were wearing your RBF, but I could tell you were into the one whom you nearly crippled with your shoe." She lets out a giggle and I huff at her display of amusement.

Resting bitch face.

Yeah, I wear it well.

And Ash always notices it.

"They were just some guys who wanted to meet with Nate. You know he's thinking about expanding this place. They own, um, a construction company." She doesn't need to know the truth, especially since she didn't see me canoodling with Sergio last week, focused on my spy game.

"And you impaled the hot one with your heel because…?" She quirks a brow at me, egging me on.

I shrug. "He got a little mouthy."

"Ha!" Ash snickers. "And in this scenario, were you the pot? Or the kettle?"

"I'm a businesswoman," I say in a stiff voice. "I don't appreciate it when men act like condescending assholes, thinking that just because they're dealing with a woman that they can make, you know, innuendoes. And that the women will just melt at their feet." I can feel a heated flush creep up the sides of my neck, and Ashleigh can't help but point it out with a hint of glee in her voice.

"You're getting kind of hot and bothered over this 'guy,'" she says with a knowing wink. "Maybe you weren't as offended as you'd like me to believe."

"Please!" I snort. "And anyway, it won't happen again. Nate wasn't interested in hearing what they had to say." I turn away from Ashleigh, berating myself for allowing Sergio Villani to burrow under my skin. I figured if I stomped on his foot, he'd go running and I could forget about how he backed me up against that column, how warm and demanding his hand felt as it clutched my hip, how his rough touch scorched every inch of my skin and made me feel things…bad things…dangerous things.

Things I can't ever act upon.

Things I no longer have the freedom to feel.

I clear my throat. "The reason I pulled you out here was just to let you know that I need you to keep an eye on those two tonight. If either one of them starts anything, I'll make sure they never headline again." Good God, sometimes I feel like a glorified babysitter keeping these girls in line.

I let out a deep sigh as Ashleigh hurries back into the dressing room after giving me a quick salute. So many hormones, so many ruffled feathers…and I'm not talking about costumes either.

I deserve a raise. A big one.

And hot new shoes with a handbag to match.

I think I'll go up to my office and email a list of demands to my brother.

Yes, something to focus on other than Sergio and his big…ego.

I square my shoulders, pushing through the sweaty, writhing throngs of people grinding against each other in one of the rooms off the main club area.

At what point in my life did I ever imagine I'd become the manager of this pussy parade?

I bite down on the inside of my lip.

Then again, let's be realistic.

I never thought I'd live long enough to see my twentieth birthday after that disaster raged back in Miami years ago. I dig my fingernails into my palms as I stomp toward my office, the only place where I can get any bit of peace and quiet. It's not in the basement like Nate's. Mine is upstairs, tucked away from the rest of the club, and the only way you can get to it is by using a hidden staircase. I force a smile for the patrons guzzling expensive liquor and champagne, swaying into each other, drunk, high, and without a single care in the world.

I wonder what that feels like.

Freedom.

I wonder if I'll ever know.

I unlock the door leading to my private staircase, kick off my heels, and stagger up the steps barefoot. I reach the top and slink into my office, the plush carpet thick and warm beneath my toes. I cross the room and collapse on the large leather sofa, my eyes on the plasma screen hanging on the wall across from me, my reality show du jour looping on the screen.

I am a reality television junkie. I think it's because I'm so fascinated by the fact that these people openly welcome millions of stranger into their lives, for better or for worse. Good decisions, bad decisions, they let it all hang out.

They hold nothing back. They are exposed and vulnerable for the whole world to see.

Must be so liberating, to not give a fuck what people think, to not worry about who's watching, to be on perpetual display.

It's a luxury I will never be able to afford.

I watch the people on the screen bicker about the best way to sell some insanely expensive mansion in the Hamptons, and I allow myself to be swallowed up in the shallowness of it all. It sure beats the hell out of worrying about our cover being blown to bits.

That's always the biggest threat that looms over us on a daily basis.

It's one that Nate doesn't usually acknowledge, at least in front of me. He keeps so much to himself, never really trusting anyone around him. He has no friends because the closer people get, the more they see, the more they hear, the more they ask. He has a crew but they don't know who he really is, what we did, and how the hell we ended up in the middle of the desert sitting on a cash cow of epic proportions. Our last name is different now, which is the only thing that gives me any peace at all, but realistically, how long can we really hide? Is a different last name going to give us the protection we need to survive?

I have my doubts, but I keep them to myself. I'm sure Nate shares them but we've just learned to peacefully cohabitate with our big ass pet elephant.

I let my eyes flutter shut, crossing my legs at the ankles as the reality show drones on in the background. It's not loud enough to drown out the police sirens, or the screaming, or the gunfire that loops through my mind on forced repeat, though.

Because I have zero control over the darkness that consumes my brain when I drift off, far away from my new reality, however temporary it may be. When my eyes close, it's like an open invitation for the wounds that afflict my heart and soul to burst open, exposing the grief, guilt, and panic like a nerve.

I bury all of those useless emotions, the ones that perpetuate weakness, down deep, way below my sharp-tongued, prickly exterior. It makes people less likely to want to peel back my layers. I may look like one of the club's dancers, but I can give a better beatdown than all of the bouncers put together.

My personal defense mechanism has served me well for the past few years. Nobody gets close because I simply don't let them.

They have no choice.

I make the rules, strict ones that weren't made to be broken.

They were made to keep me…*us*…alive.

I squeeze my eyes shut even tighter to block out the horrific images wallpapering my mind. They are ghastly, blood-soaked, and haunting memories of the life we left behind. My pulse throbs harder with each passing second that they bubble up in my conscious, dragging me back into the murk that I fear I will never be able to claw my way out of, the murk that holds me captive, the murk that will swallow me whole if I let it.

The events leading up to that night at my parents' house still haunt my dreams. I'll never get a second chance to make things right with them. Sometimes I think I've landed in this shitty predicament just so I can suffer the consequences of my actions and words. Sometimes I think I deserve it.

I swallow hard.

It feels like I'm caught in purgatory, in limbo, just waiting and wondering and hoping for a reprieve that may never come.

Every day that I wake up is borrowed time.

There will come a point, hopefully later than sooner, where those last grains of sand slip through the hourglass, signifying that our time has run out.

And when that happens, we have to be ready.

For anything and everything.

I can't ever make things right with my parents, but I can make sure the people who hurt them suffer the same fate, my last conscious thought as a thick, sleep-induced fog blankets my mind and consumes my body.

I smooth down the front of my denim miniskirt and do a little side twirl in my mirror. Then I slip on my thigh-high, black patent leather boots, stepping back to examine myself. I flip my long, dark hair over one shoulder and narrow my eyes at my reflection. Then I jut out my hip for good measure, puckering my deep red lips.

A tiny shiver of anticipation runs down my spine, making me quake with glee. I clasp my hands together, shrieking into them as I dance around to the music pouring out of my speakers.

Tonight is the night I give myself to Eli.

It'll be my first time.

Our first time.

I bite down on my lower lip, scouting my bedroom for my overnight bag. I've already told my parents I'm staying at my best friend Maria's house and that I'll be back in the morning since they aren't exactly Eli's biggest fans. And Eli made up some bullshit excuse to give the club, an excuse that I heard my brother Nate swallowed hook, line, and sinker.

It's going to be absolutely perfect!

I hum along to my favorite song as I pull open my bottom dresser drawer, fishing around the t-shirts for something flimsy and lacy and red.

A special surprise in honor of the night.

Red is my favorite color.

The color of love.

I'm in love!

Oh my God, who would have ever believed that me, Jaelyn Ramirez, would have ever fallen in love with a nerdy, spectacled, skinny guy like Eli Wilson? Eli, whose nose is always buried in a sci-fi novel or an issue of Omni *magazine or something equally geeky when he's not tinkering around with his bike. Eli, with his unruly curly blond hair, kind eyes, and sweet smile. He's not the typical biker dude, that's for sure. He's definitely not the type of guy I ever pictured myself falling for. I mean, he's smart, for one. I'm smart, too, but in a street sort of way. Definitely not the bookish type. And Eli can actually string together whole sentences without profanity, unlike the other guys in the club.*

He ended up at the clubhouse when Nate helped him ward off two guys from a rival club one night. They were hassling him where he worked as a busboy at a local diner, a real shithole in the worst part of Miami.

Nate saw the bikes as he was passing through the neighborhood and smelled trouble.

He was right. And sure enough, it stank.

So he did what any decent do-gooder would — he kicked the crap out of the guys as a message to their club, and gave Eli a job at the auto body shop he runs to keep him out of harm's way and employed at the same time. It was a win-win for everyone. Eli got out of his dead-end job, making more money than he was at the diner. Nate solidified his control over his territory by sending those two guys running back to their own club with their dicks between their legs.

And I fell in love.

Hard and fast.

Suddenly, my life-long aspiration to become a mechanic grabbed hold, and I spent every waking hour at the shop, pretending to learn every last detail about servicing bikes and cars. I spent hours every day poring over engines, changing filters and oil, topping off fluids, diagnosing faulty transmissions.

I didn't give a damn about any of it.

I only did it to be close to Eli.

Nate isn't stupid. He knew the deal and never called me out on it.

I guess it's because he didn't ever see Eli as a threat.

I wish everyone in my family shared that opinion.

Unfortunately, that's not the case, hence the reason why I lied to my parents about where I'm going tonight.

Where I go pretty much every night.

I rub the back of my neck. The guilt knots at the base of my spine, tense and tight and always present. I don't understand why they just can't accept Eli, why they have to be such snobs about the fact that they want better for their only daughter. Yeah, he doesn't have much, but he's brilliant and funny and loving.

At the end of the day, aren't those things way more important than money or status?

A light knock at the door makes me jump, and I let out a breath when I see my mother's head pop into my room. I suck in a breath, prepared with my story. I really hate how uncomfortable things have gotten with us since Eli appeared on the scene. We used to be so close that I'd tell her everything. But lately, I keep everything short, sweet, and surface-level only. We don't have those heart-to-heart talks I loved so much where we'd sip tea and giggle for hours anymore. I miss that. I miss hanging around with my dad at his golf club, playing nine holes and then going to lunch so he can coach me on everything wrong with my swing.

And trust me, there's plenty wrong with it. But still, he was always so patient, determined to get me on the WPGA tour.

That is, before Eli came into the picture.

Things shifted when we started seeing each other. I know how they feel about him, but they're going to have to learn to accept him.

Not that I plan to have that debate tonight.

Tonight is going to be the most amazing night of my life, and I don't want anything to overshadow it.

Mom's eyes narrow when she sees me. "Interesting outfit, Jae. Where exactly are you and Maria headed tonight?"

"Oh, we're just going to a party. One of the guys from school. It's not a big deal. We won't be out late, I promise." I talk fast, hoping she doesn't ask too many more questions and hurries the hell out of here. I told Eli to be here by seven and it's almost that now!

She nods, pursing her lips.

"Why haven't you guys left yet? You were supposed to be at the benefit already, weren't you? Are you excited? It's such an honor for you both!" *I keep up the flow of chatter hoping that if she can't get a word in edgewise, she won't ask me any more questions that she really doesn't want to hear the answers to, anyway.*

"Yes," *she says slowly.* "It is an honor, one that your father and I really expected you and your brother to be present for." *Mom looks at me with a disapproving expression on her face.* "I think your father is really disappointed that you aren't joining us. It's supposed to be a family event."

"I didn't realize..." *I furrow my brow in confusion.* "Mom, why wouldn't you say something about it to us? We just assumed it was something you were going to celebrate together."

Mom lets out a sigh. "You know, Jae, sometimes it would be nice for us not to have to coerce you both into doing something. Sometimes it would be nice for you to just offer on your own."

"Oh, um..." *My eyes flicker over to the clock. Two minutes to seven. And Eli is never late.* "I'm sorry. I guess I just didn't, ah, think about it."

She nods again, her eyes traveling over my outfit one more time. "I just hope there isn't another reason why you're staying back tonight, Jae."

"I don't know what you mean," *I say, hoping like hell that the look on my face actually reflects true confusion.*

Mom sighs. "I know we haven't exactly seen eye to eye about this whole Eli business, sweetie, but I'd hate for you to use that as a reason for hanging back tonight. You know we only want the best for you. And lately, things have been so tense between us. I feel like we're drifting apart, and I don't want this to come between us." *She reaches* out and takes my hands in hers. "I love you, honey. I will always love you. I just want you to be happy."

"I know, Mom," I whisper. "And I know you'd never want to hurt me."

I just wish I could be honest with you. But I can't. I know better even if you don't.

She smiles. "Have fun with Maria."

I force a return smile. "I will."

Mom turns to leave and my eyes dart around my room for my phone. I can stop Eli before he gets here. He won't know they're still here because my father always parks his prized BMW 7 series in the garage.

In a few minutes, they'll be gone and our night can begin.

But a nagging feeling in my gut tells me to do the right thing for my parents, go to the benefit, and to forget about my plans.

Stop the lying, Jae. It's destroying your relationship.

I tap the toe of my boot on the floor for the couple of seconds it takes me to decide.

I stab a message into the keyboard on my phone, tossing it on my bed before I run over to my closet and grab a black cocktail dress.

"Mom, Dad!" I yell, poking my head into the hallway. "Don't leave yet! I'm coming—"

But my words are drowned out by the loud chimes of the doorbell.

And with each chime that sounds, my stomach drops lower and lower into my boots.

Oh, no...

"What the hell are you doing here?" Dad bellows from the front hall, the sound echoing throughout the foyer. "I thought I told you to stay away from my daughter!"

I race down the steps, gripping the banister tight as I skid to a halt at the bottom. "Daddy, please!" I yelp as he steps closer to Eli with a menacing look on his face.

My father looks at me, his lips twisted into a grimace. "I trusted you. How long have you been lying to us, Jaelyn? How long has this been going on? We told you to stay away from that clubhouse, away from those people!"

"Those people are my friends!" I yell, balling my fists. "They care about me. Yes, they're different from you and Mom, but does that make them bad?"

"You don't understand how the world works. I've tried so hard to give you the best life possible, and now you just want to throw it all away, just like your brother did when he joined that...that motorcycle gang?"

"He's not throwing anything away!" I scream. "He is a business owner! At only twenty-two! Why can't you just be proud of him instead of tearing him down every chance you get?"

"Because I wanted more for him! And for you!" Dad looks at Eli. "You will never be good enough for her!"

Eli nods, staring right at my father. "You're right, sir. But I love her."

Oh, Jesus. I can see the smoke billowing out of my father's ears. "You what?" he hisses. "You love her? Is that what this is?" He creeps closer to Eli. "You meet a beautiful girl who comes from money and follows you around like a puppy dog and you think you can convince me it's love that you feel? Do you think I'm some kind of an idiot?" he roars, the vein in his forehead pulsating as rage courses through his body. He keeps his fists locked against his sides, and even though I know my father would never hit him, a tiny part of me knows he desperately wants to tear Eli's head from his body.

"You don't love her," he hisses. "You love what she can do for you. What my family and my money can do for you!"

"Marco, that's enough," Mom says, pulling him backward. Her eyes dart over to me and she gives her head a little shake.

Dad swivels around and narrows his eyes at my outfit, making me cringe. "So this is the choice you've made. You've decided to go against our wishes and slum it with this...this..." He looks at Eli, his face beet-red with anger. "This piece of trash!"

"He's not trash!" I yell. "And you can't tell me what to do! This is my life!"

"The hell it is!" he shouts. "You're eighteen years old! You're a child. My child! And as long as you live under this roof, you will do what I say!"

"Well, then, maybe I shouldn't live under this roof!" I cry.

Mom gasps. "Enough, both of you!" She tugs at my father's arm. "Marco, just leave it alone. If you let it go too far—"

"What?" he demands, turning to sneer at Mom. "She'll leave?" His eyes are wild when he looks back over to me. "Then leave! Go! You think you can do a better job of taking care of yourself than we can? Be my guest!" He stomps over to me, shaking a finger in my face. "You're finished. The lies, the deceit, the sneaking around. It's over. All of it!"

"You can't make me stop seeing him!"

"I can give you a choice," he says, his voice dropping to a growl. "Make it, Jaelyn! Right now!"

"I hate you!" I shriek without thinking, stomp my foot on the polished wood floor, tears of anger streaming down my face, my teeth chattering uncontrollably.

Eli's jaw drops and Mom clamps a hand over her mouth.

Dad's expression slowly morphs from one of disdain to one of utter helplessness and despair. He recoils slightly at my words, blinking fast as if he questions whether or not they are really hanging in the tense air between us.

As if he questions whether or not his little girl, his only daughter, just said the very worst possible ones imaginable.

Reality smacks me in the face like a rubber glove.

I did.

And from the look on his pale, shocked face, they brutalized him like spikes slicing right through his flesh, shredding him from the outside in.

I'll never forget the look on his face in that moment...

In the instant I broke my father's heart.

Chapter Eight
SERGIO

I stare at Enrico's pale face, a deep sigh shuddering through me.

He's a kid, dammit. He should never have been dragged into the shit that we call real life.

Enrico ended up on my crew after I picked him up trying to steal food from one of our restaurants back in Sicily a few years ago. He was trying to take care of his family as the man of the house since his father died. But the guy was barely a man himself and he didn't have two sticks to rub together for fire.

As soon as I figured out we were being robbed, I stood watch in the shadows to find the person who was responsible. I saw him show up night after night, taking whatever he could carry when he thought nobody was paying attention. I admired his will and his stealth, which never faltered, even in the face of starvation.

And when I finally confronted him, making bullshit death threats I knew I'd never carry out just to see how he'd react, he accepted his fate. He apologized for disrespecting me. He didn't beg for his life or cry like a bitch. He just asked me to let him take food to his family one more time…the last time…so at least they could eat that night.

I knew right then and there that he was a guy I wanted to have on my crew. He wouldn't crack under pressure, he'd stare adversity in the eye and do whatever it took to protect what was important.

He was a guy I could trust. I mean, as much as I can trust anyone.

I gave him a job on the spot and he hasn't disappointed me once.

But I sure as hell failed him tonight.

He survived the bullet wound. Thankfully it wasn't a kill shot. Doc was able to dig it out and stitch him up. I eye the IV funneling fluid into his body, my chest tightening.

That bullet could have punctured any number of organs as it ravaged his insides, all because I was dead-set on making a nonexistent deal.

Because I was greedy and looking for approval from the other families.

And because I wanted to build my own future, not have it assigned to me by anyone else.

I convinced the families to let me negotiate, figuring that cash is always king.

I was wrong.

Maybe not everyone can be bought after all.

Torres didn't care about my offer. He has no intention of selling. He only wanted to get me in there, face to face, so he could tell me that the power I'm desperate to claim will never be mine.

He played his hand like the sneaky, cutthroat bastard he is, and I didn't call his bluff in enough time to salvage my own.

My blood simmers as his smug smirk flashes in my mind.

Did he really think he could get away with that fucking stunt? That we'd scatter like cockroaches after the hit, running into the darkness without a look back? That we'd let him fucking live after unsuccessfully trying to kill us?

Not such a brilliant plan, Torres, especially when we could crush you without breaking a sweat.

He really needs to work on his messaging skills because they're complete shit.

Maybe he didn't realize who he was dealing with.

Neither did his sister.

Maybe it's time they both found out.

I press my fingertips to my temples, the blood now rushing between my ears as I look down at Enrico sleeping peacefully.

This could have gone a very different way tonight, a much more deadly one.

And I always take care of my own. Enrico may not be blood, but he's done enough for me that I consider him family.

And you always take care of family.

"What do you think it means?" Bruno asks me in a low voice as he walks up behind me.

"It means that I underestimated our target," I grumble, sweeping a hand through my hair.

"And you're sure the target is Torres, right?" Bruno asks.

I furrow my brow. "Who the fuck else would it be? And don't say Becerra. I only cut off Javier's hand. It's not enough to warrant an all-out assault!"

Bruno nods. "True. Okay, so how do we fight back against Torres? Do we go and shoot up the club? Do we pop him?"

I shake my head. All of that is messy. Very fucking messy. "I don't know enough about his inner circle. If we go after him, we might be taking on a much stronger enemy. There's no way he's working alone. There's someone behind the scenes feeding him cash and Christ only knows what else, I'm convinced of it." I pull my eyes off of Enrico and push Bruno out the door, closing it behind us. The least I can do is give the guy some peace. "There's no way they just deal in pussy. On the surface, that's the big draw, but there has to be plenty going on behind the scenes. Drugs, guns...they must be funneling money through there constantly. Did you see those cars in the VIP lot? They weren't there just to get their cocks sucked. I mean, yeah, that's their sideshow, but not the main event."

I walk over to where Matteo is sitting at the kitchen island with Heaven leaning against him. Heaven gives new meaning to the words 'badass bitch.' Months back, after her father married her off to Matteo as part of a deal, she executed a rival boss. Then she broke ties with her father and subsequently, her brothers, when she found out that the old man sold her out to protect his own ass. Yeah, my sister-in-law is pretty damn fierce, although marriage has mellowed her.

A little bit.

She and Matteo started out hating each other, but they're pretty gaga over one another now. I guess that means she's my saving grace and the reason why he doesn't lash out at me with the same amount of ferocity as he used to before he was so pussy-whipped.

And now they're out here to strengthen ties with the other families in our recently formed syndicate, the one that's gonna take over the gambling industry in the United States, city by city. Hotels, restaurants, casinos — it's our fledgling empire. And with the manpower of our crew, along with the brutal Russian Severinov family and equally vicious Marcone family, also out of Sicily, we're unstoppable.

At least, I thought we were before that damn meeting with Torres went sideways.

We got a lot more than we bargained for when we tried to finger that damn-near lethal pussy.

But I'm not settling for a portion of the crown. I want the whole goddamn thing.

"Sergio," Heaven says, a warning tone in her voice. "You can't go back after Torres. If what you said is true, and he's working with one of the cartels to run drugs through his places, it's no wonder he won't sell. He's got too much to lose, and the cartels won't be happy if we take an axe to their pipelines. And it's also very possible the guys who tried to take you out are his part-ners. Cartel scumbags who wanted to scare you. Maybe Becerra?"

I shift my weight, stepping down hard on my injured foot as a sharp tinge of pain shoots up my calf. Dammit. Just when I thought I was free from the memory of Jaelyn Torres, it all comes rushing back, sucking me into her funnel cloud of chaos. I take in a sharp breath, the seductive-slash-sinister glare on Jaelyn's face flooding my mind. In the past few hours since we escaped that ambush, I tried to forget her, to forget the sensa-tions swirling through me when she'd fire that death glare in my direction, to forget the disdain in her voice and in her gaze. She probably meant to freeze me out, but her efforts had the exact opposite effect. I can still feel the heat of her body singeing my palms as I gripped her bare flesh, the warmth of her breath against my face, the speed of her heartbeat pressed against my chest.

She didn't try to push me away.

Keep your friends close and your enemies closer.

In that moment, she declared war on us…on *me*.

And I'm ready to go to battle.

"It was definitely Torres who wanted to send the message, Heaven. Becerra wouldn't try to partner with us and then finger Torres. Besides, I didn't outright tell Becerra that we wouldn't work with him. And I didn't kill anyone. I just sent a message to let him know that if he wants to work with us, he'd better show up at the bargaining table and leave his asshole soldiers home," I say, gritting my teeth, my skin prickling as visions of Jaelyn lying spread-eagle on my bed in her fuck-me heels flood my mind. Oh Jesus. How the hell did she end up *there*? How am I not able to think about anything other than her gliding her fingers along her wet slit, moaning as she flicks her thumb against her clit? Enrico was almost killed tonight. I have more fucking important things to worry about right now!

But my body is on an entirely different page than my brain. My pulse throbs against my neck, my chest growing tighter by the second. "Someone fucked with my car to run us off that road. And Torres made the threat!" I grip the granite countertop tight, my knuckles turning white against the black stone.

"Sergio, you can't just declare war because of a hunch. You don't know for sure that it was Torres behind the hit!" Matteo walks over to me, his eyes narrowed. "That's not how this works. We take it to the families and discuss how we will handle it as a group!"

My fingertips tingle, bright spots flashing in front of my eyes as white noise consumes the space between my ears.

Instead of focusing on the issue at hand, I'm back in the club, lost in her eyes…clear green ones taunting me, with sparks of fury glittering in the depths. I'm envisioning her deep red lips that twisted into the sexiest of scowls, clamped tight around my dick and those luscious tits bouncing hard as she rides me.

"Are you listening to me?" Matteo says, his voice muffled as if he's speaking underwater.

My mind races in time with my rocketing pulse.

Risks, there are so many risks to this plan…

I can't.

I won't!

It isn't fair to go into battle without consulting with the troops first.

Right?

Right!

I know the rules. I know how the game is played.

But something happened tonight.

Something I couldn't control.

My breath catches as I see Jaelyn turn away from me with that one real smile, swinging her hips, that tight dress barely covering her ass as she walks back into the club, swallowed up by the lights.

What in the *fuck*?

I can't think. I can't breathe.

"Serge!" Matteo barks, jolting me. There's an expression of concern on her face. "Where the fuck did you go? It looks like you just blacked out there for a second."

I blink fast, rubbing the back of my neck. What the hell is happening to me? Am I having a fucking stroke right now? Why can't I stop seeing her? Feeling her? Smelling her?

Matteo's voice fades away, my heart thumping faster and faster. I don't know if it's the rage coursing through me, the guilt over Enrico, or the frustration of not knowing for sure what move to make next, but my brain is spinning out of control like a goddamn top.

And I'm about to snap like an overstretched rubber band.

"Fine, we take it to the table," I rasp, limping away from them. I slam the door to my bedroom, collapsing against the back of it, gulping in as much oxygen as my lungs can hold.

I don't lose control!

I don't let emotions command me, like my brothers Dante and Roman!

But even as those words thunder between my temples, I fumble with my belt, shove my pants to my knees, and grab my cock. Thanks to the salacious highlight reel that's been looping through my mind for the last few minutes, it's already stiff as steel against my palm. I lean my head back, squeezing my eyes shut as I imagine Jaelyn handcuffed to my bed.

Naked. Gagged.

Writhing as my tongue delves into her slit, plundering her soft folds.

I stroke my dick harder and faster, my chest heaving.

She's the enemy…

A sexy and devious one, equal parts erotic and deadly.

My breath hitches as I feel her pussy tighten around my throbbing cock. So wet, so greedy as it pulls me deeper. Her legs lock around me, her hips thrusting against me as she digs her heels into the mattress.

I plunge deeper and deeper, sparks firing in my groin as my cock erupts with a vengeance, hot cum spurting out the tip, slipping down the sides of my shaft. I grip it tight, blinded by the sparks of light exploding behind my eyes. My labored pants eventually turn into shallow breaths, and it's not long before my vision clears and the irritation of not knowing my next move dissipates into the thick fog around me.

Torres's message begs for a response.

And I know exactly how I want to reply.

Chapter Nine
SERGIO

I'd hoped a good night's sleep would rid me of the demon otherwise known as Jaelyn Torres.

And it might've worked if I hadn't woken up twice to whack it to her in those X-rated porno fantasies fucking with my head. After the last time, I ran straight into the bathroom and dunked myself under an ice-cold stream of water in the shower, the only thing that could give me some peace from the erotic curse she'd put on my body.

It worked for a little while, until my body temperature skyrocketed yet again at breakfast.

"Are you sweating?" Bruno asks as I walk up to our regular table in the coffee shop. He stuffs a forkful of pancakes into his mouth as I slide into a chair next to him.

"I just came from the gym," I lie.

"You didn't shower?"

I shrug. "You the hygiene police or something?"

He smirks. "I don't give a shit what you smell like, Serge. I ain't fucking you. Just don't sweat in my espresso, yeah?"

I let out a sigh and dab my napkin against my forehead. I'm damn close to overheating here. This is ridiculous! How in the hell?

"Did you see Enrico this morning?" he asks me.

"Yeah, but he was sleeping. I didn't want to wake him. The Doc came by to check on him and is hanging around until I get back." I avert my eyes, knowing exactly what question he's going to ask next.

"Where are you going?"

It's the only one I don't want to answer.

It's also the one I don't want him to guess the answer to.

"I have a meeting."

"With?" He lifts an eyebrow at me.

"With a guy about a place." I take a large gulp of coffee and swallow hard, the searing liquid scorching a path down my throat where it sloshes around in my empty stomach.

"Oh, is that supposed to be a riddle or something?" Bruno snickers, shaking his head. "Or code for you're gonna get laid?"

He had to say it, didn't he?

I clutch the tablecloth in my hand, my heart hammering in my chest. "This isn't about sex," I hiss, almost like I'm trying to convince myself that it isn't. I hope Bruno believes me more than I believe myself.

Bruno's eyebrows fly upward. "Sore subject? You going through a dry spell now?"

He has no idea.

"Look, sometimes I like to take meetings to find out if there are opportunities for us. I don't need to hand over my calendar so you can see where I am at any given hour of the day!"

"Jesus, cuz," Bruno says, holding up his hands. "I just wondered if you were gonna take the shit show from last night to the table like you guys agreed last night."

My lips stretch into a tight line. "You mean like Matteo and Heaven agreed."

"Sergio, don't tell me you're gonna try to handle this by yourself," he says, the warning evident in his tone. "The families will be pissed and you'll end up getting yourself killed. And we still won't get those nightclubs!"

I force out a chuckle. "You really think I'm gonna deal with Torres on my own? Nah, I'm letting the families handle this one. They'll figure out a way to make him pay, and then I'll be happy as a pig in shit to deliver the punishment."

Bruno just stares as me as he stuffs scrambled eggs into his mouth. "You sound pretty convincing. You think everyone else will buy that line of bullshit?"

My eyes narrow. "That's how it will be handled. How Torres will be handled. He tried to kill us, Bruno, and he will be handled." A tight smile lifts my lips. "In the exact way that the families decide. As of right now, I'm stepping out of this Torres sinkhole." I shove the chair away from the table as I stand up. "And I'm going to my meeting so that I can figure out another way for us to take over nightlife in this goddamn city since nobody has come up with any other brilliant ideas."

"Hey, Serge," Bruno says, putting down his fork. "Look, I get that you want a win here, but maybe stop going around on your own to put deals together? I mean, it didn't exactly work out for you last night. Definitely didn't work out for Enrico." He sighs. "I know you feel like you have a lot to prove, but—"

"Don't tell me what I feel," I say, my voice choked. "I've done plenty for our family. I jumped in when Matteo needed me in Manhattan months ago. I fucking went with Heaven to take out that drug lord and break up their sex trafficking ring while Matteo was lying in a hospital bed after getting shot! But because Matteo is next in line to Papa, *he* gets to make the decisions and the plans on our behalf. Fuck that! I've done plenty to prove myself and I'm done. I'm ready to write my own goddamn rules! I don't need Matteo dictating shit to me, telling me how to do my job. I've done just fine for myself and for our family!"

"Easy," he says, looking around. "You're getting a little crazy about this. You guys will go to the meeting and figure out a new plan. This isn't about Matteo or about you fucking up." He smirks. "I mean, *this* time it's not about you fucking up."

I roll my eyes.

"Torres is clearly a wild card, and nobody expected things to go down the way they did. This isn't on you—"

"The hell it's not."

I twist around to see Matteo's lips curl into a sneer. He steps toward me, dressed from head to toe in black. Suit, shirt, shoes. But no tie.

Never a tie.

I guess he doesn't need anything else choking him on a daily basis.

"Don't sugarcoat this for him, Bruno," Matteo says, still staring me down. "Shit went sideways last night because you couldn't handle Torres. You think you have what it takes to sit at the negotiation table, but clearly you don't. Anyone who knows anything about business, about people, could have gotten him to agree to our terms." He stands toe to toe with me. We're both about the same height but he's darker — everything from his skin to his demeanor. More menacing all around when he's talking business. He barely smiles. Never laughs.

Yep, Matteo can be a real dickwad.

"You talk a big game about getting an earned seat at the table," I hiss. "But what the hell did you ever do to get yours? Be born first?"

Matteo lifts an eyebrow at me. "Careful, brother," he growls. "I have no problem making a recommendation to have you shipped the fuck out of here if you don't watch your ass. See, that's the difference between us. I deliver on what I promise." He leans toward me, his eyes turbulent and volatile.

That's the only sign of what's going on behind his chaotic gaze.

If you don't know him, you'd never see it, or him, coming.

And when the devil comes knocking, you're already too late to escape.

But I've been dealing with this my whole life.

Buttons?

There are plenty to push.

This one is the hottest, though.

Insinuating that he got his role because of birth order instead of skill always gets his dick in a twist.

It's not entirely true, but it pisses him off regardless.

I hold up my hands with a nasty smirk on my face. "Sorry, I know how sensitive you are about…*role play*."

His nostrils flare, and if we were behind closed doors right now, he'd take a swing. Or three.

Of course, he'd land on his face because I'd use my ninja-slaying powers to slice through his cocky ass attitude.

Courtesy of me being a trained assassin.

"Don't test me, Sergio. Papa brought me out here to close the deals you can't. And now we need to fix things with Torres," Matteo says in a tight voice.

Adrenaline floods my veins when Matteo speaks his name.

Tiny mewls amplifying in my mind send a jolt to my groin.

No, no, no!

Christ, not again. Not now!

"There is no fixing anything," I say in a choked voice. "He put a hit on us after we left his place. There was no conversation, no discussion, no invitation to negotiate. There was only a power play. His. On *us*. There is no fucking way we have another conversation with that tool."

"Who says anything about you having the conversation?" Matteo asks, tapping a finger against his stubbled chin.

"What, you think you're gonna just walk in there and try to—?"

"There is no try. Only do." Matteo's lips curl into a sneer. "Something you obviously couldn't handle."

"Fuck off, Yoda," I snip. "The guy wanted to stake his claim last night. To show us he's not gonna bend over for any amount of money. What the hell do you think another meeting will accomplish?"

"Everyone can be bought," Matteo says. "Everyone wants something. You just have to figure out their price. That's how you really negotiate. I guess they didn't teach you that in Sniper School."

"The way to get to him is to push him out, to show him that we can outmuscle him! We need to beat him at his own game, to smother him with our resources!"

"See, that's why you're never going to be taken seriously by the families, Sergio. You have all of these plans, but you can't seem to make them a reality. You're a dreamer, but the reality never seems to follow. You've got plans, but where's the fucking money, bro? Where's the opportunity? Can you do anything beyond maiming? Or will that be your only claim to fame?" He shakes his head. "This is exactly why Papa sent me out here. At the end of the day, he knows who can get the job done."

I stick my fist in my mouth to keep from pounding Matteo's smug face. His words thunder between my ears. He's right. I always have a plan, I'm always full of ideas. But the one big chance I have to put it into action almost gets me killed. The Torres deal was my idea, my future! And Matteo is right, I fucking shat the bed. I walked out of there without finding out what he really needs.

What he really wants.

I don't deserve a seat at that table if I can't secure my own deal.

I don't deserve a seat if I can't prove that I'm a fucking power player, too!

Thump, thump, thump!

My throat tightens, my pulse hammering with increasing force.

Matteo thinks he can do it by talking, by charming the guy, by manipulating him into believing that we can run his clubs better than he can.

He's got a proven track record, I'll give him that.

And really, I don't know why I keep resisting. Let him go in there and attempt to make a deal. Let him get his ass shot up like Swiss cheese!

But I don't want his seat by default.

I wanna earn mine.

Torres doesn't need to have his dick stroked.

He needs to feel real fear.

He needs to feel, period.

"Enrico is lying in a bed right now because of that guy. You fight fire with fire, Matteo. Not with fucking cannoli cream and espresso!"

Matteo rolls his eyes. "If he wanted you dead, you'd be dead right now. He's just playing a game. It's our move. And you're gonna tag me in." He glares at me, his eyes narrowed. "And just so you're clear, it's a rhetorical statement. You don't have a choice."

A hammering in my chest reverberates between my ears, but yeah, I heard him loud and clear.

And he's right.

I don't have a choice at all.

Chapter Ten
JAELYN

I stir my coffee, shifting in the wooden chair at my favorite little diner on the Strip the next morning. I wonder how much longer they're going to sit here and gossip. I have a ton of work to do at Sapphire and all of this…I don't know, I guess it's girl talk…is getting to me and my head feels like it is slowly being filled with oatmeal.

Apropos since we just finished breakfast.

Nate is always telling me to make friends and to socialize.

I tell him I have Ashleigh and I don't need anyone else.

I guess I've just never been used to having a whole gaggle of girlfriends. I always spent all of my time at the clubhouse back in Miami, and then when Eli showed up on the scene, he filled my hours.

I never really did well with other girls.

Catty bitches.

Case in point, the near-disaster at the club last night between Velvet and Cassia. Although, since both of them made an insane amount of cash last night because of their impromptu tag team act, they're pawing at each other like long lost lovers this morning. Testing some material for their next performance?

Maybe.

It just means more green for Sapphire, so I'm all for whatever it is.

"Jae!"

I blink fast and turn to Ash. "Yeah?"

"I said your name three times!"

I shrug. "Okay, and now you finally have my attention. Or did you expect Beetlejuice to appear?"

Ash rolls her eyes. "Well, good, because I have a great idea!"

"Listening…"

"Well, you saw how amazing things went last night having Velvet and Cassia together on stage," she starts.

Velvet and Cassia exchange a look and suddenly, their joyous expressions morph into resting bitch faces.

It's clearly an occupational hazard of working at the Sapphire Lounge.

At least, that's what I tell myself.

They're obviously anticipating the reason for Ashleigh's excitement and wondering how much it's gonna cut into their profits for the night.

"I was thinking, why don't we do a show where we bring all of our headliners together for one night and also invite a few others who will draw in their own crowds?" Her lips curl upward. "You know that the porn convention is being held in Vegas next week, right? So why not invite a few of the heavy hitters to join the party? We can even invite one per club and rotate them around the other nightclubs throughout the week! It would be amazing for business, don't you think? You always have to stay ahead of the curve, right?"

I love Ashleigh's enthusiasm. Really, I do. But Cassia and Velvet look like they want to leap across the table and shred her with their multicolored talons.

"Ash, there's a lot to consider with that. Contracts, agents, added security." I give her shoulder a little squeeze. "I think this idea would be great, but I need to run it past Nate. You know how he can be. He'll blow a million holes into the idea before he'll ever entertain it."

"You don't need porn stars. You have us," Cassia purrs.

"Even the hottest pussy gets tired," Ashleigh snaps.

"Are you calling me old?" Cassia squeals, slamming her hands on the Formica tabletop.

"I'm just saying that the audience gets tired of the same old thing!"

"She said old again!" Velvet hisses. "You wanna get cut, bitch?"

Ashleigh lets out a frustrated sigh and flips her blonde hair over her shoulder. "You two don't know anything about running a business! Let me tell you this, if we can't give people new reasons to come and sample the talent, they will go somewhere else! Somewhere they can see something new and fresh and shiny!"

"So I'm fucking tarnished?" Cassia yells, jumping up from her chair and launching back a fist.

I leap up and grab her wrist before she lets that fist fly at Ash. "Hey!" I say in a warning voice, twisting my head left and right. "People are watching," I hiss. "Hold your shit together, Cassia. I don't think you want to spend all of that hard-earned money bailing your ass out of jail, am I right?"

She yanks her wrist out of my hand, her eyes narrowed to slits. "I don't share the spotlight, Jae. Last night was great, but my pussy can command its own huge audience, you got that? Any other club would love to have me!" She grabs her bag, and with one final death glare at Ashleigh, she flounces out of the diner, Velvet on her heels.

I rub my temples, collapsing back into my chair. Guys wouldn't have this kind of exchange. They'd just be like, "You wanna add another cock? Yeah, great. Can I get more beer in the dressing room?"

And the conversation would be over.

But this?

Jesus Christ.

My head is splitting and it's barely eleven o'clock in the morning.

Ashleigh slouches in the chair. "I thought it would be good for business."

"You know, business is really rocketing, right?" I say.

She throws up her hands. "So you just sit back and ride it out? No! You have to keep doing new things, different things, exciting things!"

"Listen, I know you want to have a voice at the club, but you have to know who you're dealing with. These girls are territorial and vicious. I don't want them to jump you in the parking lot because you're trying to steal their cash."

"But I'm not trying to steal it! I'm trying to get them more!"

I shake my head. "More competition to them means less money. They don't think strategically with their heads. They think with their pussies. And pussy say, shine the spotlight on me!"

Ashleigh giggles, spitting orange juice on the table. "You need to get Nate onboard with a new plan for the club. We need new ideas!"

"And this is exactly why we hired you. Don't worry about those old bitches," I say, making Ash smile. "Let me talk to Nate and we'll come up with a plan. For what it's worth, I like your angle. I think it could work really well. Guest porn stars. Classy." I wink at her as I stand up and grab my handbag. "I'm heading to the club right now, but I'll talk to you later tonight. Maybe we can get some time with Nate and present your idea."

Her mouth opens. "Really?" she asks.

"Definitely." I give her shoulder a squeeze and toss a few bills onto the table before hurrying out of the diner.

Nate will be happy.

I socialized *and* stopped an assault as an added bonus.

He'll be proud.

That's more than I can say for his reaction to my version of girls' night last week.

I fling my bag over my shoulder and trudge to my car. My whole body aches from falling asleep on the couch in my office last night. When I finally dragged myself out of the club, under Nate's supervision of course, it was almost six.

And it felt like I had been in traction.

He followed me home, like always, and I collapsed onto my bed for another few hours. But just like my time on the couch, my sleep at home was splintered with memories…some good, some bad, some erotic as hell.

The erotic variety are the ones I remember the most clearly.

And they all starred Sergio Villani, the arrogant, self-centered prick who thought he could come into our club swinging his Italian stallion dick around with all kinds of threats about what his family could do to us if we don't accept his bullshit offer to sell.

Why wouldn't they just spend their money bailing out their own nightclubs and keep their grubby hands off of what *we* built?

Fucking mafia.

Vegas is like a breeding ground for those greasy bastards who think they can own every square inch of this city. Not that Nate rattles easy. The last thing he wants is to get in the middle of their crosshairs. We don't need any more enemies.

He played it cool, though. Exactly as I planned.

And Sergio's reaction was perfect. He's desperate and hungry, which means he needs Sapphire.

And us.

That means we have a chance to battle the Becerra Cartel head on, just as soon as Sergio's need for our business makes him so crazed with greed that he's willing to do anything to get a piece.

But for as angry as I was that he thought he could waltz into Sapphire and expect us to just bend at his will because of his family influence, I can't forget how his fingertips scorched the surface of my skin, insistent and greedy. I can't forget how his eyes bore into me, heating my insides to the point of boiling. And I can't forget how his cock pressed against me, long, thick, and hard. It was damn impressive.

I wasn't lying when I called it an Italian stallion dick.

I pull open the door handle of my car and hop into the driver's seat. I love it so much. My Mercedes is ridiculously expensive and impractical, but one I have fantasized about having for as long as I can remember.

Nate got it for me for my last birthday, courtesy of the nightclub circuit. It's technically a company car, but call it what you want, it's still my ass driving it.

I head toward the club, which is on the opposite end of the Strip. It's still pretty early for Vegas, so traffic is light. I like getting to Sapphire early in the day. It's quiet and I can think without having to deal with whiny divas and pulsating music.

It also gives me a little bit of peace and privacy. Nate doesn't show up until later, and it's nice to have the place to myself for a little while.

To not have him hawking me.

I know why he does it, and I'm grateful for everything he's done to keep us safe for the past few years. But it's not a life.

Not one I want to lead long-term, anyway.

I pull off the main road, making a left turn off of the Strip, headed in the direction of the club. This road is one of the reasons why Nate picked the location for Sapphire. It gives it an air of exclusivity since it's off the beaten path. You don't just find Sapphire. You go because you're in the know, because you're a VIP, because you're one to be seen.

It's a whole mental thing with our patrons.

And it works well for us.

The sun blazes in the sky, heating me through the windshield even though I have my air conditioner on full blast. I'd love to feel the wind whip my hair around but in this heat, I'd be drenched in seconds if I opened the window. I speed down the road, taking a deep, calming breath after my unsettling breakfast, determined to put all of the angst and drama behind me.

Nate was so hell-bent on me having my own life so I can find a way to fit into this new normal, but I don't. Not that I really want to. A tiny part of me is convinced that it's all temporary anyway. I mean, how realistic is it that a powerful drug cartel can just 'lose' targets? Targets who dare stay in the country? Targets who do the unthinkable…like make a name for themselves and even worse, tons of money?

That's just asking for trouble.

And since our enemies are now here in Vegas, we're screwed unless we come up with a battle plan.

My brilliant partnership strategy.

Imagine having the backing of not one, but several, brutal mafia families.

Becerra will be shitting hash bricks.

My ninety percent of the time level-headed brother usually dismisses my concerns about the cartel tracking us any time I bring them up. I know he's trying to make up for what we lost. According to Nate, his decisions forced us out of a life we loved and destroyed our family. I say he was in a no-win situation and did what he needed to do to survive. He made a call that was supposed to protect everyone and instead, it went sideways because drug lords don't like to hear the word 'no'. Nate has been trying to make up for it ever since and wants to make sure he positions us so that we can battle whomever we need to.

The mafia dudes are our answer.

Our salvation.

I let out a deep sigh. Of all the things I saw for my future, leading this pussy parade was definitely not one of them. I had plans. I had dreams. I had Eli.

Although, if I'm being honest, there wasn't a single second I spent with Eli where he made my stomach knot like a pretzel or make my heart slam against my chest like a jackhammer or made me drip with desire in places that have never been properly plundered.

Like, and I really hate to admit this, Sergio Villani does.

I loved Eli but he never made me hot to the point of sweltering. He was sweet, respectful, and gentle, so different from the typical guys in the club who were only out for rough, dirty, and meaningless sex. I loved that he was my friend first and that he made me feel beautiful and wanted. That he made me feel ooey gooey on the inside anytime he'd flash those big brown eyes at me.

Maybe I just liked the way we complemented each other. He grounded me. Since I already had enough of my own fire, I guess I liked that he could bring me into the calm. It was different from the turbulence that was my life.

That turbulence was nothing compared to what I've experienced over the past three years.

And a nagging feeling deep in my gut tells me it's about to bubble up again.

Because you just can't run forever.

But drive? In my beloved car?

I relax my shoulders, a smile plastered on my face as I feel the engine purr when I accelerate.

I could do this for a lifetime.

I could follow this road and never stop.

I could keep going, and going, and—

My cell phone pings, and I press the button on the dashboard to answer.

"Hey!" I say to my brother.

"How was breakfast?" he asks.

"Eventful, as always," I say with a chuckle. "But Ash has a really cool idea I want to run past you later."

"Okay," he says. I bite down on my lower lip because I can totally tell he has a thing for Ashleigh. He thinks he hides it well, but I can see it clear as day. And I love to hassle him about it any chance I get. Sometimes I need to rattle him with something fun to think about since his days and nights are overshadowed by his fears of impending doom and gloom.

He needs to smile more.

Hell, so do I.

"I'm on my way to the club. What time will you be there?" I ask.

"Probably in a couple of hours," he says. "But, Jae, be careful, okay? Get inside, set the alarm, and call me immediately. I'll be watching on the cameras, too."

"When does the electrified fence activate?" I say with a snicker.

"Smartass," he grunts. "I'm trying to keep you—"

"I know, alive," I finish his statement. "But don't worry. I've got eyes everywhere, too. I'll be fine. I promise."

"Okay, later."

I click to end the call and sing along to the song on the radio at the top of my lungs when a loud crack explodes into the still air around me.

And just as suddenly, my car jerks far right, skidding into the dirt on the side of the road.

"What the hell?" I screech, trying with every ounce of strength I have to steer the car the opposite way to straighten it out before I crash head-on into one of the nearby palm trees lining the side of the road.

Another pop follows, and now the back of the car is fishtailing out of control, spinning out before it finally comes to a screeching stop. I'm jolted and jerked around in my seat, panic snaking through me. Pants mixed with expletives spew from my mouth, my shoulders quaking as I clutch the leather steering wheel. "Oh my God! What the fuck is happening?" I cry out.

My chest heaves as I fumble with the lock for the glove compartment. I need my gun, dammit!

Visions of the Bowman brothers splattered with blood streak across my vision as I dig around for my weapon.

I knew this would happen.

I told Nate it was coming!

My fingers are shaking so badly that I can't even grip the handle for longer than a second before it slips out of my hand and onto the floor. In my periphery, I see a tall figure approaching and I bend down to grab the gun, checking that there is a full cl—

Fuck!

It's empty!

I toss the gun to the ground since it's useless to me now. I grab a pen from the console, ready to impale anyone who gets too close.

The man's image gets sharper as he closes the distance between us, my spine stiff, my pen hand ready to lance.

I blink fast.

Wait…I know him!

Dark hair.

Killer body.

Harsh, penetrating gaze.

It's Sergio Villani.

And he's pointing a gun right at my head.

He pulls it away for a split second, just enough time to pop off a shot and deflate the front left tire, making the bottom of the car crack against the pavement under it.

I let out a piercing scream until he has the gun back on me. He pulls open the door, motioning for me to get out. This is my chance. I can at least take out an eye!

I keep my arm at my side, pen wrapped tight in my fingers as I glare at him. "What the fuck do you think you're doing?"

"Get out of the car, Jaelyn," he says, his lips twisted into a grimace that makes him look hotter than hell, if that's even possible. God, he does the menacing thing really well.

Must be all that mafia boot camp shit.

I leap out of the car with a guttural scream, launching my hand at his jugular at the same time a brief sting in my left arm jolts me. Sergio doesn't even blink as he sidesteps my attack. The sting quickly replaced with an icy cold sensation that slithers down to my fingertips, numbing them almost instantly. It winds through my insides, rendering me completely immobile in seconds. I try to swat at him, my already-weak attempt useless since the pen is now on the ground at my feet. I sway left and right, my knees buckling as I collapse against him.

I can't move. I can't yell. I can't do a goddamn thing except lay in his arms as whatever he just injected me with sucks the consciousness from my body.

As numbness spreads through me, quickly replacing the panic, a heavy black fog consumes my conscious and I spiral hard and fast into the sinkhole that has suddenly become my life.

Chapter Eleven
SERGIO

*F*uck, fuck, fuck!

That happened way faster than I thought it would. Doc Arlo said it takes a few minutes to feel the effects of the drug when injected. I'd asked for it just in case Enrico needed a little juice to ease the pain today. I didn't think that when he gave it to me I'd be using it for something else, a plan that really didn't start percolating until after my blowout with Matteo.

Jaelyn went out like a light in a fucking blink. Christ, I hope I didn't give her too much. The Doc said the dosage was enough for Enrico, but he's a big dude and she's about half of his size. But time wasn't really on my side. It was either shoot her up, or get stabbed in the neck with a pen.

And if I'm going out with a pen, it's gonna be something like a Mont Blanc. Not a fucking Bic.

A hot flush snakes up the sides of my neck as I press my ear against her throat. "Thank God," I mutter when I hear the faint thumping of her pulse. I can't prevent my fingertips from grazing her high cheekbones as the relieved breath expels from my mouth.

I do manage to yank back my hand before my traitorous fingers start tracing the outline of her full, pink lips.

I'm still in control of myself.

My situation on the other hand?

Completely fucked unless I do something other than ogle her unconscious form.

Sweat drizzles down my back as I scout my surroundings. I can't dick around here for much longer.

Even though I had the needle in a case next to me, I really only wanted to talk to her. To reason with her. To convince her why it was in her best interest to take the money and run.

But not too far since I wanted a chance to dig my fingers into her hips again, rubbing myself against her curves, making her moan and scream my name…

My eyes fall back to her face, her skin stained a deep pink from the heat pounding us from overhead.

I am so full of shit.

Talking was the last thing on my mind, tied with incapacitation.

Thoughts pop between my ears like bullets.

What the hell have I done?

I swallow hard, my skin prickling with some combination of lust and angst. Conversely, Jaelyn looks so peaceful, her body limp as I wish I could say my cock is right now with her chest pressed against me. I expected her to be wearing the same expression she had painted on last night, her whole face twisted like she'd just taken a bite of the most sour lemon.

But instead, she looks relaxed, despite recent events…namely me, stabbing her with a needle right after destroying her G wagon.

I figured she'd show up early in the day. Call it a hunch. And after that verbal firefight with Matteo at the hotel, I needed to get the fuck away, to clear my head before I pulled my gun on him and blew off his head. That's when my not-so-brilliant plan took shape.

Note to self…never try to plan when you're about to erupt like Mount St. Helen's.

I thought if I got out for a little while, came up with a new and more convincing way to get Torres to listen to my terms, I could salvage things by going through his sister first.

Going through her, under her, over her, behind her…

Jesus, I wanted her every which way.

Except the way I have her right now.

A whiff of Jaelyn's perfume teases my nostrils as I back away from her car with her in my arms. It smells light and fresh, not like the heady, sexy scent that wafted around her last night.

It makes her seem softer than she was only hours earlier. Less like a viper. More vulnerable.

Well, yeah, considering she's knocked out right now and I'm about to stick her in the back of my car headed…somewhere.

I quickly wipe off the door handle to rid it of my fingerprints, and carry her over to my car on the opposite side of the road. The tall grasses were my big advantage when I sent her careening off the road. I glance back at her car, my throat tight.

Torres will find it.

He'll flip the fuck out and come looking for us when Jaelyn is nowhere to be found.

Because he'll know we delivered on our threat, exactly the way he did.

I take in a deep breath, staring down at her bronze skin, her dark hair splayed over my arms, the wheels in my mind circling furiously with no destination in sight.

For hours and hours, I dreamed about holding her close, fantasized about having her plastered against me.

Be careful what you wish for...

That's when an eerie calm settles over me. The fact that I have Jaelyn in my arms right now should scare the shit out of me. This stunt will have my ass in front of a firing squad, and at this point, it could be anyone pulling the trigger, including my own family.

I open the back door of my car and slide Jaelyn into the leather seat. I grab a pair of handcuffs from the floor and slap them on her before jumping into the driver's seat. I press the ignition and the engine roars to life. I slam my foot on the gas, spin the steering wheel around, and tear back down the road toward the Strip.

Away from the Sapphire Lounge and toward…

I grip the steering wheel tight.

Where the hell am I even going? Am I really doing this? Am I really kidnapping Jaelyn Torres?

Jesus, this was not what I had in mind when I said I wanted her lying on my bed, spread-eagle.

I take a few breaths, trying to calm my heart so it doesn't explode out of my chest while muttering to myself. "Where can I go? Not back to the hotel. Not back to the Sapphire Lounge." My fingertips thump on the steering wheel, harder and faster until I get an idea. A fucking brilliant one.

The Severinovs, the notorious Russian bratva that we've partnered with here in Vegas, are about to become my saviors. They have a safehouse outside the city. Away from everything and everyone. Completely off the grid.

But better than that?

It's under renovation, and the crews won't be back to work for another week. That should give me plenty of time to figure out what in the hell I'm going to do with Jaelyn. From a business standpoint, that is. I already have plenty of ideas about things I can do to her that have nothing to do with work and everything to do with pleasure.

And it definitely won't take me a week to exhaust *that* list.

My eyes dart left, right, forward, and backward as I drive into the desert and far away from the Excelsior. If you need anything in this life, it's fucking three-hundred-and-sixty-degree vision.

It's critical to your survival.

Last night, we got lucky and escaped death.

And today?

I check the rearview mirror, my lips curling upward. My tongue sweeps over them as I catch a glimpse of Jaelyn's tits peeking out of the neckline of her tight shirt.

That's the moment clarity shines light on my otherwise murky predicament.

Matteo is always bitching about the fact that I don't make moves that have any value for the family.

Well, fuck that, bro!

I have a ton of value in my grasp right now, about a hundred-and-twenty pounds of it, wrapped up tight in spandex that highlights every luscious curve.

She's not just the epitome of carnal pleasure.

She's our bargaining chip.

An incredible hot and fuckable one, if I say so myself.

Her asshole brother thought he could scare us away with bullets, but he's about to find out you don't fight fire with fire. You fight fire with a nuclear fucking bomb.

And when it drops, when he realizes exactly who he's turned into his most lethal enemy, he'll realize he has only one move to make.

The one we dictate.

Put that one up your ass and smoke it, Matteo.

Chapter Twelve
JAELYN

I slowly crack open my eyes, and damn, my eyelids feel like cement shades that insist on staying closed. After a brief struggle, they let in the blinding light that shines overhead. I blink fast to clear my blurred vision, struggling to lift my pounding head from…I look to my right and left to figure out where I am.

What in the hell?

I'm in a bed.

Shit.

Who's fucking bed is it?

And where is said fucking bed?

I open my mouth to scream, but all that emerges is a raspy squeak.

Pebbles of sweat gather on the back of my neck as my head sinks farther into the fluffy pillow under it, so heavy I can't imagine my shoulders being able to hold it up for even a split second.

Okay, if I can just get leverage, maybe I can sit up.

Relax, Jae. Just put your hands on the mattress and push off—

I choke out a gasp.

Fuck!

I jerk my wrists, straining my arm muscles with each flail, my hands hanging limply from their position.

No, please, no!

Silver handcuffs have my arms firmly attached to the bedposts, holding my body prisoner in the center of this mattress. Sharp breaths slice at my insides as I struggle against the metal cuffs that show no signs of loosening or cracking open.

"Help!" I sputter in a weak voice, still jiggling my wrists. "Help me!"

I grit my teeth, trying like hell to remember how I got here… what happened, where was I, how did—?

And then fragments of the terror I felt come flying back at me with a vengeance. My tires exploding, my car spinning out uncontrollably across the desert road, a dark-haired man coming toward me, the needle he stuck into my arm…

But it wasn't just any man.

Goddammit!

I kick my feet out as far as I can reach, knocking over a tray sitting at the foot of the bed. A loud crash reverberates between the walls as I try once again to screech in anger. But my mouth is so damn dry, I can barely make out a syllable.

"Villani!" I grunt through gritted teeth, clanging the handcuffs to the head of the bed as hard as I can.

The door opens a minute later and once again, my breath hitches.

This time it's because he's holding a glass of water with a straw in it.

I'd give my right arm for a sip…

Oh yeah, I've already given him that limb as well as my left one.

He walks toward the bed, holding the straw to my lips and despite my raging desire to claw out his eyes, I gulp down as much of the cool, clear liquid as I can without choking.

When I've guzzled most of the glass, I pull away, leveling him with a searing glare. I have no weapons except for my mind and unfortunately, I can't gut him like a fish with brain waves as my only tool.

He's standing close to my head, too close for me to launch my foot at his groin. I mean, if I was a gymnast or a contortionist, *maybe*?

But in my reality, I'd end up in a full body cast.

"You shot my tires," I mumble. "And drugged me."

"Your memory is still intact. Good."

"Where is my car?" I ask in a groggy voice. "I loved that car…"

"You should be more concerned with other things right now." He folds his arms across his broad chest, staring at me taking in my new surroundings. The walls are stark, bare, and in need of paint. And there's dust in the air. A lot of fucking dust which is doing a great job of choking me right now.

Well, dust and fury.

A dull ache settles between my temples, but it's not enough to stop me from unleashing the pent-up animosity festering in my gut.

"What in the fuck are you doing, Villani?" I hiss, shaking my wrists. "Are you going to kill me to teach my brother a lesson? Is that how your people handle this kind of thing?"

"Nah. I believe the world is a lot more interesting with you in it." His blue eyes flash with a hint of mischief, and I'd be lying if I said I didn't feel tingles erupt in my belly when his lips curl into a cocky half-grin.

But good that he's not planning on fileting me.

My life hasn't exactly turned out the way I planned, but that doesn't mean I'm ready to give it up without a fight!

"You can't take no for an answer so you figured...what? That you'd kidnap me to convince my brother to take you up on your pathetic offer? Or is this the way you get girls to fuck you? By drugging them and chaining them up?" Bitterness mixed with disdain drip from my lips as I spit out those words.

He lifts an eyebrow, but his mouth remains closed as he rounds the bed and picks up the tray from the floor.

"Oh, now you stop talking?" I shriek now that my mouth actually works. "Do you have any idea who you're dealing with? What my brother will do to you when he finds out that you're holding me hostage?"

"I haven't even begun to execute my plans for you," he seethes. "And so we're clear, your brother is an arrogant piece of shit who's gonna find out very soon that we don't bend after a fucking ambush like that. We attack right back!"

I furrow my brow. Ambush? Uhh. When I try to focus too hard, my stomach clenches tight and a wave of nausea washes over me. I take a few deep breaths, letting my eyes float closed before I launch my next assault of scathing rhetoric at him. "What the hell are you talking about? You came in with three guys last night! How the hell did we ambush *you*?"

"You're either ignorant as hell or a crap ass actress. I don't have to explain myself to you or anyone else!" He narrows his eyes. "And for your information, I don't need to chain women up to sleep with me. They fucking beg for it, sweetheart."

"Beg, my ass! They're just completely incapacitated from all the wine you need to pump into them to get them to open their legs!" Rage bubbles deep within my core, rushing to the surface and when it explodes…well, I won't be able to do a goddamn thing about it since I'm chained to this fucking bed!

Sergio crosses the room, fisting my hair and yanking my head back. A hot flush creeps down my neck and over my prickled skin. I hate myself for even thinking this, but his whole 'I'm the powerful and all-controlling alpha' kitsch is way more sexy than it is scary. I gasp as his head dips lower, his lips hovering so close to mine.

Wow, am I a headcase and a half or what?

Heat pools between my own legs right now while here I am, trying to convince him that he has no carnal pull on me.

Jesus, any woman with breath in her body would react in the same way if his muscular body was pressed against them.

On a bed.

Handcuffed to the posts.

Legs open.

Oops. About that…

My ankles fly together like a magnet against steel.

Then he does the absolute unthinkable.

He smiles, trailing a fingertip down the side of my face while my traitorous body shudders. "Yeah, that's what I thought," he murmurs, backing away from me as I kick and scream like a banshee.

"Scream all you want, gorgeous." Sergio smirks as he leans against the doorway. "There's nobody around to hear you. But I'll warn you now, that screaming will get on my nerves fast so if you don't want to have a piece of duct tape slapped over those lips of yours, either you're gonna suck my cock with them or you're gonna shut the hell up." He winks at me. "Your choice."

Chapter Thirteen
SERGIO

"I wouldn't suck your cock if it was the only one on Earth and I needed it to breathe!" The dark pink color that floods her cheeks makes her eyes pop even more than normal against her bronze skin. She glares at me so hard that I believe she's trying to kill me with her mind right now.

It's hard not to chuckle, especially since she thinks she had the last word last night at the club.

Look who's in the driver's seat now, Jaelyn.

How does it feel to be Miss Daisy, in a very erotic, very compromising position?

Just looking at her — long, dark hair spread out on the pillow below her, shirt riding up to expose taut, smooth abs with a hint of boob, shapely legs thrashing about — fuck me.

She's the sexiest captive I've ever seen.

The only one I've ever had, actually.

That's when reality smacks me across the face with the force of a big beefy hand.

I kidnapped this woman.

Stole her from her life.

And her beloved car.

I'm holding her prisoner in a safehouse that's not mine.

I have her chained to a bed, also not mine, though it's one I'd very much like to share with her, handcuffed or otherwise.

I scrub a hand down the front of my face.

Forget about her sucking your cock and figure out how you're gonna fix this situation so nobody slices off said cock!

Jaelyn's head suddenly drops to the pillow like she's just succumbed to extreme exhaustion and her breathing gets more and more shallow. Tiny mewls escape her lips as her arm and leg muscles tense and seize.

Fuck, what the hell is happening to her?

I grit my teeth, watching her transform from raging bitch to one step above a vegetable in only a few seconds. I stand still, staring at her, willing her to light me on fire again with that mouth, but she only moans louder. Blood rushes between my ears as I rub at the stress knot tight against the base of my spine. Are these side effects? What if she's having a reaction to the injection? What if she's allergic? What if she convulses and fucking dies on me?

In the Severinov's goddamn safehouse, of all places?

I'd have to chop her up and bury her somewhere in the desert!

Otherwise, I'll end up in my own grave next to hers.

With a throbbing pulse, I walk back toward her, concern outweighing all primal urges at this point. Beads of sweat dot her forehead as her whimpers get fainter and fainter.

I lower my head to her chest, her pulse double the speed of my own.

Her eyelids flicker and flutter as if she's about to black out, her skin clammy.

Holy shit, I need to call an ambulance!

"Hey, Jaelyn," I murmur, smoothing back her hair. "Are you ok—?"

But before I can even utter the words, a paralyzing shock of pain erupts between my legs and before I can catch myself, I collapse right on top of her. My stomach leaps into my throat and the anguish resulting from her shin colliding with my balls roars through my groin like a wildfire incinerating everything in its path. "Goddammit!" I roar, doubling over as I roll off of the bed.

"Fuck you, Sergio!" she sings, alert, awake, and most importantly, alive. Sure, she may have just sterilized me, but death would be much more painful.

For me, I mean.

"You can chain me up but you'll never hold me down, dickhead!" She giggles as I clutch myself, staggering toward the open door, gasping for air.

Jesus Christ. She fucking played me and I let myself get sucked right into her twisted and sadistic game.

She may be gloating now after crippling my manhood.

But there's no piece of ass on this planet hot enough to cripple my goddamn livelihood!

"You do realize that if you put me out of commission, you'll still be handcuffed to that bed, right?" I gasp, doubled over. "No ability to move or escape?"

"It would be worth it just to see you suffer!" she shrieks. "I'd rather starve to death or lay in my own waste to see you crumbled on the floor like the weak, pathetic asshole you are! Oh, so powerful and scary," she mocks in a voice dripping with disdain. "You couldn't even get me here without sticking a needle in my arm! You knew I'd fight and that you'd lose!"

Her eyes blaze, her jaw so tight I think it might crack from clenching so hard. She's right. I knew she'd fight. Like a fucking hellcat.

I just didn't want to have to fight back.

I needed to keep my leverage intact.

The corners of my lips lift as I slowly rise to my feet. "Well, I'm not on the floor, sweetheart. But don't worry, I'll make sure the rest of your requests are granted. Enjoy your stay."

I slam the door, my pulse throbbing against my neck as she flings out the harshest expletives that would even make a prisoner's ears bleed.

I lean against the door and push back my hair. I have Jaelyn Torres on her back, which is exactly where I'd fantasized she'd be if I had my way.

But now that I have her, there's the tiny little detail of what the hell to do with her. I didn't think that part through very well.

Okay, not at all.

And what was my plan for work? How many damn meetings can I say I have that'll keep me away from the hotel and out from Matteo's thumb?

I need backup.

Someone to run interference.

I walk through the mess of construction and pull out my phone, as far away from the bedroom door as possible so she can't hear the panic in my voice.

I'm reserving that for one person.

I stab Bruno's number into my phone and he answers after a couple of rings.

"How's Enrico?" I ask in a choked voice.

"Good. He just woke up a little while ago. I brought him some food."

I nod. "Okay, glad to hear that."

"How'd the meeting go?"

"It, ah, didn't go as planned."

Bruno snickers. "Did you shoot someone?"

"Not exactly." More like shot someone up. "Where is everyone?"

"You mean where's Matteo? I try to keep away from him, so I don't really know. Don't wanna know, either."

"Bruno, I have a job for you to do." I take a deep breath. "My meeting kinda went sideways and I'm going to be out for longer than I planned. I need you to cover for me."

Another high-pitched shriek emerges from the bedroom and I squeeze my eyes shut.

"Dude," Bruno says with a chuckle. "If you wanted to get laid, you coulda just told me. And why would you need me to cover for you, anyway? It's not a hooker, is it? Jesus, Serge. Not again. There's plenty of pussy right here that you don't have to pay for."

"Bruno," I hiss. "There is no hooker. And there sure as hell isn't any sex. I just…I have to take care of a few things today. You know, figure out how to fix things with, ah, Torres."

"The only thing that guy is fixing for is an opportunity to kick your ass, you know that, right?"

"I might have come up with a way to get through to him," I say through clenched teeth.

"Oh shit, that's not him screaming, is it? You gonna ass-ram him or something until he agrees to sell?"

"No," I hiss. "I don't have time to play Twenty fucking Questions now!"

"Sergio!" Jaelyn shouts again. "I have to pee!"

"Serge, what the hell is going on there?"

I mute the phone and yell back to her. "You just said you'd happily lay in your own waste! So be fucking happy, yeah?"

"Serge?" Bruno asks again. "You wanna tell me what the hell is going on? Where are you and who the hell has to pee?"

I suck in a breath. "Bruno, I did a fucking bad thing. I mean, I didn't think it was bad at first. Well, actually, I didn't think about anything at first except talk—"

"Sergio!" Bruno bellows.

"Fine," I say, expelling a sigh. "I'm at the Severinov safehouse."

"The one under construction?"

"Yeah."

"Do I wanna know why?"

I rub the back of my neck. "No."

"But you're gonna tell me anyway, right?"

"Yeah." I lean my head back against the wall. "I came here because I knew nobody would be here to use it."

"And you needed privacy because…?"

"Because I kidnapped Jaelyn Torres from her car this morning and needed a place to keep her."

"Fuck me," he mutters slowly. I can see his expression in my mind, eyes wide, beefy hand scrubbing the stubble of his beard.

"Yep."

"And by kidnapping her, just to be clear, you, ah, what exactly?"

"I gave her a shot of whatever Doc Arlo gave me for Enrico. It was strong enough that she passed out. I pulled her from her car and brought her right here."

"You kidnapped her in broad daylight?"

"Yes."

"And left her car on the side of the road."

"Yeah." I pause. "But I wiped down any area I touched so there wouldn't be prints."

"Mm-hm," he mumbles, silent for a minute. "And you thought that drugging and snatching Torres' sister was the best way to negotiate a fucking deal, Serge?" Bruno shouts.

"Easy," I mumble. "I don't want anyone to hear you and ask what you're grousing about."

He lets out a dry laugh. "Sure, I'd get why you want me to keep my dipshit cousin's meathead plan to salvage the deal with Torres quiet!"

My mouth twists into a grimace. "If you were here, I'd shoot you for saying that shit."

"But I'm not!" he sings out. "I'm not the fucking idiot who just committed a kidnapping and left all of the goddamn evidence out in the open for anyone to find!"

"There weren't any eyewitnesses," I grunt. "Don't be so dramatic. It's not like you're a Boy Scout, Bruno."

"True," he says. "But I am a planner, though. I strategize before making a move, especially one that would have Torres all over us. Not to mention the shit you brought on us by cutting off Javier's hand! What the hell is with you, Serge? This isn't like you! This screams Dante and Roman!"

I shift against the wall. He's right. I don't make sudden moves like this without thinking them through. But my life…starting from when Jaelyn walked into my nightclub…has become a very dangerous and destructive funnel cloud. It just spins with lightning speed, sucking me deeper with every passing day. It continues to wreak havoc at every turn and I don't know how to stop it.

I wanted to talk to her. Really.

I figured I could come up with something to say that might get her to change her mind about me, the offer, all of it.

But then Matteo's words rang out in my head and I just lost it.

All of it.

The anger charged through me when I saw her car coming down that road, and I wanted to show Torres how short-sighted he was for attacking us like he did.

"He tried to kill us," I seethe. "He deserves nothing less than to have his precious sister's body hand-delivered to his club in a crate of dry ice!"

"Please tell me that's not part of your plan."

"Not yet it isn't." I scowl as Jaelyn's whining gets louder. "I can't say it won't become the plan, though."

"So how long are you planning to keep her locked up?" Bruno asks. "And are you going to stay there with her? You do have a job here, you know. I can only cover for you for so long before Matteo starts asking questions. And it won't take long for him to jump down my throat if you're not here to distract him."

I roll my eyes. "Thanks. And yeah, I know I have things to figure out."

"Look, let's be real here. You made a dumbass mistake by taking her. No doubt about that. We could have figured out another way to deal with the situation. But if Torres finds out, Matteo will be the least of your problems. By then, you'll be earless, handless, and dickless. Probably on your way to being headless."

"Thanks for the vote of confidence."

"I'm just telling it like it is."

"You're not helping."

"Do you want me to kidnap some other chick from the club to keep her company? Would that be helpful?"

"You're flicking my last nerve."

"There will be a lot of lasts for you when Torres finds out you hijacked his sister. Your nerves should be last on your list of concerns."

"Just don't blow my damn cover, okay?" I say through clenched teeth.

"Just figure out how the hell you're gonna fix this situation you've created, okay?"

I click the end button without saying goodbye and fight with everything in me to not hurl it at the unfinished sheetrock.

Jesus Christ, what the hell have I done?

My eyes flicker toward the closed bedroom door.

Jaelyn would know the truth.

But would she tell me?

She'd never sell out her brother, and would I be able to trust her if she said it wasn't them?

Another round of screams explodes into the air. I hear the headboard of the bed slam against the wall as she flounders on the mattress.

"Sergio!"

I clutch the sides of my head. "*What?*" I shout back.

"I have to pee!"

I drag myself off the wall and fling open the door. "What part about making you suffer wasn't clear the first time?"

"Look," she seethes. "I don't know why I'm here or what you plan to do to me, but the least I'd expect is to be treated with a little bit of goddamn dignity! And that means being able to use a bathroom! Cuff me to the freaking toilet, but get me in there!"

I let out a sharp breath and stare at her. The second I uncuff her, she's gonna attack me like a rabid lioness. I search the room and then wander into the foyer for supplies. A roll of duct tape sits on one of the half-walls. I grab it and bring it into the bedroom. I wrap it around her ankles first so she has nowhere to run, and kicking will be quite the challenge since I've basically turned her into a mermaid. Then I uncuff one wrist and pull her loose arm over to the still-cuffed one. I snap the handcuffs on both of her wrists and bend down to gather her in my arms. I swing her upward as she wiggles around.

"You think you're so smart, don't you?" she mutters as I carry her toward the bathroom.

"Well, seeing as how I'm not the one who's so trapped she needs to be carried to the toilet, yeah. I think I'm the smarter one in this scenario."

I deposit her inside the bathroom and she glares at me.

"Pull down my pants, you dickhead."

I can't fight the smirk and she curses me before collapsing on the seat. I turn around to give her some privacy because I'm not an animal, after all, and when she's done, she calls my name. With a sweet smile, she asks me to wipe her and pull up her pants again.

This time when I lean over, she clocks me in the side of the head with her knee. I make sure to pull her panties up so high, they're in her throat when I carry her back to the bed and cuff her again.

"You can't keep me here forever," she says in a low voice, squirming on the bed. "Nate needs to know that you have me."

"Oh, he will. When I'm goddamn good and ready!"

She shakes her head, her eyes fluttering closed for a minute. "I would do anything to protect my brother."

"I know that. It's why you came to my club last week, to fuck around with my business and figure out a way to get the upper hand. You fucking played me!"

She lifts an eyebrow. "It wasn't that hard."

I narrow my eyes. "Well, guess what? It didn't work. Your brother doesn't get the last word. I do!"

"So you think you're just going to babysit me until he changes his mind?" She shakes her head. "You don't have any idea what you're up against, Villani. You want Nate to change his mind? Well, he needs to be alive to make that deal. There's so much more to this than you know, and the longer you hold me here, the less of a chance you have of that happening."

I stomp over to her, hovering low against her face. "Jaelyn, I'm gonna tell you something right now that you need to remember because I won't say it again. Fool me once, shame on me. Fool me twice, you are completely fucked. See how that works?" I trail a finger down the side of her face, tilting her chin upward so she has no choice but to look at me. "I do not and will not believe a single word that comes out of your smart-ass mouth. That's what happens when you try to play someone one time too often. You lose their trust. Now, you can cry me whatever the hell river you want, but to me, it's all white noise. I have an objective and you're my way of achieving it. I don't need to hear anything more from you. Anything that you say is complete bullshit and will be ignored, do you understand?" I pull my finger away. "Don't think for a second that you can actually win this. You will fail. I promise you that. And when you fail, guess who pays the price?" I flash a nasty smile. "That's right. Big bad brother Nate. You wanna be responsible for that?"

Her nostrils flare and she twists her head away from me. "If you don't tell him you have me, it'll be too late for him to pay you anything," she rasps, her voice choked.

Chapter Fourteen
JAELYN

"You can't leave my feet taped up like this," I say as Sergio storms toward the doorway after my last cryptic comment. "Please. It will drive me absolutely insane if I can't move my legs apart. And it's not like I can go anywhere if my hands are cuffed together."

He stands still for a long minute, like he's trying to decide whether or not I've been tortured enough today. As if it wasn't bad enough to have been assaulted, kidnapped, and then humiliated in the bathroom like that.

"Why the hell should I make you comfortable?" he growls. "This isn't a sleepover party, princess."

I grit my teeth. "You said you needed me as leverage, right? Well, what kind of leverage would I be if I was dead, huh? Not a real effective bargaining chip. And if you come in tomorrow morning and find me blue because the lack of circulation killed me in my sleep, then what hope do you have of using me to get what you want?"

Sergio glares at me, his lips parting and then slamming shut once he realizes that I'm right. I would be useless to him.

"Please," I say again, hating how my voice takes on a slight whimper. I wiggle my toes, the urge to spread my legs overwhelming. And not just because I'm fighting a massive internal lust fest with my captor.

He walks out of the room and returns with what looks like a box cutter. With a flick of his wrist, he slices through the tape, and my ankles fly apart. I am so overwhelmed with relief that I can move some part of my body that I don't even think to give him another kick.

He does have the box cutter, after all.

And even though I know he wouldn't kill me, he might just cut off a finger or toe out of spite.

No, thank you.

I'll behave.

For now.

"Thanks," I say, breathing out a deep sigh as blood returns to my feet. The tingling sensation eases up as soon as the circulation returns, the tips of my toes again tan instead of stark white.

"Are you hungry?" he asks in a gruff voice.

"No," I say with a hint of defiance. The truth is, my stomach is still in knots, I guess from whatever drug hangover I'm still suffering. I pushed through the head and body aches, refusing to let them encumber me, but the nausea is still in force.

Not that I want him to see me in that compromised state.

I won't.

This time when he walks out of the room, I let him go without another word.

What's the point?

I can bitch and complain and lash out at him, but it won't change the fact that I'm pretty much at his mercy right now.

All because Nate played his part so well the other night. We made him desperate, just as we intended. The problem is, we didn't anticipate how very desperate he actually is.

Or that he'd resort to kidnapping in an attempt to take over our business.

He doesn't strike me as the type of guy to pull such an impulsive stunt. He seemed unruffled each time I saw him. Sure, he got a little heated, but nothing that would indicate he'd snap like a rubber band.

And that he did.

I sigh, using my feet to slide myself higher up on the bed so that I don't suffer dislocation of my shoulders as a result of being handcuffed like this.

I wonder how people into BDSM do this kind of shit for fun. I mean, they chain themselves up and use all kinds of contraptions during sex play…at least, from what I hear. I bite down on my lower lip, a shiver slipping down my spine. I never thought about it before, but now…

I swallow hard, my breath hitching. An image of Sergio walking back into the bedroom flashes across my mind and I shift on the bed, slamming my legs together as tingles in my core ignite.

Dammit. What in the hell is happening right now?

He crawls onto the bed and slides my leggings down to my ankles, pulling them off one foot at a time before flinging them to the floor. He forces my knees apart, his hands running down the inside of my thighs, grasping the flesh hard with his fingertips.

I gasp, squeezing my eyes shut and allowing my mind and body to succumb to the fantasy.

His head dips lower, his breath hot against my wet pussy. When his tongue slips inside, my stomach clenches, my hips driving upward against his mouth.

I can feel his palms cup my ass as he lifts me upward, dragging his tongue out and flicking it against my clit before he sinks back into me. He sucks my clit between his teeth enough for a ball of electricity to fizzle and spark deep within my core.

A tiny mewl slips from my mouth as I wiggle and writhe on the mattress, the imaginary scenario causing a slew of tremors to erupt within me.

My eyes fly open.

Cue the record-scratch-sound effect.

Good God, I am a sick and twisted woman.

I'm lying on this bed in crucifixion position by a guy who clearly wants to torture me, and I may have just gotten off on nothing more than an erotic daydream about him?

Okay. I get the BDSM hype now.

Jeez. And that was just a quick little mind sexscape.

Imagine how the real thing would go down.

Pun very much intended.

My breathing finally calms and I let my eyelids flutter closed while that fantasy loops through my cluttered mind.

Maybe it will bring me peace while I sleep.

That would be a welcome first.

Chapter Fifteen
JAELYN

I roll over onto my side, a smile playing at my lips as Eli strokes my bare shoulder.

"I didn't hurt you, did I?" he asks, a look of concern in his eyes.

"No," I whisper. It's a total lie, but there's no sense in making him feel bad about it. After that disastrous face-off at home with my parents, I couldn't wait to get away and to lose myself in something other than the anger coursing through me.

Sex was the act of choice.

And regrettably, my first time wasn't one that will go down in the books as one of the most romantic experiences of my life.

But I needed a different memory, a new one that could be powerful enough to replace the one I'd just suffered. I forced things with Eli, practically assaulting him once we got to his apartment instead of letting him take the time to prep me for what was to come, but that was just because I needed to eradicate the toxic scene from my brain. I wanted a distraction, something that would help me focus on anything other than the altercation now forever branded into my memory.

I told my father that I hated him.

A shiver runs through me as those heated words creep around my heart, making it clench. I'd forced them to the back burner, putting Eli at the center of my attention after we sped away from my house earlier tonight.

I can't ever take those words back.

And I won't ever forget the look of shock and horror on Dad's face once my screams pierced the tense air.

His little girl. His baby.

Hates him.

Although I keep the smile plastered on my face, tears sting my eyes as I avert my gaze from Eli's pensive one.

"We didn't have to do this tonight, Jae," *he murmurs, rubbing my back.*

"Yes, we did," *I sniffle.* "Because I love you and you love me."

I wait, but he doesn't affirm.

I narrow my eyes and look back at him.

"But it was bad timing, you know, with your parents and that whole mess at the house." *His forehead pinches and he rubs the back of his neck.* "You think your dad will tell Nate what happened?"

Warning bells sound in the recesses of my mind.

"Is that what you're really worried about right now? What my brother will think?" *I sit straight up, gripping his bedsheet in my fists. I just basically told my parents to go fuck themselves, that I choose Eli over all, and he's worried about Nate's reaction?*

That's his big concern? The fucking club?

Not me?

I just gave him my virginity! My whole self! I would have walked to the ends of the Earth to be with him if he asked!

Now I get why he didn't.

Eli shrugs. "Well, the club comes first, right? I don't want him to think my loyalty is in question just because we're together."

My eyes widen and all at once, the tears are forgotten. "So, you told me you loved me and got me into bed. Now, you're afraid my parents are going to blow the whistle on us and compromise your future with the club?"

"Wait," he says, also sitting up. "You're twisting this all around. I'm just saying that I don't want Nate to—"

"Oh, no, I hear exactly what you're saying. And not saying, by the way." I jump out of the bed and start pulling on my hastily discarded clothes. "I told you I loved you. I chose you! Over my family!"

"I never asked you to choose," he says in a small voice.

"So is that supposed to mean you'd have chosen differently if push came to shove?" My pulse rockets with each passing second and my throat is so tight, I can barely breathe right now. He doesn't respond, but the look on his face speaks volumes.

I throw my head back and let out a dry laugh. "I can't believe what an idiot I was! What I gave up for you!"

"Jae, you're making this into more than it is. All I was saying is that I don't want there to be static between me and Nate!"

"Well, don't worry about that. I can assure you that static between you and me will be much more damaging!" I twist around the room, searching for something, anything to hurl at his head. I grab the television remote and fling it at him. It narrowly misses his head and crashes against the wall behind him. "Thank you for an amazing night. It's one I will never forget," I say, sarcasm dripping from my words.

"Jaelyn!" he says again, rolling out of the bed and rushing after me. He reaches out to grab my wrist as I pull om my boots and I stare at his fingers for a split second before I use my other fist to launch a punch straight at his nose.

He groans, doubling over as he tries to catch the blood with his hand. "You're a fucking crazy bitch, do you know that?"

I smirk at him, flinging my handbag over my shoulder and flipping him off as I pull open the door to his apartment. "Yes, so I've heard."

"Jae," Eli rasps, chasing me as I stomp over the threshold. "Please don't tell Na—"

But I don't let him finish his pathetic plea before I slam the door in his dumbass face.

The most book-smart guy I know is also the most fucking stupid one.

I don't bother to wait for the elevator. I fly down the stairs, trying to put as much distance between us as possible before angry tears spring to my eyes.

My first love.

Ha!

What a fucking joke!

My skin crawls, like tiny spiders are creeping up and down my legs and arms. Bile rises in my throat as I rub my hands up and down my sleeves, trying to squash the sense of impending dread that immersed me right when Eli's priorities became painfully clear.

But I loved him!

I run down the last flight of stairs and explode out of the building, collapsing against the brick wall next to the entryway before I allow the sobs to quake my body. And dammit, I hate every tear that falls from my eyes. This isn't me. I'm not this girl!

Or am I?

I clench my fists, gritting my teeth as I swipe a hand under my eyes.

I was going to give up everything for that jerkoff!

So this rejection is more than just a little sting. It's a full-on incineration of my heart.

I dig through my bag for my phone so I can call an Uber, scrolling through the screens for the app. I jab at the screen, typing in my destination. I'm about to select an Uber X when Nate's name flashes across my screen.

Shit.

He knows, doesn't he?

Mom or Dad must have called him to drop the bomb.

I close my eyes for a brief second before I accept the call.

"Hey, what's up?"

"Jae, where are you?"

I bite the inside of my mouth. "Ah, well, I'm...by Marlins Park," *I say slowly, my eyes darting left and right. Well, at least I will be by the baseball stadium in about fifteen minutes if I get walking now. A shudder runs through me. It's dark, and strutting through this neighborhood isn't my most brilliant plan, especially in the outfit I'm wearing.*

"Okay, get there and I'll pick you up in a few minutes," *he says in a choked voice.*

"Nate, what's wrong?" I ask, hugging my arms around myself. I don't know why. It's seasonably scorching hot.

"Just...get there," he rasps, struggling to keep his voice even. "I'll see you in a few minutes."

"I'm not at Marlins Park," I blurt out, my teeth chattering uncontrollably for some reason. "I lied. I'm sorry. I'm outside Eli's building."

I just hear deep breaths through the phone lines. "Stay there," he says in what sounds to be a defeated voice. His tone is sad, broken, and completely uncharacteristic. "I'm close."

"Nate," I whisper, my heart thumping as blood rushes between my ears. "You're scaring me. What happened?" I squeeze my eyes shut. "Did something happen to Mom or Dad?"

"Stay put," he says, not answering my question. "I'll be there soon."

Click.

That's when the impending dread morphs into my soon-to-be reality.

I stare at the phone for a few seconds, the screen again black.

Nate is on his way here, to pick me up for some reason that he couldn't croak out over the phone.

He didn't respond when I'd asked about our parents.

I press a hand to my forehead, swaying against the building. My breaths slice into my lungs like tiny shards of glass, sharp and shuddering. I sink to the ground, hugging my knees as shadows move past me along the sidewalk.

Something bad is coming.

I felt it before but pushed it aside, chalking it up to the blowout with Eli and the shattering of my heart.

But there's more to come that will shatter the rest of me, I just know it.

I sense it.

It hangs in the air around me like a thick, dark ominous cloud.

My head falls into my hands as I cry silently into them.

I sit there, the pavement rough and cool against my skin, for what feels like hours, even days. Prayer has never been my thing since I'm not an overly religious person, but it's the one thing that springs to my mind as I tremble in the balmy air.

Please, God. Please let my parents be safe. Please don't let them be hurt.

And please let them know how much I love them and how sorry I am!

Bright headlights finally light up the patch of concrete I'm huddled against as Nate's car pulls up to the curb.

I jump to my feet and run over to him, yanking open the car door and crawling into the front seat, afraid to speak the words. He turns to look at me without a response to my silent question, his eyes red, tears streaming from the corners.

No words are spoken.

They don't need to be.

His face tells me everything...none of which I want to hear or accept.

I fall into his arms, sobs quaking my body as he holds me tight against him, his sorrow mixed with mine.

My prayers were futile.

And now the guilt and heartache are all that's left to swallow me whole.

Chapter Sixteen
SERGIO

I pace in front of the tall, floor-to-ceiling windows on the far end of the apartment, trying to dissect Jaelyn's words about Nate.

"If you don't tell him you have me, it'll be too late for him to pay you anything."

I shake my fists in the air, trying to keep from blowing like Old Faithful, but it's hard. Tormentingly so. She's so goddamn infuriating with all of her venomous words and cryptic warnings.

What in the hell is that supposed to mean?

And why do I even care?

She's proven before that she'll say and do just about anything to protect her brother, so why should I think there's anything credible behind that statement, especially when she's the one chained to a bed and is looking for any way to get out of here?

I pace for a few more minutes, my stomach growling.

Shit. I really didn't plan very well at all.

I walk into the kitchen, push aside the tarp covering the refrigerator door, and pull it open. The appliances are still hooked up, so maybe there's some food here.

I frown at the almost-empty space.

Stoli vodka and a jar of pickles.

Fantastic.

We can get drunk on vodka cocktails with pickle garnish.

I slam a hand down on a slab of plywood, sending it flying into the air.

My ears prickle after it crashes to the floor.

Is that…?

I step closer to the bedroom where Jaelyn is staying, my brow furrowing.

She's crying?

I quietly push open the door and find her twisting around on the bed, her hair a mess of tangled strands around her face. She's at battle with something as she sleeps very fitfully. Her mouth moves, only the faintest of sounds emerging, different than the whimpers I just heard from the kitchen. I can see the tears streak her cheeks as she flips left and right, seemingly trying to escape whatever is corrupting her mind.

I move toward the headboard, my fingers fumbling in my pocket for the handcuff key. I slip it into the lock and twist it to release the cuff. Her hand drops to the mattress and with a loud gasp, she sits straight up, bringing her hand to her heaving chest.

She looks around, her eyes unfocused as she takes in her surroundings.

That dream must have really fucked with her since she doesn't seem to have any recollection that she's here.

It isn't until she turns her red-rimmed eyes toward me that I see what's lurking within the depths. My breath hitches. It's the first time I've seen her without the protective mask, the one that keeps everyone out and all of the pain inside.

She uses her free hand to wipe her eyes, her lips still trembling. Her labored breaths sound like shallow rasps, and she trembles as she sits in the center of the mattress, still staring at me.

I can see the anguish.

I can feel the grief.

And so I don't think much in this moment.

I just act.

No questions, no lies.

I hold out my arms and she falls into them, the whimpers becoming full-fledged cries…pleas for forgiveness and mercy, apologies for not being the daughter they deserved.

My throat tightens as I stroke the back of her head.

This is bad. This is very fucking bad!

She's still chained to the bed. I haven't let her go completely, not that she seems to be in any shape to make false moves on me.

But I can't be comforting her like this! Her brother tried to kill me, for fuck's sake!

As far as I'm concerned, any ploy to bring me in here is one that's gonna put my whole plan at risk.

I should let her go.

I should re-cuff her.

I should walk right out of this room and let her drown in her tears, dammit!

But I don't do any of those things.

I stay right where I am as she nestles as far as she can into my chest, her other arm still suspended above the bed.

And this kind of shit is exactly the kind of thing Matteo would jump on me for because he doesn't have blood running through his veins.

He has cyanide.

Pure poison.

Completely lethal.

We sit together as the minutes drag on, neither one of us making any moves, which, I guess for me, is good since both times I got too close, she nailed me with her flying limbs. This time she doesn't seem too anxious to let go or to sterilize me.

Both are good signs, in my opinion.

It feels like we've been molded together for days by the time she lifts her head and pulls away to look up at me. Her eyes are still watery and a little bit puffy and her face is dotted with red splotches.

She's never looked so gorgeous.

Or so broken.

I was shocked to see it the first time.

This time is plain surreal.

Little body.

Larger-than-life attitude.

And we can't forget that huge chip sitting right on her shoulder.

I can't help but ignore the question of why.

She sniffles, flexing her fingers. I instinctively move away from her, just in case she's getting ready.

With a small smile on her face, she drops her hand to the mattress. "I'm not going to hit you."

"I don't know if I should believe you," I say with a quirked eyebrow. "Past experience dictates something very different."

"Yeah, I know." Jaelyn lets out a sigh, pushing her hair, matted with tears, away from her face. "So why did you uncuff me?"

I shrug. "Because I was afraid I'd kill you if I kept you locked up that way. I took a chance that you wouldn't run or attack me if I freed one of your arms."

"Well, I appreciate you saving my life."

"I, uh, also heard—"

She holds up her free hand. "No. Don't go there."

I rake a hand through my hair. 'Why? Because you don't want it to get out that, contrary to popular opinion, you're not a complete bitch twenty-four-seven and that you do actually have a sensitive side?"

With a roll of her eyes, she collapses back on the mattress. "You're a big gangster-type guy. You know emotion is for the weak."

"Yep, and the weak ones get the ice pick to the head. I know the story well." I smirk.

"Good, so then let's just agree to drop it."

I nod. "Okay, it's forgotten. Anything else off limits that I should know about?"

Her eyes take on a glower. "You've already made it clear that anything I say is worthless, so why even ask?"

"Look, Jaelyn," I say, sliding off the bed and walking over to the far wall. Jesus, I really need to keep my distance from this girl, for a lot of reasons. "I know you don't understand what's happening, but there's a good reason why you're here. A very good reason."

"What's *happening* here?" she asks, her voice rising. "There is nothing happening here! You kidnapped me for this alleged 'good reason' but you seem to have no plan for what to do to me or with me. That tells me your 'good reason' is actually total crap."

I clench my fists at my sides. "I know exactly what I'm doing! Don't fucking challenge me!"

Jaelyn lets out a huff. "Okay, so first, you're getting pretty defensive for a guy who has everything figured out. Second, I heard you on the phone with one of your idiot friends! So don't feed me that garbage! Admit it, you don't know what the hell you're doing! Maybe you should just stick to running strip clubs into the ground! You're fucking great at that!"

I stomp over to the bed and grab her chin so she has to look up at me. I also make sure I grab her free hand to keep myself alive and unmaimed. "You don't know what the hell you're talking about!"

"Don't I, though?" she snips, wrenching her face out of my grip. "You wouldn't be so pissed off if I was wrong. You'd laugh it off, thinking the joke is on me. But it's not, is it? You didn't think this through and you don't know what you're going to do next!" she shrieks. "And my brother could die because of it!"

That's when her feet flail, one of them coming dangerously close to my groin.

"I don't really give a damn what sob story you think you can sell me. It won't fucking work! And your brother's death would be fucking justice served!" I thunder.

Her eyes widen and she gasps. "What the hell are you talking about?"

"You play dumb pretty well, but I'm not that stupid, sweetheart." I lean over her, our foreheads almost touching as I hiss my next and final words. "This is about taking an eye for an eye, Jaelyn. An eye for a fucking eye!" I grab the handcuffs and cuff both of her wrists again, this time together. At least she's not being stretched apart again.

Although the cracks running through my merciful side are starting to spread, and pretty soon I'm gonna just give it all up and hang her out the window by her goddamn ankles to keep her mouth shut.

And to prove to her that I do have a plan.

To win!

Chapter Seventeen
JAELYN

I slam my feet into the mattress, letting out a shrill yell. Frustration and panic grip me, and I'm torn between wanting to tell Sergio the truth and keeping my mouth shut because then I'd have to tell the truth, further exposing me and Nate.

But I know that every second that passes brings Nate closer and closer to the edge. Even if the alarm bells don't sound when he can't get a hold of me by phone, I'm sure that seeing my car abandoned on the side of the very road he'd take to the club will put him in killing-spree mode.

I haven't seen that version of my brother in three years, and we barely escaped within an inch of our lives when the ambush on the Bowman brothers unexpectedly went sideways on us.

I always suspected it was Eli who tipped them off that Nate and I were coming. We couldn't stick around to prove it or to punish the jackass, but deep down, I knew it was him.

Nate forced him to patch out of his charter after that horrific night, and Eli never forgave either one of us for uprooting him and voting him out. And since he still had friends in the charter who didn't agree with him being forced to leave, it was pretty clear how word got out about our revenge plan against the Becerra Cartel and their dipshit drug mules.

The idea was to cripple them in the most brutal way possible, and we did.

But the bullseye on our backs has just gotten bigger and bigger with each passing day.

Nate already knows the cartel leaders are here looking for us.

He won't assume I've just fallen off the face of the Earth because I took a wrong turn into the desert.

He's going to assume they're the ones who snatched me.

And he's going to storm the lion's den to rescue me.

It would be a suicide mission.

They'll never let him get out alive, not after everything he's done to their organization.

They've waited too long and their hate for us runs too deep to let him slip through their grubby fingers.

I squeeze my eyes shut. If I don't speak up now and show my hand, I risk losing my brother, the only family I have left. Sergio has made it pretty clear that he wants Nate dead, so it's a big risk telling him what I'm certain Nate is about to do. He might just make a call to his pal Becerra with that information and kill two birds with one stone — secure his partnership with the cartel and sacrifice my brother.

"Argh! No!" I swing my arms back over my head, slamming the metal cuffs against the headboard.

Sergio flings open the door and stands there with a glass of clear liquid in his hand. "You're giving me a goddamned headache with your screaming. If you don't shut the hell up, I'll slap the duct tape over that mouth of yours."

I struggle to sit up, floundering around like a fish out of water as I try to get leverage against the soft mattress. "Listen," I say, gritting my teeth. "I need to tell you something."

He lifts an eyebrow and gulps down the liquid. "I hope it's not that you have to pee again. I've had about enough of your knees, Jaelyn. And there are a lot of hammers in this place," he says. "Just remember that."

I roll my eyes. "Fine, be a badass. Whatever. Does it look like I'm afraid of you or whatever stupid ass scheme you're trying to run using me as bait?"

His eyes flash and he slams the glass against the wall across from me, and with a loud crash, ice cubes and shards of glass fly into the air. Then he stomps toward me, closing a hand around my neck. It's not too tight and I can still breathe, but I won't lie. It startles me a little bit. He seems so calm and cool all the time, except in these fleeting moments when he just completely loses his shit and lashes out.

It's a little scary.

And hot, if I'm being honest.

But I need logical Sergio right now, not psycho Sergio.

"You're not going to kill me," I whisper.

"You're doing a good job of making me want to," he seethes, his blue eyes darkening like a turbulent storm is about to ravage the otherwise calm pools. But he loosens his grip nonetheless, and the crashing waters begin to recede.

Thank fuck.

"I can offer you something, Sergio. But in return, I need your help," I murmur in a choked voice.

"Why would I want to help you? You're a lying, double-crossing, manipulative bitch."

"And that's all bad because why? Because I got one over on you? Beat you at your own game? Isn't that what's driving that pole further and further up your ass?"

"For someone who wants my help, you're doing an awesome job of convincing me to tell you to fuck off." He pulls his hand away from my throat and I drink in as much oxygen as possible before speaking again. I really need to work on my timing.

Note to self: Don't incite the monster just before asking for his help!

"You're right," I say, coughing a little bit. "Okay, forget that I just insulted you. I really need you to hear this."

"Listening," he growls. "So make it good."

I expel a sigh through my lips. "I know you want the nightclubs."

"Yeah, I think I made it pretty clear the other night that I did." He snorts, backing up from the bed and folding his arms over his chest.

"So much that you'd be willing to kidnap me in order to get your hands on our business?"

His lips twist into a grimace. "Don't bullshit me again, Jaelyn. You know that's not why you're here."

"Look," I say, struggling to keep my voice even. "We're losing time dancing around here. Okay? You are, I am, and so is Nate! So let's just be honest with each other and see if we can work together to fix things. I'm scared for my brother. That's the only reason why I am willing to come up with a trade."

He narrows his eyes. "A trade?"

"Yes, your help for a share of the nightclubs."

"Why the fuck should I help you or Nate when he tried to kill me and my guys the other night?"

I gasp. "What are you talking about?"

He grabs the duct tape from the plastic-covered dresser and walks over to me, shaking it over me. "If you're fucking with me, Jaelyn…if you're not being straight with me…I will wrap you up like a damn mummy in this tape!"

"I don't know what you're talking about!" I shout.

He grips the back of my hair, forcing my head upward. "When we were leaving the club the other night, we were ambushed by a van. Shooters opened fire on us. They got one of my guys."

"I-I didn't know," I rasp, the pain from his tight grip shooting to the roots of my hair follicles. "But it couldn't have been Nate. He wouldn't have done that. I mean, I know I told him to—" I muse out loud, stopping before the rest of it slips out.

"Told him to what?" Sergio snarls, tugging my hair harder.

"Ouch!" I snap. "Let me go and I'll tell you!"

He pauses for a second and then releases my head. It stings so badly but I can't even rub the sore spot because my hands are cuffed together.

"He threatened me," Sergio says. "In front of my guys. Disrespected me, and then to prove his point, he sent his crew after us to show us that he's not intimidated by the families we're aligned with. You heard all that, too, sweetheart, so don't play it like he's innocent. Maybe he didn't tell you what he was planning, but he fucking did it. And that's why you're here, not because I'm hard up for your nightclubs."

"Look, the only reason he acted that way was because of me. It was my idea to shut you guys out. We wanted to make you desperate!"

He waves his hands around him, a disbelieving chuckle tumbling from his lips. "Well, look around, Jaelyn. This whole thing screams desperation, yeah?"

"So you only took me because you thought Nate tried to kill you?"

"Direct retribution." He lifts an eyebrow.

I shrug. "Kind of."

"What the hell does that mean?"

"Well, none of you guys are dead. So it isn't exactly an eye for an eye."

He narrows his eyes. "Enrico's arm is all shot up and in a sling. Should I bust yours up, too? Then, will we be even?"

I sweep my tongue over my dry lips. "I'd rather offer you a partnership stake in our clubs for your muscle."

Sergio's eyes glaze over for a second, and a mischievous smirk tugs at his mouth. "*Which* muscle, exactly?"

"This is serious," I say. "Nate didn't try to kill you, I would stake my own life on that. I don't know who did, but—"

"No," Sergio mutters, turning away from me. "No! That whole 'eye for an eye' thing is really coming back to bite me in the ass."

"Yeah, I'm beginning to see that you don't quite get the gist of that saying."

He fixes a murderous glare on me. "I didn't think cutting off someone's hand would warrant a revenge murder," he says through clenched teeth.

Uhh, exactly how much of that clear liquid did he drink before he threw the glass against the wall? "I don't understand what you're trying to say…whose hand did you cut off?"

"Javier's."

I furrow my brow. "Who?"

"The guy who attacked you outside of the club the other night."

"You cut off his hand?" My mouth drops open. "I thought you were working with his organization."

"Why would you think that?"

"Because of the meeting you were supposed to have! You were pissed off that his boss didn't show up? You said something about partnering?"

Sergio scrubs a hand down the front of his face. "What the hell is happening here? Why do you care so much about that dipshit Javier's organization and my business with them?"

A throbbing erupts between my temples, my pulse picking up speed as the seconds tick by as an image of Nate stepping into the demon's lair flashes in front of my eyes. A red haze clouds the picture, a harbinger of what would become of him if he went to battle in the pits of hell otherwise known as ground zero for the Becerra Cartel. My throat grows tighter and tighter with the knowledge that Nate will be at death's door unless he finds out the truth, that it wasn't the cartel who took me.

It was the fucking mafia.

And they're the only ones who can save my brother now.

I squeeze my eyes shut, flipping over my cards because there's no other out for me or my brother.

Sergio, ironically, is my only hope.

"Because they killed my parents!"

My words pierce the air, reverberating in the space. I can't swallow them back. Hell, I didn't even know they were there on the tip of my tongue, just waiting to spew.

I didn't mean to tell him that.

I didn't want to tell him that.

This isn't about them.

It's about Nate.

My skin prickles as if tiny needles are dancing over the surface of my body. Memories swirl through my mind, commanding air time that I've tried so hard to preserve and protect. Deep breaths become impossible, and only slivers of air can make it into my lungs. Short, sharp pants quake my shoulders and I close my eyes to block out the terrifying scene playing out in my mind.

Images flash across my eyes as the sounds of my screams rupture my ears and the scent of burnt rubber assaults my nostrils. It's like I'm there again, immersed in the aftermath of horror.

"Jaelyn," Sergio says slowly. "Tell me what the hell is going on."

I blink fast, keeping the tears at bay, my own words about emotion resonating in my mind. "Javier works for the Becerra Cartel."

Sergio nods. "Yeah…"

"That cartel was responsible for the murder of my parents in Miami three years ago." My eyes open, brimming with unshed tears. "And they're here in Vegas now because of us."

"Keep going," he mutters.

"First, you have to believe me when I tell you it wasn't Nate who tried to hurt you. He wouldn't do that. He was only putting on an act because we didn't know any other way of getting your attention, and we need your help against the cartel, now more than ever." I take a deep breath and a hiccup slips out. "Look, you're right about the night I went to your club. I was spying on you. We'd heard that the Becerra Cartel was here in Vegas and were afraid they were closing in on us. The offer from you and your organization seemed strange because you have so much money and backing." I let out a sigh. "I thought you were just using it as an excuse to get close to us, that you might be working with the cartel to take us down. It wasn't until I saw Javier's tattoo when your guy dragged him away from me that I knew for sure it was them."

"So that's why I could freeze ice on your ass the night we came to Sapphire. You thought we were the enemy."

"And then you kidnapped me, so I'm not entirely convinced you're not," I huff.

"So the cartel, what do they have to do with your parents?"

"It's a long story."

"We have time." He grins. "No food, but time. And vodka."

"Are you going to uncuff me now?"

"I still don't really trust you. Lemme hear the rest of the story and I'll decide if you deserve to be released."

I make a face. "Can I at least have a drink? I'm fighting a hangover from whatever the hell drug you shot me up with. I may as well do myself in completely with some booze."

"Pickle garnish is all I can offer."

"I'll take it."

He disappears and returns a minute later. "No mixers either."

I take a sip of the clear liquid. It goes down so smooth, landing coolly in the center of my empty belly. "Nate used to be President of a motorcycle club in Miami. His guys did some illegal stuff, mainly money laundering through the club's businesses. I wasn't privy to too many details, but one night, he told me that the head of the Becerra Cartel approached him to do some drug running and distribution. It was big money, he said, but Nate didn't want to do it. It was dangerous work and he didn't want to put the club on the radar of the cops and the Feds. So he turned down their offer. They didn't like that answer and sent him a message," I finish in a choked whisper, taking another sip of the vodka.

Sergio nods. "I know all about those kinds of messages," he says in a low voice. "I'm sorry."

"Yeah, well, the guys who did it got off without so much as a week of community service. They walked. My parents were murdered and they got to leave the courthouse as free men."

"Why are you still on Becerra's radar? You fuck with his business?"

"Crippled it," I say. "Me and Nate. We went after the guys who killed my parents. Torched their warehouse and popped them both. Then, we disappeared." I manage a small smile. "See, *that* was direct retribution. Two lives for two lives."

"But the debt ain't paid, is it?"

"No. And they're just aching for the day they can collect the total. Do you see why we have to warn Nate?"

Sergio rubs the back of his neck. "I just wanted your fucking pussy," he groans.

"Excuse me?" I squeal, sitting straight up.

"Relax, I meant your nightclubs." He snickers. "Don't flatter yourself, sweetie."

A hot flush blankets my body and floods my cheeks.

He tips his head back and drains the rest of his drink.

"So, you're going to let me go now, right?"

He stands up and walks over to the door, turning briefly to wink at me. "I still don't trust you, princess. I want my share of your places if I'm gonna help you. This is gonna bring a lot of heat on me, and I'm not sticking my neck out for anyone without a guarantee. In writing. There's no pussy out there that's hot enough to distract me from what I'm owed, you hear me?"

"But, Nate—"

"Is a big boy. And I'll take care of him while you sit tight. You're still my leverage, Jaelyn. I can save your brother, but my help doesn't come for free. It's gonna cost you. Plenty."

"Can't I at least call him—?"

"And risk you telling him where you are so that the cartel, who most likely is already watching him, tails him here and turns this place into a fucking warzone?"

"I don't even know where we are! I was drugged when you brought me here, or don't you remember?" I scream. "I should have known you would be a complete dick about this! It's who you are!"

"Hey, easy. I may be a dick, but I have what you want, Jaelyn, what you *need*…strong fucking muscle."

"You're infuriating! I never should have trusted you!"

"Maybe not, because now my leverage has become much more valuable. I'm gonna get a partnership share for a much lower than asking price when I make my counteroffer." He grins. "But, hey, you can at least be happy I'm not gonna kill you. I need to trade you for what I want in return so you get to live and we'll get to work together. That's something, isn't it?"

"Did I say the head of the cartel was evil incarnate?" I yell. "Because I was fucking lying! It's actually *you*!"

"Evil incarnate. I like the sound of that. I might put it on my new business cards."

"Only you would take that as a compliment!" I shriek, wanting so badly to fling a shoe at his head. But I have no shoe, or the capability to use either of my arms right now. "You are the fucking *worst*!"

"Have another drink. You might feel differently."

"I can't hold the glass when both of my hands are cuffed together!" I glare at him, fury rising from deep within me as I see the smug look settle into his features. He stares down at me like I'm a sizzling steak and he's a predator who hasn't eaten in a week.

"I love your fire, you know that? You have to admit," he murmurs, dragging a finger down the front of my shirt as he leans over me. The scent of his cologne intoxicates me, making my head instantly dizzy with pent-up lust. I've tried so hard to keep it bottled up since that night in his office, tried to ignore how my body instinctively hums with week-old aftershocks when it's anywhere in his vicinity. But as much as I try to convince myself otherwise, the truth still comes back to haunt me. I want him with every cell of my being. On top of me, behind me, below me. Any and every which way. And dammit, I hate myself for that more than I claim to hate him.

"We blazed that night in my office. It was fucking hot." He grins at me, his half-hooded gaze making my pussy tingle.

Goddammit! It's the harshest betrayal I can imagine at this moment.

He tugs at the neckline of my top with his thumb. "You remember it. I know you do. And even though you think you hate me right now, you're torn because you want me to fuck you again. Isn't that right, Jaelyn?" He leans both of his hands onto the mattress, his body straddling me. His warm breath flutters against my cheeks like feathers and I close my eyes, turning my head away from his magnetic gaze.

"I do hate you," I grumble. "So much."

"Hate sex," he says in that low, growly voice that makes my toes curl. "Is the best kind of sex. You wanna test the theory?"

"I want to call my brother," I hiss, my eyes flying open again and spewing disgust. "And you're a complete pig!"

"Why? Because I know what I want? Or because I know you want the same thing?"

"Don't be stupid. I want nothing to do with you!"

"Well, we'll have to figure out a way to get past our little issues if we're going to work together."

"Work with you?" I snort. "I wouldn't walk to the end of the street with you!"

He slides his hand between my legs and I gasp, my back arching as his fingers brush against my pussy. "Uh-huh, that's what I thought. You want more. I want more. We should get more."

"I want…" I let out a sharp breath. "N-nothing!"

"Let's see about that," he says, looping his fingers into the waistband of my leggings and sliding them to my ankles. I lock my knees together to keep him from finding out my evidently worst-kept secret, but it's a futile attempt. He slides his fingers against my slit, letting out a low groan as he dips his fingers inside of my wet folds.

"You liar," he hisses, fisting my hair and pulling my head back so he can drag his tongue down the side of my neck. "You're so wet. We both know what that means."

My head drops back onto the pillow as he slides them deeper, rubbing against my clit with his thumb at the same time. "It d-doesn't mean a-anything," I rasp, clenching my toes as the fingers of one hand move faster and deeper. His free hand pulls off my leggings and pushes open my legs. Suddenly, his fingers are replaced by his lips and hot coiling tongue, his fingertips digging into my ass and forcing my hips upward. His teeth nip at my clit, electricity charging through my insides with each flick and tug. I want to drag my nails down his back to make him feel even a shred of what is coursing through me right now. I want to draw blood, I want to make him scream, I want to hear him feel it all!

"Ahh!" I scream, my ass clenching as he assaults my pussy with his lips. "Oh, God, that's it! Don't stop! Please don't stop!"

That's when he pulls away.

The very minute I scream out.

My chest heaves as he lifts his head, a self-satisfied smirk on his asshole face. "I told you what you wanted. Why'd you deny it?"

I can barely squeeze out a breath, so I flip him off with both of my hands over my head. "Fuck you," I seethe when I can speak again. "I want out of here! Now!"

"I bet you don't wanna go anywhere, sweetheart. You wanna stay right here. With me. And even though you hate yourself for it, that's what you need." He sits back on the bed and digs his phone out of his pocket. Then he reaches up and uncuffs one of my hands. "Call your brother. Tell him the Becerras didn't snatch you and that you're with me until tomorrow morning. When he draws up the partnership paperwork for us, he'll get you back and I will take care of the cartel in return for my shares. That's when he'll get what he wants. But I'm gonna take something I want first, though. And I know you're not gonna stop me."

I swing my hand at his face, my palm stinging as it makes contact with his stubbled jaw. He doesn't even flinch. He just smiles. The fucking nerve! I want to poke his eyes out! "You're a sick bastard!" I hiss.

"Maybe so, but it doesn't stop your pussy from dripping when I'm close to you, does it? And these nipples." He yanks my shirt up to my neck, exposing my bra. With a flick of his fingers, he reaches behind me and unhooks it. The air hits my breasts and I gasp as his fingers massage my flushed flesh. "They're so hard, they can cut glass, and all I've done is breathe on them. What does that tell you, sweetheart? Because it tells me a hell of a lot."

He raises an eyebrow at me. "Number?"

I tell him the number through gritted teeth and when he clicks the green button and drops the phone in my hand, I put it to my ear. It rings once, twice, three-*yah, my God*!

I swallow a squeal as my brother's deep voice comes on the line. "Who the fuck is this?" he growls.

"Nate," I rasp, clutching the phone tight as Sergio's tongue sweeps down the slit of my pussy before sucking on my swollen clit like a fucking kitten at her mama's teet. He tugs and teases and toggles my nub with his devious tongue, his teeth getting in the center of the action.

"Jae!" he yells. "Thank God! Where are you? Are you hurt?"

"No," I whisper, clawing at the pillow over my head when what I really want to do is scream my bloody head off. "I'm not hurt. I'm fine. We're fine," I murmur, my eyes sealed shut as his mouth works me from the inside out. I almost black out, the intensity of pleasure too much for my brain to process.

"Jae!" Nate says again and my eyes fly open.

"Oh God, oh God, oh God," I whimper as Sergio's tongue probes deeper and deeper. I clench tight around him, squeezing my legs together so tight, they are fused to the sides of his head.

It only spurs him on, making him work harder.

Oh, lucky fucking *day*!

"Tell me where you are and what the hell happened! I saw your car and went straight to the cops!"

"N-no….no cops," I mutter, my mind in a state of the most blissful euphoria. "N-no danger."

"Jae, what the fuck is wrong with you?" His voice gets higher and louder with each passing second that I fall deeper under Sergio's salacious spell.

"Nate," I mumble, my head rolling left and right as I thrust my hips into Sergio's mouth, his mouth fucking me like a voracious lion who can only be sated by my throbbing pussy. "I'm good. Don't go after….oh God…no cartel!" I cry out, electricity zipping through me, exploding out of every limb.

"What about the cartel? Jae, talk to me! Is someone there?"

"Yes!" I screech at the top of my lungs. "Yes, oh my God, yes!"

"Who is it?" Nate shouts. "Put me on speaker! I wanna talk to the fucker!"

"No," I whisper in a breathless voice as Sergio crawls up to me with the typical shit-eating grin on his face. "No, just promise you won't go after the cartel. They had nothing to do with this. Don't go after them. Please, promise me!" I breathe as the aftershocks settle in and my body deflates like a balloon, sinking farther into the mattress as if it's been weighted down by bricks.

One of Sergio's hands creeps over my breasts, kneading them as he grinds himself against my pussy. His cock is thick against his pants, hard enough to explode through the fabric.

And the other hand decides to create an entirely different form of action.

He grabs the phone from my hand, and I immediately fumble with the button on his jeans to free him…and myself.

"Torres, this is Sergio Villani."

And then he must put the phone on speaker because I can hear the disgust in my brother's voice.

"Villani," he snarls. "What the fuck is going on?"

"Listen, here's what you need to know," he says as I give up all hope that the button is going to cooperate, and I just dig my hand into the front of his pants until I close my fingers around his thick, throbbing shaft. He bucks his hips as I stroke him, but his voice never wavers as he delivers his list of demands to Nate.

My God, I am a horrible sister and partner.

I should fight this with everything in me!

I shouldn't let him take advantage of us like this!

I should…I should…I should….

Oh, fuck it.

What I should do is *him*.

"I had a nice conversation with Jaelyn. She told me all about the bait and switch you had planned, and I told her I'm willing to make a little trade instead. I'll take care of your headaches with the Becerra Cartel, and you sign over controlling interest in your nightclub circuit.

Even though my brain is fogged with lust, I pull my hand out of his pants and gasp. "What the fuck?"

"Jae, did you agree to that shit?" Nate demands. "And why the hell wasn't I invited to this little meeting, huh?"

"Look, Nate, here's the deal. I kidnapped your sister because I want your business and I needed to talk some sense into her. She told me about your past with the Becerra Cartel and I think the head of the cartel is a piece of shit who needs his goddamn head blown off. We came to an arrangement, and get this…we both fucking win. So now that you have the story, let's save all the details for tomorrow because I'm about to fuck your sister. Trust me, if we can just move on and end this call, it'll be good for everyone. I mean, better for me than you, for sure." He snickers, winking at me.

Jesus Christ, I don't even have words. I shake my head, my mouth falling open.

"Your takeaway from this is to leave shit alone with the cartel. I've got that covered." Sergio smirks. "So what do you say? Breakfast? Ten o'clock at your place?" He licks his lips as he stares down at me, sweeping his other hand over my pussy and then licking his fingers.

My traitorous pussy clenches with need.

God, I hate her.

"You think you're gonna come to my place tomorrow and leave it alive?" Nate roars. "You motherfucker! I will cut off your balls and shove them up your goddamn ass! Then I'll stick my hand down your throat and pull them out of you again!"

"That's an impressive visual. But it sounds unnecessarily violent. It might be something the cartel does to you when I give up your location to them. I don't think you want to have that much heat on you, right? Those assholes have a pretty serious beef with you and your sister. Now, don't worry about Jaelyn. She'll need a lot of comforting if they kill you, Torres. But I'll be there to take care of her, owning my controlling piece of *your* pussy pie. Either way, I get what I want. *Everything* I want," he hisses. "You need to make the call for yourself. What's better? Me getting to fuck your sister six ways from Sunday and being your boss, *or* you dead after being tortured in a pretty fucking excruciatingly painful way? Think about that and tell me your answer tomorrow."

He stabs the end call button and tosses the phone onto the mattress.

"Are you insane?" I scream, pounding on his chest with my one free fist.

"Easy or I'll cuff you again," he says darkly.

"How could you tell my brother…I mean, how would you like to hear that kind of shit about your sister?" I say. "You're a total sicko! And he's going to kill you tomorrow for what you just did! You do realize that, right?"

Sergio crawls up the bed and unlocks the second cuff. My hand drops to the mattress like an anchor to the bottom of the ocean, it's so damn heavy. I wiggle my fingers to get the blood flowing and the color slowly returns to the tips. I rub my wrists, rolling them out as I glare up at him. "So you're the face of this family operation, huh? They put you in front of prospective partners and clients? Are they also completely and fucking deranged?" I roll my eyes. "Stupid question. Of course they are, because who else would sic *you* on the underworld?"

His lips curl upward. "You think you're insulting me, but it's actually kind of a compliment. My job requires this, sweetheart. You don't get anywhere in life by bending over and waiting for someone to shove their fist up your ass. You shove the fist, you have the control."

"This exchange is really about a million steps beyond disturbing," I mutter.

"I agree," he says, pulling off his shirt and tossing it to the dusty floor. Then he gets off the bed and shoves his pants and boxer briefs to the floor, kicking them off one foot at a time.

Gulp.

Yep.

That's right.

A big ass gulp follows.

I don't know why. I've already had it buried inside of me, but seeing his perfect pink cock standing straight at attention, rock hard and so thick I can't wrap my fingers around it fully, makes me forget how deranged he is and how certain I am that Nate is going to beat his ass tomorrow.

It makes me forget a lot of things.

And makes me remember one…how he used that cock to launch me into the stratosphere only one week ago. It was a place I'd never visited before, and one I want to experience again.

And again.

And again after that.

"You say you hate me," he murmurs, dipping his head between my thighs. "But why are you so wet for me, Jae? Why are your legs quivering when my mouth comes close to your slick lips? You say you hate me, but your body tells a different story. So stop fighting it and let me make you come like I did before, hard and fast, all over my dick."

I raise my arms and he smirks, getting my message. He brings himself to his knees and slides my shirt over my head, straddling me as he runs a hand down the front of my torso. "You're mine tonight, Jae," he says in a thick voice. "All of you."

I nod, the knot in my throat too tight to even croak out a reply.

I hate that my legs fall open for him.

I hate that I mewl at the sensation of his cock grazing my slit.

I hate that my heart beats with all of the crazy he emanates when he's this close.

Oh, God.

I hate it all!

And yet, here I lie, beckoning him, urging his body to connect to mine in the most primal way possible.

I want him.

I need him.

And judging from the way he's staring at me right now, I know he feels the exact same way.

He laces his fingers with mine and kisses the inside of my wrists. "Still sore?"

I nod.

"I'm gonna make you forget all about that," he whispers.

"Aren't you afraid I might try to stab you or something since my hands are free?"

He hovers over me, the head of his dick grazing my opening. "No."

"You're a pretty trusting guy."

"Nah, I just know what you like. And when I deliver, death is the last thing you're gonna want to inflict on me."

"You are such a cocky assh—"

But he doesn't wait for me to finish before he covers my mouth with his, his tongue pushing into my hungry mouth, swirling with mine. He wraps his arms around me, digging his fingers into the small of my back as he sinks into my pussy, stretching me wider with each thrust of his hips. The delicious burn when he first penetrates me makes me simultaneously drip with desire and yelp with need.

He feels so amazing as his cock slides in and out of my slickness, the fact that he doesn't stop to put on a condom barely registering through the blissfully erotic cloud hanging over us. He grips my ass, pulling me into him so he can drive harder and faster.

I dig my fingers into the globes of his ass and he takes a sharp breath before plundering me like a man possessed. I guess he likes ass play. Well, that's all he's going to get. I'm not prepared for anything mo—

"Holy shit!" I scream out.

"It's called the shocker," he says, burying his face in my breasts as his finger presses into my tight hole, the ring of muscle aflame from the pressure. "Good name for it, yeah?"

Shocker, indeed.

Sergio slows down his movement, fucking me with long, deep strokes as his finger drives into my ass.

Double the pleasure is a gross understatement.

Tingles in my groin morph into a full-fledged fireworks show in my core, blasts ricocheting and sparks flying. Heat floods my insides as the explosions rumble and roar, erupting from deep within my pussy and shooting out to every extremity.

My body seizes from the intense pleasure consuming every inch of me, sizzling my skin as well as every nerve ending in its path.

Oh my God…that finger…it's like insta-orgasm!

I don't hear myself scream. I think I've shattered my own eardrums.

All sounds are drowned out by the static fizzling between my ears.

So it takes me a second to fall back to Earth and into my current reality where there is a very tall, very hot, and extremely menacing man standing over us with a gun pointed at the back of Sergio's head.

"What the fuck is going on here?" he roars in a deep, gravelly voice.

Sergio puts his hands behind his head, staring down at me. "He's got a gun on me, yeah?"

I nod because I'm too startled to even speak.

This day.

Seriously.

Surreal as fucking hell.

Chapter Eighteen
SERGIO

Jaelyn's eyes narrow after a few seconds. "Yeah, and why am I *so* not surprised that some random person tracked you here to shoot you in the head?"

I raise my hands up. "This isn't a break-in." I sneak a look over my shoulder, my stomach dropping when I realize who's standing over me.

While I'm naked and mid-fuck.

Alek Severinov, boss of a very lethal Russian bratva that is part of our family syndicate.

I swallow a groan.

Matteo finding me would be so much better.

He sees me and rolls his eyes, dropping his hand with the gun. "Jesus Christ…" he mutters.

"Look, Alek—"

"No," he says, holding up a hand. "Just stop right there. Fucking put yourself together and then get outside. I can't focus when

I'm staring at your ass."

I smirk. "I know. I hear that a lot."

He glowers at me and puts the gun to my temple. "I won't hesitate. You're just a business partner, always remember that."

I give a quick nod. "I'll be right out."

He slams the door shut and Jaelyn pushes me off of her while she scurries around to grab her clothes. "Seriously, Sergio? Where the hell did you bring me? And who is that guy who just saw me completely naked?"

"Relax," I mumble, pulling on my pants. "We work together. I'll take care of everything."

"Don't get shot in the process," she hisses, pulling on her leggings. "Or I'll have to ask your hot friend for a lift home."

I narrow my eyes at her. "You think he's hot?"

Her lips curl upward. "Oh *yes*. So hot. Does that bother you?"

"No," I grunt, my lips twisting. Alek is happily married with kids, but that's beside the point. Just the thought of another man's hands on Jaelyn is enough to make me go all Incredible Hulk and pound the shit outta him.

"You have a lot of hot buttons, and damn, they are so easy to find, you know that?" she says with a smirk.

I grab her around the waist and pull her close. "It doesn't mean I want you to stop pressing them, you got that? I just need a few minutes and then you can press them all you want."

She sits on the bed, resting her head against the pillow. "I'll be waiting."

I pull on my shirt and run a hand through my sexed-up hair before opening the door and joining Alek in the kitchen. He holds up the bottle of vodka. "I guess you got hungry."

"Listen, I know this looks bad, but let me explain—"

"Quiet." He glowers at me. "You do realize that anything you do isn't just on behalf of your family anymore, right? This whole syndicate we've formed means that your business becomes my business and vice versa. And I don't like it when your business fucks in the middle of my business. You get that?"

I nod, rubbing the back of my neck.

Alek folds his arms over his massive chest. He's got about six inches on me height-wise and he's broad and built like a brick shithouse.

The head of the brutal Severinov family.

The man who sat in a restaurant in Monaco and stabbed a drug lord in the chest with a fork and pretty much split him in two with it.

He's a king among men in the underworld.

I do not want to be on his bad side.

We haven't really spoken much since the families banded together months ago. He's out here to help build up his family's interests in Vegas, and Matteo is his counterpart, not me. So, I take a backseat most of the time. I'm looking for Alek's approval, yeah, but I don't want to get it with my head coming out of his mouth.

Anyway, the guy has created an international empire over the past years since he took over his family, and I know I could learn plenty from him…that is, if he doesn't kick my ass for executing my latest brilliant plan without anyone's knowledge or approval.

"You wanna tell me who she is?" He cocks an eyebrow and gulps down a shot of vodka. "From what little I know of you, it doesn't seem like you lack places to screw women. And a guy in your position wouldn't take one to a fucking construction zone."

I lean my head into my hands. I may as well tell him the truth. It's gonna get out soon enough that the Becerra Cartel is targeting me.

All of us, really.

"The Becerra Cartel tried to kill me and my guys the other night. But we're not their only targets." I nod toward the closed bedroom door. "Turns out she and her brother are on their radar, too. But we worked out an arrangement — controlling share of their nightclub business to take out the cartel leaders."

"That's a big plan coming from the guy who's trying damn hard to get a seat at the table." Alek shakes his head. "Matteo knows about this?"

"Only about us getting shot up. Nothing else."

"So you made this decision on your own to take on the cartel?"

"To get the deal I wanted for the nightclubs, yeah." I say.

"Did anyone give the approval to take over those clubs? Do we know anything about their operations and associates?"

"I checked out their operations. They look solid. Trust me, I got a good deal for us. It'll make a shit ton of cash.

"At what cost, Sergio?" Alek grunts. "Matteo is your representative. He's supposed to bring decisions like this to the group."

"He didn't think I could make the deal in the first place."

"But you did."

I yank my eyes away from his icy blue stare. "Not the first time I tried, but when I realized what they needed and how I could help, I knew we could land it. And we just did."

"How'd you get them to change their minds? How'd you know about their issue with the cartel?"

"I, uh, kidnapped the girl." Heat creeps up the sides of my neck because even as I say it, I know it's grounds for Alek hitting me over the head with that glass jug of vodka.

His eyes darken and he takes another gulp of his drink. "I assume Matteo doesn't know about that, either." He claps an enormous hand on my shoulder and squeezes. "You know what, Sergio? I could put a bullet in your brain right here and now for opening us all up to your own personal shit."

"I really don't want you to do that," I say. "I made some pretty stupid decisions over the past week, but I can fix everything. If you kill me now, I can't take care of the problems I caused."

He gives a swift nod. "You know, the static between you and Matteo…I've had the same thing with my own brothers. They were a lot like you, making stupid choices that didn't get us very far, but caused a lot of headaches. Most of the time, it was because they were rebelling against me. They either didn't like my plans, thought they could direct family business better, or they just didn't appreciate my not-so-subtle way of telling them that they're fucking morons when they screwed up." He shrugs. "It's not easy being the boss."

I scrub a hand down the front of my face. "This isn't on him. It's all on me and I'll accept the consequences."

"That's not how this works, Sergio. It's like I said before, one person's decisions impact all of us and our interests."

"I'm going to fix this," I repeat. "Tomorrow. It'll be handled. I'll do it by myself. I'll swallow all the risk."

"Again, not your call." He rolls his eyes. "You really aren't getting the whole syndicate concept, are you?"

"Look, Matteo can be a prick, but he and the others shouldn't be punished for a bad move on my part."

Alek stares at me for a long minute. "You want to know what I think you should do?"

"What?"

"Talk to Matteo. Tell him the truth about what you did and why. Level with him."

"You at least spared my life before," I grumble. "I don't think he'd hesitate to shoot me if he knew all of this."

"Maybe so, but if this syndicate is going to work, it requires each family to be united. That means no more petty bullshit. Christ, if I could reel in my own brothers, I'm sure you can fix things with Matteo."

"This is feeling a lot like therapy," I say with a snicker.

"I'm no stranger to family drama. And trust me, it doesn't stop with my own immediate family. My in-laws, the Marcones, are worse." He grins. "My wife included."

I lean into the counter with a deep sigh. All for a goddamned seat at the table with the bosses.

But it's what I want, so yeah, I'm going after it.

"Talk to Matteo. Take control of this. Own the dumbass moves you made. He'll respect you for it. Eventually, maybe not tonight." Another smirk. "Convince him that you made a smart move for the group and I'll consider backing you up against the cartel. And if you ever think of fucking another woman in my safehouse, I will castrate you."

"Thanks, Alek." I stick out my hand and he pumps it hard.

"Now get the hell out of here. I've got work to do, and the images of you two are giving me a brain bleed. I don't want to accidentally see or hear anything else out of you tonight, got it?"

A knock from inside of the room sounds and Jaelyn's voice floats out into the hallway. "Is it safe to come out now?"

"Yeah," I say.

She steps out, hugging her arms around herself but staring straight at Alek with a defiant look that tells him she doesn't give a damn that he just saw her in a pretty compromising position. The bright pink spots in her cheeks tell me something different.

I want to get her back into that compromising position as quickly as possible.

After tonight, who knows how many more people are gonna want me dead?

And the more appropriate question is, will any of them actually achieve that goal?

"I'm going to leave you to the rest of your night, somewhere else," Alek says with one final glare in my direction. He grabs the vodka and heads for the back of the apartment.

I grin at Jaelyn. "Pretty eventful day, huh?"

She sticks a hand on one hip and cocks her head to the side. "And it's not even over. Do I want to ask what happens next?"

"I can tell you some of my ideas," I say, nuzzling her neck. "But I don't like spoilers."

"Listen, I really think we need to find Nate. He's pissed as hell and I don't want him to do anything stupid, like try to blow up your hotel."

"I'm a big boy and I can handle your brother. You, on the other hand," I say, smacking her ass. "Still need to be tamed. And it's gonna take a long time, lots of grueling hours. He'll just have to sit tight while he waits for our meeting tomorrow."

"He's not one for waiting," she says, biting her lower lip. "If I were you, I'd be afraid. Very freaking afraid."

"Look, right now there's no shortage of people in Vegas who want to cut my wrists and throw me into a tank of man-eating sharks. I should be doing a lot of things to protect myself, but what I really want to do is *you*. So we're going back to the Excelsior where I'll come clean with my brother Matteo about what's happening right now since he's topping that list of people. Then I'm gonna take you up to my place and fuck you until you black out from coming so hard."

"I should make you drive to Nate's place," she breathes as I nip at her ear. "So you can apologize for being an ass."

"But?"

"But I'm a little afraid of what he might do to me after he takes care of you." A teasing smile lifts her lips and she tightens her arms around me. "So I'm thinking that a blackout is a far superior option."

I take her lower lip between my teeth and suck it gently before dipping my tongue into her hungry mouth. "Mm," I mumble against her lips. "Let's go because I'm starving, and the only food I want is *you*."

The car ride back to the Excelsior is fast, mainly because Jae's hand was stuck down my pants, tag-teaming with her lips. My cock swells against my jeans, dying for release as we pull up to the hotel and hordes of people are crowded at the entrance.

I groan. Great, I love walking around with my dick ready to explode out of my pants.

A blue haze clouds my vision, and I decide the meeting with Matteo can wait until I can see clearly again.

I jump out of the car, drop the keys into one of the valet's hands as he salutes me, and pull open Jaelyn's door. I shift her around so that she's in front of me as we walk since I have nothing else to hide what's happening below my waist. I trail kisses along the back of her neck as we get into the revolving door and push into the ornate lobby.

It's packed with people loitering, drinking, and generally enjoying their night at the hottest hotel on the Strip.

Sorry, Alek…

I snake an arm around Jaelyn's waist as we make a path for ourselves.

"Private elevator is at the back of the casino," I murmur. "Just a few more minutes and we'll be—"

"Jaelyn!"

A deep, angry voice yells her name from somewhere in the vast space. The harsh voice not only startles us, but everyone around us. I turn to the right to see where it's coming from and I roll my eyes when I see Nate stomping across the polished marble tile floor.

I hold up a hand. "Listen, Nate, just calm down, okay? Let's talk about this like—"

Whack!

It happens so fast, I don't even see it coming. I only hear the whizz in the air as his fist cracks against my jaw. I fly backward into a tall potted plant near the entrance and it tumbles over, the ceramic pot shattering as it hits the ground. I stagger around as I try to get my footing, finally swaying to my feet as he approaches.

I step left and right, not finding balance at all before he takes another swing. This time, I manage to duck under his fist, collapsing against one of the reception desks.

Hotel goers have formed a circle around us to watch the bullfight.

Except in this case, the fucking matador is the one who's getting killed.

I blink fast to clear my vision, diving at Nate and tackling him to the ground. We roll around on the floor, grunting and swearing as Jae's screams pierce the air. Bright flashes blind me as pretty much all of the spectators pull out their phones to take video of us grappling, with our limbs flailing and fists flying. My head slams back against the hard tile as Nate hurls himself over me again, my jaw on fire from where he repeatedly punches me.

"You didn't really think I was gonna wait until tomorrow to do this, did you, you piece of shit?" he roars as I slide out from under him. His fist connects with the floor instead of my throat.

Score one for me.

I struggle to my feet, hunched over and panting from the repeated punches to my midsection. The guy has some serious pent-up rage. I wipe my upper lip, my fingers bright-red with blood.

Okay, maybe it isn't so pent-up anymore.

He lunges for me again, but this time I'm ready for him and I land a shot right into his chest. He stumbles, caught off-guard, and crashes into a nearby slot machine. I leap at him and pound the shit out of his face. "My back's not turned this time, Nate! I'm right here, so fucking give it to me!"

"Nate!" Jae yells running over to us. "Sergio!" She pulls me off of her brother whose face, I'm happy to say, is bruised and bleeding profusely. "Enough of this! You're acting like animals!"

"Did you expect something different from this fucking guinea?" Nate roars, charging at me again. I ball up my fists at my sides, ready to attack until Jae shoves him backward.

"No!" she yells. "Not here! And no more fighting!"

Nate glares at her. "This is between me and the fucking incompetent godfather wannabe. I'll deal with you later!"

"No," she seethes, grimacing at him. "You'll end this right now and then we can talk."

Nate grumbles as he rises to his feet, pointing to me. "You have some fucking nerve talking to me like you did. You're lucky I didn't cut off your tongue. Or your dick."

Jae's eyes widen and she turns her back on us, addressing the rapt audience. "There's nothing more to see here! Leave now!"

Her shrill scream is enough to make everyone scatter and once they do, she turns to us, her eyes blazing. "Nate," she says, her voice shaking. "We have a lot to discuss. But you need to cool the hell off first!" She looks up at me, bringing a hand to my split lip. "Are you okay?"

I nod, and Nate lets out a thunderous, animal-like sound.

"Are you kidding me, Jae? You're asking if he's okay?" Nate shakes his head. "Is the gangster made of fucking glass or something?"

"You didn't fight fair," she says with a warning look. "And I was going to call you to talk like adults before you came in here like a bat out of hell."

"Talk?" he snarls at her. "A replay of the conversation we had earlier? Because you see how well that one ended, right?" He lets out an incredulous laugh, running a hand through his hair. "I don't believe it. You actually *like* this jerkoff, don't you?"

She sneaks another look up at me and shrugs. "Maybe."

"Jesus, Jaelyn!"

"What the hell is going on here?"

I bite back a groan as Matteo and Dante rush over from the casino. Anyone else gonna join in the ambush? Is my father waiting in the wings, too, looking to take his shot?

Matteo narrows his eyes at all of us while Dante hangs back, a smirk on his face. Must be nice to not be the guy who's about to get leveled.

"Who are you people?" he says, looking at Nate.

"Nate and Jaelyn Torres," I mumble.

He flips around to look at me and I can't help but enjoy the shock seeping into his features. "Torres as in Sapphire Torres?"

"The one and only."

"Why are they here?" he mutters, very aware of the people still hanging around us, pretending not to be eavesdropping on this very heated exchange. I'll bet some are still filming.

Dante had better start confiscating some phones before this shit ends up on YouTube.

"I think we need to take that conversation somewhere private."

"You're really stretching my patience, Sergio," he hisses, grabbing my arm. "Get in my office. *Now.*"

I shake off his arm. "Just so we're clear, I'm only going because I have something to tell you, not because you ordered me to."

"Yeah, he doesn't take instruction very well," Jaelyn snips, her arms folded over her chest.

I'm gonna punish her for that later.

I wink at her and flip off Nate before I follow Matteo into his office. He storms inside and slams the door shut so hard that the walls shake and one of the framed pictures clatters to the floor, the glass shattering into a million pieces.

Well, that's good. He can't stab me in the heart with a shard of glass.

He could stuff a handful of them in my eye, though…

"Are you fucking insane?" he shouts, pounding his fist against a wall. "Bringing them here and brawling with Nate Torres? I told you I'd handle him! Do you have a death wish? Because I'll just kill you now! It'll save me some goddamn grief!" He shoves me backward but I stand my ground, refusing to falter.

I shove him back harder. "This is my space. Don't fucking invade it or I'll cut off *your* hand, too."

Matteo's eyes glow with a demonic sheen, his lips turning up into a sneer. "You've got a lot of nerve making threats against me."

"Who said it was a threat?"

We stare at each other, circling like predators and prey.

At this point, I'm not sure which roles we're even playing, but still we skulk.

"Are you going to tell me what's going on, Sergio? Or do I have to beat it out of you with a tire iron?"

"I need you to chill the fuck out first. There are some things I have to tell you, and if we're gonna take on the car—"

"Whoa!" He holds up a hand. "Take *on*? As in battle? Who are you to make that call?" he bellows. "I thought you were convinced that Torres was the one who was out to get you, not the cartel?"

"I might have gotten it wrong," I say, stretching my lips together.

"Oh, those words!" Matteo grouses as he stalks around his desk. "You might have gotten it wrong? *Might have?*"

His voice reverberates between my temples, making them throb louder and harder with each passing second. The punches I took to the head aren't helping with the pounding in my skull, either.

"Listen—"

"No, you fucking listen!" he screams. "Do you know how long I've worked to get the respect of these other families, Sergio? While you were fucking around with cocktail waitresses and any other women who flashed their pussies at you, I was trying to make a name for us! I was working with these guys, convincing them that our backing, connections, and money would be worth their trust in us!"

"That was a good thing," I say. "Nice work."

"And then you come along with your big plans to take over a string of nightclubs when you can't even run the one you have! You made yourself, as well as the rest of us, a target for the Becerra Cartel when you cut off Javier's fucking hand, and you shit the bed with Torres! Do you know what that all means?"

I let out a sigh of frustration. "Why don't you just tell me?"

"Fine," he seethes. "It means all of my work is fucking destroyed! You crapped all over it with your dumbass ideas and plans. You wanted to prove yourself, right? Well, what you've proven is that you're an incompetent jackass."

"Fuck you!" I roar, kicking over a chair. "You know, maybe I'm tired of being stuck in a no-win spot. You have me working on shit that isn't worth my time or effort! I have ideas, ideas that I want to put in play. You hang this seat over my head like a set of tits, for Christ's sake. 'You almost have them. Almost, Sergio. Just reach a little higher…higher…higher, and get ready to motorboat those fuckers!'" I snip. "Well, guess what? I'm gonna get them, okay? And they will feel fucking amazing!"

"All talk," he grumbles. "No action."

"I kidnapped Jaelyn Torres this morning," I blurt out, biting back a smile when I see Matteo's jaw drop. "I found out that the Becerra Cartel has them on their radar, too. So got on a call with Nate and volunteered to pop the heads of the cartel in exchange for controlling interest of his nightclubs."

"Jesus…" he groans. "I think I'm gonna have a stroke."

"No, but hold that thought. There's more."

He rolls his eyes. "Why is Torres so pissed off at you that he needed to come here and tear you apart in my lobby?"

"Because I fucked his sister like a prisoner on death row and I told him so."

Matteo's head falls into his hand. "Is there anything else you want to pile onto this shit sandwich?"

"Just one more little thing." I take a deep breath. "I brought her to the Severinov safehouse because I didn't know where else to go. Alek walked in on us, ah, well, you know."

Matteo's eyes have bulged to the point where I could probably just pluck them out of their sockets.

"But don't worry. I smoothed everything over," I say, hurrying to finish before Matteo grabs the spear next to his desk and impales me with it. "I told him everything."

Matteo presses his fingers together and watches me for the longest minute of my life. I'm convinced when he opens the desk drawer, it's to grab a gun but instead, he pulls out a joint and lights up.

"Can I have a—?"

"No!" he rasps, sending out a thin stream of smoke. "You can't."

He takes a few more drags and I know he is furious right now because he only lights up when he is so far beyond anger that it becomes the only way to make sure he doesn't murder someone.

That someone being me in this scenario.

"What did Alek say?"

I shrug. "He told me to talk to you. He knows I fucked up. I know I fucked up."

Matteo nods. "And what should we do about that? I have ideas."

"Look," I say, sitting in front of him. "Things between us haven't been great, but I'm not trying to mess this up for you or for us as a family. But I want a voice. I've earned a fucking voice!"

"You've earned a butt-fucking by one of the trannies upstairs at the bar," he grumbles.

"Yeah, probably." I snicker. "Although I don't plan on collecting that punishment."

"What do you want, Sergio?"

"I want to fix things with the Becerra Cartel. They almost killed Enrico and they tried to kill me and Bruno. Those guys are toxic to our organization. I want to run them the hell outta Vegas, but I can't do it alone. If they stay here, they're gonna come after us. It'll be a bloody war that we don't need right now. We have our own backup with the other families, but the cartel will try as hard as they can to destroy us. You know it and I know it."

"And why should I trust you after all of the shit you just caused? How do we know that Torres isn't going to come after us out of revenge for your snatching his sister? Or for trying to soak him for more than half of his worth?"

"He needs us," I say. "And we need him, too. But I need you behind it. You're always telling me to earn my seat at the table. Let me do it, Matteo. Give me a fucking break for once."

He takes one more drag before snuffing out the joint. "There's a lot on the line here. A lot of money, a lot of people, and a lot of potential death."

"I know."

"You've got a plan?"

I nod. "Sure do."

"You'd better." Matteo pushes the chair back and stands up. "You get one chance, Sergio. Don't make me regret this or I'll be the one cutting shit off next."

He flings open the office door and stalks back out to the lobby. I follow, a smile tugging at my lips. A small part of me expected to walk out of there with either a black eye or a broken nose. I'm pleasantly surprised to find out that the whole conversing thing actually works, even with two people as stubborn and self-righteous as me and my brother.

But there's still a nagging feeling in my gut that tells me this isn't even close to being over. I have to figure out a way to get to the cartel under the guise of some bullshit meeting. They have to be expecting it after their failed attempt to bury us last week on our way back from Sapphire.

We've both taken shots.

We're both at risk.

But somehow, I need to make them feel comfortable getting into a room with me. That way, I can build trust and then extinguish it with a knife blade to the jugular.

That's what I do.

I see Jaelyn talking to Nate in the corner of the lobby. He turns toward us, his eyes skipping past Matteo and landing squarely on me. There's a lot of rage in that gaze, and I have no doubt he'd try to pummel me again if we were anywhere else.

But right now, it looks like Jaelyn has talked him off the ledge.

He might let me live…tonight.

And tomorrow?

Well, like I said. There are plenty of people who want me dead, so he can just join those ranks and take his chances.

I'm still standing, so that says something.

I don't hesitate to snake an arm around Jaelyn's waist and Nate's eyes narrow to slits as she snuggles into me. I'm tempted to grab one of her tits, but that would just be begging for trouble.

And my goal tonight is to not end up in the hospital. I have plans, very carnal ones that include only one Torres, and it's not the fucking brute who's still bleeding all over the lobby floor.

Nate's jaw tightens as Jae lays her head against me. "So, you've got a plan for how all of this is gonna go down, Villani?"

I nod. "I'll share it as soon as you have that partnership paperwork drawn up. I wanna be solid on our business agreement before I do anything with the cartel."

His eyes skate to Jaelyn's and she nods at him, grasping his hand. "This is for the best. It's what we need to do."

Nate snorts. "I can't believe I'm hearing this. I expected more from you, Jae. You know what we're trying to protect."

"Look," she says in a low voice. "We all win this way, and you get to keep part of your business. It may not be exactly the way we wanted it, but at least we'll finally be free and safe."

Nate looks at me. "You make sure that not a single hair on her head is damaged or I will come after you and torture you in ways you've never imagined."

"Sounds like something Jaelyn said to me earlier today." I chuckle. "Guess it's in the blood."

Jaelyn tentatively pulls away from me and wraps her arms around Nate, giving him a hug. It takes him a second, but he pulls her tight. He's so large that her tiny body almost disappears into him. She whispers to him and he nods with one final glare in my direction.

"Tomorrow morning," he grunts. "You come by the club and we'll sign the papers. Then you execute your part of the deal."

"That's the plan," I say.

Nate straightens up and Jaelyn laces her fingers with his as we walk toward the exit. "Come on. You need to get some sleep."

He looks down at her. "And what about you?" he asks with a raised eyebrow.

"Oh, she's not gonna be getting much sleep," I say.

Matteo rolls his eyes and gives me a shove, and Jaelyn levels me with one of her icy stares.

We walk out into the dry heat, weaving our way around Ubers and cabs pulling up to the hotel as endless streams of people file into the famed revolving doors. Nate drops a kiss onto his sister's head before looking back at me.

"Just so we're clear, Villani. I fucking hate you. None of this changes *that*."

I flash a half-smile. "You're in good company, Torres."

He lets out a snort and pulls open his car door as we turn to head back inside.

"Your list of enemies is so damn long, how do you even keep track of who wants you dead anymore?" Matteo gripes.

I shrug. "I just assume everyone does. Keeps me on my toes."

"You'll be lucky if you can—"

But three loud gunshots, and the piercing screams that follow, swallow up Matteo's next words.

I flip around, searching the circular driveway as people either scatter or dive to the ground in sheer panic.

"What the fu—?"

And then I see it.

The booted foot peeking out from the side of Nate's truck.

Attached to his jean-clad leg.

"Nate!" I bellow, running over to his truck as a blacked-out Range Rover peels out of the driveway and loses itself in the traffic running up and down the Strip.

Jaelyn shrieks and dashes past me, crumbling next to Nate who is face-down on the cobblestones. "No, no, no! Nate, wake up!"

I press my head against his chest, listening for his heart. Using two fingers, I find a pulse, albeit a weak one. I look up at Matteo. "We need to get him to the hospital now! Help me get him up. We'll take his truck."

Jaelyn's body quakes with sobs, tears streaming down her face. It's the first time I've really seen her crack and it shatters me. Nate is her world and I have to do anything I can to keep him in it.

Between me, Matteo, and one of the valets, we manage to get him into the back of the truck with Jaelyn. I jump into the driver's seat and Matteo slides in next to me. Minutes later, we pull up to the Emergency Room, and a couple of orderlies rush out with a gurney. After loading him onto it, they take him inside with Jaelyn grasping his limp hand.

I lean my head back against the seat. "Fuck," I breathe out. "This is bad fucking news, Matteo."

"Yeah, no shit," he grunts, rubbing the back of his head. "This is hitting too close, Sergio. If we wait to handle the cartel, Christ only knows who else we'll lose? Hell, we might have just lost Torres."

"Don't say that," I grunt, scrubbing a hand down the front of my face. "She can't lose him," I murmur.

"Since when did you become so sentimental?"

"Fuck me if I know." I sigh. "Okay, so my plan was to have a meeting with the head of the cartel and surprise! Ambush his ass."

"We can't wait," Matteo says.

"No," I agree. "It has to be tonight. They're tracking us and they know we're aligned to Torres. If we don't make a move now, we're going to be sitting ducks."

"What about Jaelyn?"

"I'll talk to her. She has to stay here with Nate, so at least she'll be safe." I look at Matteo as I pull the truck into a parking spot. "Can you give the guys a call? We'll meet here and figure out what to do next."

"I've got it. You go inside and see how Nate is doing. I'll get a location on Becerra." He claps a hand on my shoulder. "You shit the bed with this one, Serge, but lucky for you, I'm used to cleaning up your messes."

"Just don't slip and fall into it. That stench is damn hard to wash off." I hop out of the truck and jog into the hospital to find Jaelyn. I find her hunched over in a chair, quietly sobbing into her hands. I run over to her and drop to my knees in front of her. "Jae, what happened?"

"H-he's back there now," she whispers. "They took him right in, but nobody has come out to talk to me yet."

"It's only been a few minutes." I squeeze her hands. "You have to stay positive."

"I c-can't lose him, Sergio. He needs to come out of this. Oh, God! I knew this was going to happen eventually. I knew they'd find us and come after us." Her shoulders shake as she covers her tear-streaked face with her hands.

"Look, I promise you I will take care of them, Jae. They're gonna pay for what they did to Nate, do you hear me? And they will never get close to either of you again."

"He lost so much blood," she weeps, as if she didn't even hear what I just said. "I saw the looks on the doctors' faces when they wheeled him back. I could see it in their eyes!"

"Hey," I say, giving her a gentle shake. "This isn't you, Jae. You don't give up on anything, so why are you so ready to give up on Nate? He's a strong sonofabitch, and I know he's sure as hell not gonna give up on himself, not if he knows you're by his side rooting for him."

She nods. "You're right. I know you're right. It's just that everything with my parents…and now Nate…these people have taken s-so much from me," she murmurs, her teeth chattering. "They can't have him. They can't!"

I pull her up and drag her to a corner of the waiting room, which is surprisingly empty, even for a weeknight. "Listen to me," I say in a low voice as we sink into two empty chairs. "You're one of the strongest people I've ever fucking met. You don't crumble, you fight with everything in you. And Nate is the same way. Don't ever doubt that he won't fight like hell to stay here with you." I tilt her head toward me. "If for no other reason than to pound my face in the next chance he gets."

She lets out a little chuckle. "Oh yeah, there will be plenty more where that came from."

"Right. So let's focus on my getting the shit kicked out of me by your brother. There's a hell of a lot of rage inside of him, too. Must be the genetics." I pull Jaelyn close and she buries her head in my shirt, letting out a deep, shuddering sigh.

"I know I need to stay positive," she says. "And I know he's a fighter. He never takes things lying down. It's why he's here in the first place. And why we're being hunted by those assholes." Jaelyn raises her face up to mine. "I know I never told you the full story. But now you need to hear it." She takes a deep breath. "They killed my parents…slaughtered them…all because Nate refused to work with the cartel, and Becerra doesn't like to hear the word 'no'. It was their way of saying *our loss.*" She sniffs and swipes at the tears under her eyes. "The men they used to kill my parents got off without so much as a few hours of community service," she murmurs. "They walked out of the courtroom smiling when the verdict was delivered. They murdered my parents, shattered my world, and they got off scot-free because Becerra's attorney managed to get all evidence disregarded. Fucking slimeball bastards," she says in a dark voice.

"I'm sorry," I say. "I can't imagine how hard it was to deal with all of that."

"We went after them, Sergio," she whispers. "Later that night. Just me and Nate. We found the guys who killed my parents." She stops, her hands shaking in mine. "It was our message back to Becerra. I'd never killed anyone before that night. And I don't think I ever really got over it, even though they deserved it.

Making them suffer didn't make me feel better. It didn't help me move past the death of my parents. It just created more of a void. A hole I was hoping to fill with vengeance."

"That never works," I murmur. "I know from experience."

"I found that out the hard way. And for three years, we've been looking over our shoulders, waiting for the other shoe to drop because we made it clear that night was about retaliation. We almost didn't make it out of Miami, either. Becerra's guys came after us and…" Her voice catches. "One of them grabbed me just as I was making a run for our car and threw me down, his hand tight around my throat to hold me down. I fought like crazy, kicking and punching and screaming. But he had one knee pinning me to the ground. I couldn't land a shot with him on top of me. Then he pulled out a machete, and just as he was about to swing it into my chest, Nate shot him in the throat." Her voice catches. "I thought I was going to die in that second, Sergio. When I saw that blade coming at me, I was sure it was the end." Her eyes flash. "But Nate took care of me, just like he always has. The whole plan to bait you was my way of helping him for once." She takes a few deep breaths and pushes her hair back, squaring her shoulders. "They can't get away with this," she hisses. "We need to find them and make them suffer."

"I'm not gonna sit here and pretend I know how you feel because I don't. I get that you want revenge, but your brother needs you here, with him. You need to focus on him right now."

She grips my shoulders. "They will keep coming back until they finish the job if I don't destroy them first."

"Jaelyn," I say. "You're fucking brutal, and I have no doubt that you could wreak your own brand of havoc on those guys. But this war is bigger than you. Becerra won't get away with what he's done. He's hit us, too. And now he knows we're aligned. So you need to stand down and let me do what I do best."

"You can't take him on by yourself!"

"Who said I'd be by myself?" I grin. "I have a whole fucking army, sweetheart. And it's time to lead the troops into battle." I tilt her chin upward. "You need to stay here with Nate where you'll both be safe."

"I don't like to take orders."

"Yeah, I'm well aware of that." I roll my eyes. "But this isn't up for negotiation. You can unleash all of that sexy, dark fury on me later for grabbing the reins. Right now, I need to make sure you're protected." I wave my hands around. "And what better place than a hospital?"

"You do realize I'm probably better equipped to go up against those cartel thugs than your own guys, right?"

"Trust me, gorgeous. Nobody on my crew has the fight that you do. But they have guns, so that gives me hope." I wink at her.

Jaelyn sits back in the chair, expelling a deep breath. "I can't believe this is happening." Her eyes flick over to me. "And I can't believe that you, the guy I despised up until a couple of hours ago, is now my partner in taking down our mortal enemy."

"You despised me?" I say in a joking voice. "I didn't get that vibe at all."

"Don't worry, I'm sure you'll do something to piss me off again. And then I'll make sure you feel it."

"I can't wait," I murmur.

A tall man in a white coat walks toward us, his eyebrows knitted. Jaelyn springs out of the chair and rushes over to him. "Miss Torres?" he asks.

"Yes," she says in a breathless voice. "My brother Nate…is he okay?"

The doctor's shoulders sag slightly. "He's in critical condition. One of the bullets is lodged in his spinal column and it needs to be removed as soon as possible. He has internal damage to his heart and lung from another bullet. He's being prepped for surgery right now."

She claps a hand over her mouth. "Oh no…"

"Can she see him?" I ask.

The doctor nods. "Yes, you have a few minutes before he goes into the operating room. I'll bring you back."

She gives my hand a squeeze before following the doctor through the heavy red doors.

I hear the swish of the revolving door and see Matteo rushing into the waiting room. "Hey, how is he?"

"Bad," I mutter. "They're taking him into surgery. Jaelyn is back there with him now."

"Shit," he grumbles. "The guys are on their way now, but I don't have a read on Becerra. He didn't go back to his compound after the shooting."

"Okay." I let out a frustrated sigh. "That can only mean one thing, Matteo."

He nods. "I know."

"Once the guys get here, we'll split up. Let's alert the families, too. See if they can get any information for us to go on."

"I'll see what I can do. Stay out of sight with Jaelyn until we're ready to go." He claps a hand on my shoulder. "We're gonna comb the fucking city until we find those bastards. We're shutting them down tonight."

"We sure as fuck are," I grunt, raking a hand through my hair. "They're gonna pay a serious debt tonight. And the interest is gonna choke them. Hard."

Chapter Nineteen
JAELYN

I squeeze Nate's clammy hand. "Do you remember when you were first learning to ride? The time you were in the driveway and thought you had it in drive but it was still in reverse?"

Nate lets out a raspy laugh. "Yeah, and I crashed right through the garage doors. Mom and Dad were so pissed at me for that. Cost me plenty to fix them, too."

"You thought you were so cool on that bike," I say with a giggle. "You were convinced you were going to be such a badass once you got a cut."

His smile fades. "Yeah. And you know what? I'd give anything to redo that part of my life. I'd have kept the club clean and made sure we never ended up on the cartel's radar in the first place."

"You're not the only one who'd have done things differently." I press my fingertips against my temples. "I wasn't exactly an easy child."

"You were spirited. Isn't that what Mom used to say?"

"Mouthy was the word she'd use most often," I mutter.

"Kind of a gross understatement."

I nod. "Yeah…"

"Don't ever lose that spirit, Jae," Nate whispers. "Never, ever."

"Well, you'll just have to make sure that I don't," I say, my voice cracking as his eyes gloss over. I guess the medication is taking effect, and I feel like I'm losing him already. "Do you hear me?"

"Sergio is an asshole," he murmurs. "I'd say he'd better not hurt you, but I know you can kick his ass."

"I can. And I will, don't worry. But stop saying shit like that. You'll be around to kick it for me if he gets out of line." I am so desperate to keep him awake and talking because it might be the last—

No!

No fucking way will I even think it!

"I love you, Jae," he mumbles, his fingers losing their grip on mine.

"Nate, I love you so much," I cry. "Please fight. Please stay with me!"

I weep into his chest for a few seconds before the orderlies come into his room to wheel him out. I stand there watching as they maneuver the gurney through the doorway, the deep ache in my chest a painful reminder of the suffering I've experienced as a result of my choices…*our* choices.

And there's no guarantee that my suffering will come to an end tonight.

I've never felt so helpless in my life, not even when that machete was hanging over my head.

I finally collect myself enough to leave Nate's room. I take a few deep breaths to calm my racing heart, the anger, guilt, and regret consuming my body and mind.

I have to be strong, for myself and for Nate.

I have to stay positive.

A chill slithers through me, telling me one other thing I need to do.

Pray.

My throat tightens because I immediately know who planted that thought in my mind just now.

I'd never been overly religious growing up, but my mother was. And she always prayed, not just when things were on shaky ground. Sure, she asked for strength during hard times, but more often than not, she wanted to thank Him for all of the good ones. She always said praying made her feel closer to God. And she believed with all of her heart that He'd always protect her and her family.

And what good did it do? She was brutally murdered!

So much for her closeness to God.

A lot of good it did her and Dad.

I despised the thought of prayer after my parents died. How could I not when my mother had believed so wholeheartedly that God would always take care of us? Of course, when I challenged it all, the priest who spoke to us afterward pointed out that God has a divine plan for all of us, and my parents were called to fulfill their part.

Total bullshit from someone who has no fucking clue about anything concrete.

That's the kind of toxic opinion I've held about prayer and God for the past few years.

My gut twists as the shiver flutters against my skin once again.

Right now, as my eyes brim with tears and my heart aches like it's being shredded inside of my chest, some unspoken force is tossing me a lifeline. A bright light shining deep within the murk is filling me with an inexplicable sense of calm, and for the first time in a long time, I feel something, something good, something positive.

Hope.

At a time when I need it most.

I squeeze my eyes shut. She's trying to talk to me. I can feel it. I can feel her.

A sob bubbled deep in my chest and I wipe my eyes, spinning around. I walk down the corridor, stopping when I see an orderly come out of a supply closet. "Excuse me," I say. "Can you please tell me where the chapel is?"

He stares at me for a long minute before nodding, the kind of stare that makes the tiny hairs on the back of your neck stand on end. "Down the hallway and to the right," he says in a thick, gravelly voice.

"Thanks." I flash a quick smile as another shiver flutters through my clothes, except this one isn't remotely comforting or peaceful. I shake it off because I don't have a shred of spare energy to worry about creepy orderlies.

I wander around the corridors in search of the chapel, and I'm sure I followed his very simple directions. But the hallways are getting dimmer and dimmer as I venture away from the Emergency Room. It's a small hospital, and there clearly aren't many people working on this floor, other than the trauma teams. I decide to backtrack. Maybe he said to go right but he meant I should go left.

I rub the back of my neck, those damn hairs still prickling along my skin, a strange sense of dread washing over me as I walk. Light footsteps tap along the floor behind me and I spin around to find myself face to face with…nothing.

Nobody.

Just me and my crazy, overworked, and overly stressed mind.

I walk a few more steps and let out a breath.

The chapel.

I pull open the door and it creaks open. It's dark, save for the candles glowing along the dark wood walls. I walk up to the first pew and take a few tentative steps inside, sinking to my knees.

I fold my hands together and press them to my head.

Taking a deep breath, I let the scent of incense fill my lungs. My eyes flutter closed and I try to connect. My heart thumps hard, my pulse throbbing out of control against my neck. Goosebumps pop up along my arms and I feel like an imposter, like I shouldn't be here because of the anger plaguing me.

Anger directed at God for letting this happen, for allowing my world to come apart at the seams.

Again.

I search for the lifeline once more, slogging through the darkness that tries to swallow me whole. I fight, squeezing my hands together and gritting my teeth, desperate to find it and to cling to it. I push through the gloom as another breeze flutters against my cheeks.

"Speak," it whispers in a voice only I can hear.

My lips quiver as they part.

"P-please," I whisper. "If you can hear me, please save my brother. Please let him live. Please keep him safe."

The words choke me as they tumble from my lips, and I wait for the assault on my heart to commence once again since I don't feel that I deserve to ask these things of a higher power I've all but turned my back on over the past few years.

It doesn't happen.

Instead, warmth radiates from deep inside of me. It's a comforting sensation that blankets me in the peace I was certain would forever evade me.

It happened that quickly.

And it may be fleeting, but it fills me now, giving me the hope that I thought was lost forever.

Someone is looking out for me and Nate.

Someone is watching over us.

Someone is going to keep us safe.

A hand drops onto my shoulder and I gasp, nearly falling over as I twist around to find Sergio standing over me.

"I figured I'd find you here when you didn't come back out." He drops into the pew behind me. "What's happening with Nate?"

"He's in surgery," I whisper. "And I'm sorry I didn't come to find you. I just needed to come here." I look around. "To talk to someone."

Sergio nods. "I'll leave you alone. I just wanted to make sure you were okay." He rises and I grasp his hand.

"No, wait," I say, patting the seat next to me. "Don't go. Stay here with me."

His eyebrows furrow but he nods and lowers himself into the pew.

"I bet you didn't think we'd end up here when you kidnapped me this morning, huh?" I ask, laying my head on his shoulder.

He gazes down at me. "End up in a hospital? Or end up with a whole lot of feelings I can't explain for a girl I was trying to extort?"

A tiny smile plays at my lips. "Both, I guess."

He nods. "Then, yeah, I did. On both counts. Guess you can say I'm a glutton for punishment."

"And, uh, what about those feelings?" I whisper.

He shrugs. "I've never met anyone like you. You're fire and ice, lethal and scorching hot. I never know what you're gonna do next to make my blood pressure skyrocket. You drive me absolutely crazy with need, like I can't breathe with you or without you. And that mouth…" He traces the outline of my lips with his forefinger.

"My mother always did say I was a mouthy one," I say.

"You make me irate one second, and then ache for you the next."

"Is all of that…bad?" I ask, tilting my head to the side.

"It's fucking horrible," he breathes, his lips hovering over mine. "And incredible at the same time."

"So, then…good?"

He nods, sweeping his tongue over my lips, dipping between them as he gently fists my hair. He kisses me deeply, his tongue coiling around mine, devouring me in a way that tells me in no uncertain terms that the someone I need is the someone pressed against me right now.

An unlikely choice, to say the least, but the warmth that infuses my heart and body confirms it.

He's the peace and the hope and the light.

And I'm going to cling to it…to him.

It's a startling realization, one I never expected.

But for the first time, I begin to think Mom was right. She prayed for us and maybe, just maybe, God did listen.

Chapter Twenty
SERGIO

We sit in silence for the next few minutes, and my body is torn between wanting to stay and wanting to find Becerra so I can cut his throat.

I realize that having a thought like that in front of God probably isn't ideal, but maybe He'll see things my way and agree with ridding the planet of that sick and twisted scumbag.

The candles on the mini altar flicker and go out in the next second.

I lift an eyebrow.

And then again, maybe He won't.

Eh.

Either way, I'm gonna do it.

I just hope God doesn't snuff me out the way He just did those candles.

My phone buzzes and I pull it out to find a text from Matteo.

I drop a kiss on the top of Jaelyn's head. "Hey," I whisper. "That's Matteo. Time to roll."

She nods, wrapping her arms around me. "Okay. Be careful, Sergio. Please."

"I will. Believe me, I'm not gonna let anything stop me from coming back to you. We have a lot of unfinished business."

"Tons," she whispers, her mouth trembling.

"I want you to stay here, okay?" I say, cupping her chin. "Lay low. I'll find you when I get back."

"Hurry," she whispers. "And good luck."

I brush my lips against hers one last time and rush out of the chapel and down the quiet hallway. Matteo and Dante are waiting for me right outside of the waiting room and Bruno is with them.

"How is she?" Matteo asks.

"Hanging in there," I say. "I told her to stay in the chapel. Out of sight, just until we handle all of this. Just give me a second. I want to let the nurse know where she is for when Nate gets out of surgery."

I push open the door and walk into the far side of the waiting room just as a man walks through the revolving doors. He has a dark red stain covering a gray t-shirt, not that it seems to impact his movement at all. There's only one nurse at the desk. I roll my eyes, knowing I'll need to wait for him to be processed before I can let her know Jae's location.

"I'm looking for a Nate Torres," the man says, his voice tight. "Where is he?"

The nurse looks at him. "I'm sorry, I can't give you any information unless you're immediate family."

What the fuck?

I stop short and flip around a column, peering out at them but staying out of sight. I give a quick look at the entrance but see nothing but an orderly loitering outside smoking a cigarette.

The man nods. "Right, because that's your job." He opens his jacket and pulls out a Beretta. "Now I'm gonna do mine."

Crack!

One single shot explodes into the air and the nurse crumples to the floor in a blood-soaked heap.

A collective scream ripples through the group of people scattered around the waiting room and I watch the man walk toward the red doors, kicking them open, his hand extended and clutching the gun. As soon as he's out of sight, people flee the room like their lives depend on it.

And they fucking do.

I slam my fist against the cinderblock wall as the guys burst through the door.

"What the hell was that?" Dante says.

"Gunman," I say, pulling out my own gun from the back of my pants. "He was looking for Nate," I say through clenched teeth. I grab Bruno's jacket. "Go and get Jaelyn. She's in the chapel. Get her the fuck away from this area, now!" I give him a push and he runs down the hallway, leaving me with Matteo and Dante.

More gunshots erupt into the air as the guy no doubt continues his hunt for Nate.

Three other men shove past the panicked people, making their way into the waiting room wearing black masks and carrying AK-47s in their gloved hands. They stomp toward the double doors firing at the lock that flipped as soon as the first gunman got inside.

I pop out from behind the column, not thinking, not breathing, just aiming.

Crack! Bang!

Gunfire erupts as one of the men goes down hard on the tile floor. The remaining two twist around, spotting me out in the open and they point their weapons at me, peppering the wall behind me with bullets as I dive to the floor. I point my gun up at them, firing off the remaining shots in my clip. Matteo and Dante crouch low to the ground, firing their guns at the one guy who's still standing.

"Fuck!" I yell, scrambling to my feet. "I'm going after him!"

I run through the doors, my brothers on my heels. The corridor is lined with bloody bodies, and I can hear gunfire in the distance. "He's in the operating room. I have no fucking clue where that is, though. We need to take these guys out fast." I smack in a new clip and jog down the hall. Anyone who was unlucky enough to be walking down the hall is now sprawled on the ground. Muffled screams and pleas for help come from behind the closed doors as more shots are fired. I tear down the hall, finding a few people huddled behind blood-splattered desks, and my throat tightens to the point where I can barely suck in a breath.

"Where the fuck is security?" I mutter, holding out my hand. "Doesn't anyone see what the hell is happening here?" I round a corner, following signs for Emergency Surgery. I pass an office tucked into one of the maze-like hallways. The windows have been shot, shattered glass is scattered all over the floor. I creep closer to see a big, burly man in a uniform slumped over a set of monitors.

My shoulders deflate as Matteo stops next to me.

"I guess that answers your question about security," he says.

A high-pitched scream nearby jolts me. "Jaelyn!" I yell, tearing down another hallway.

I run so fast, my feet skid along the polished tile floor and I race around a corner in the direction of the scream.

Pop! Crack! Bang!

I squeeze off as many shots as I can when I see the shooter with his gun pointed at a tall, blonde woman. I catch him in the leg and the arm and he pitches forward into the wall, his gun clattering to the floor. "Kick it!" I scream at the woman. I leap at him when I'm close enough, pulling off his mask and launching my fist at his pock-marked face until I've sufficiently smashed his nose and jaw to bloody bits.

Matteo pulls me off of him. "Find Jaelyn. I'll take care of this piece of shit."

I stagger to my feet as Dante leads the shaking woman into the operating room.

Nate's operating room.

One of the doctors is slumped in the corner, a red stain spreading over his chest.

The other doctor is still standing over Nate. I can see a gash in his leg, but he continues to work.

I grasp the woman's hands. "Call someone. Anyone! I don't know how many others there are, but they took out the security officer. And keep this door locked!"

"Go!" Matteo yells.

I take off again, only to stop a short time later. I strain my ears, the silence is deafening. At this point, I'm so off-course that I don't even remember where the hell the chapel is. But I have to find it.

I have to find her.

Jesus Christ, Becerra planned this whole thing.

He knew we'd all be here. That's why he didn't show up at his compound after shooting Nate.

He came here and fucking waited.

I swallow hard, running in a different direction in search of the chapel. I sent Bruno to stay with Jaelyn. He'll keep her safe until I can get there.

If I can fucking get there!

I make a mad dash down another corridor and stumble as my foot stutters against the floor. I grab onto a metal cart, taking it down with me when I lose my balance. My gun skitters across the floor as I fall on my knees. The cart crashes to the floor just as the man in the gray shirt steps out from around a corner.

I push the cart out of my way, shoving it at him as I dive for my gun.

Crack!

"Ah! You motherfu—"

Pop!

I roll over onto my back, blood and fire coursing from my body. Bastard clipped me in both arms, rendering me and my fucking gun completely useless.

"Where's your fucking boss?" I rasp. "Sending in his peons to do work he should be doing himself!"

The guy leans over me. "I don't work for anyone, asshole. I'm here to settle a debt. You're just the annoying little fuck who was stupid enough to get in my way."

I stare at my gun a few feet away, clenching my teeth as he grabs me by the back of my shirt. I flex my fingers and I bite back the scream threatening to escape my lips.

I've been hurt before, but fuck.

How in the hell am I gonna so much as grab my gun, much less fire it with two dead hands?

He must know exactly what I'm thinking, too, because he lets me go long enough to bend down and grab my gun. I slide my left hand into the pocket of my jacket and pull out a small knife, hiding it in my sleeve. When his hand tightens on my collar again, I grip the knife as tight as I can without managing to cry out in agony. I swing my arm around and drive the blade into his thigh. He drops me, grunting in pain as he grips the handle.

I jammed it in pretty deep, deep enough where it buys me time to jump up and body slam him into the wall. I shove my leg against the knife, driving it deeper and making his yelps shatter the still air.

I kick him square in the throat as he doubles over, grabbing my gun from his hand. Sonofabitch, it hurts to hold it! I squeeze the trigger, my fingers trembling like crazy, and he drops his own gun as the bullet blasts his hand.

"Where the hell is Becerra?" I hiss.

"Fuck you. You're too late anyway. You thought you could protect her by sending your buddy to look after her," he pants. "She needed to die for what she did, that fucking whore."

I grab his hair and slam his head back against the wall. "What are you talking about?" I scream. "Who the fuck are you?"

"I'm the one whose brothers were killed by Nate and Jaelyn Bennet. And I came here to collect!" He lets out a psychotic laugh. "I did, too. I got the bitch *and* her bodyguard. And Becerra is gonna handle the rest. I told him I'd clear the way for him to get to you."

I let out a thunderous roar and point the gun at him, shooting him three times in the head. He slumps over immediately, falling face-first into the floor.

I drop to my knees, my finger shaking as the gun clatters to the floor.

Jaelyn. Bruno. *Dead.*

I try to draw in a breath, bringing a hand to my heart.

Becerra.

Fuck!

My fingers shake as I dial Matteo's number.

When the call connects, I don't even wait for him to speak. "Becerra…is here. For me. For us. I got another one of the shooters. But he…he got Jaelyn and Bruno." My voice cracks. "I won't let him get anyone else."

"That's good. I like that kind of confidence." An accented voice assaults my ears, and I clench the phone tight, searing pain racing up my arm.

"Becerra," I hiss.

"Very good, Sergio."

"Unpredictable as always," I hiss.

"Yes, well, I can say the same for you. Attacking Javier like you did, disrespecting me and my offer for partnership, and then finding yourself in bed with our enemy while you plotted to eliminate me." He sighs. "I should kill Matteo, but it wouldn't be fair to him. After all, it was you who concocted this plan, yes?"

"Let him go," I growl. "Come for me, Becerra. You've got a problem with the way I do business? Handle me your-fucking-self."

"Oh, I will. Make no mistake. But was it really worth it? We could have ruled this city. Me, your whole syndicate. We'd have owned every last inch of the place."

"We have a very strict 'no shit heel' rule for new members," I seethe. "So it wouldn't have worked out."

He chuckles, a low, sinister one that boils my blood. That fucker has my brothers, and Bruno and Jaelyn are already dead.

What the hell am I gonna do?

How the fuck can I win?

I stagger to my feet, still holding the phone to my ear.

"Come to the chapel," he says. "Say a prayer. And then, when divine intervention doesn't work because it *won't*, you can take it up with your maker."

Footsteps pound on the floor behind me and I spin around to find Dante holding a finger to his mouth. I click to end the call. "Jesus Christ, I never thought I'd ever be so happy to see you," I say. "How the hell did you get away from him?"

"I told Matteo to hang tight until backup got here, but he went looking for you. Dumbass managed to get snatched by that short, fat ass."

"He killed Jaelyn and Bruno," I say, my voice hitching.

"Fuck," Dante says, scrubbing a hand down the front of his face. "Are you sure?"

"It's what he said."

"Goddammit, Bruno," Dante says in a low growl. "Fucking guy! How?"

"I don't know. But he's waiting for us in the chapel. Says he's got Matteo."

Dante looks at my bloody arms. "You gonna be okay to shoot?"

I nod, my jaw tight. "If I had nubs for arms, I'd find a fucking way to fire this gun," I grunt. "What about Nate?"

"Still being worked on. I guess Becerra assumed one of his other guys would clip him."

We run in the direction of the chapel, slowing down as the doorway comes into view. I creep up to it, pulling open the door and staring inside.

It's fucking empty.

I walk into the small space. "I don't get it. Where the hell—?"

"Shit," Dante mutters, running past me to where an arm peeks out from the pew.

I rush to the front of the chapel where I left Jaelyn…where she now lies. I turn her over to see a huge, angry-looking red bump on the corner of her forehead. I run my fingers down the front of her black shirt, but there's no blood.

Just holes…where the bullets lodged into the Kevlar vest she's wearing?!

I press my head to her chest.

Oh, holy fuck!

"Jae," I whisper, smoothing her hair away from her face. "Jae!"

A few seconds later, her eyelids flutter lift. "Sergio?" she moans. "Oh my God, are you okay? What happened?"

"You were shot, but you're wearing a vest," I say. "How? I didn't give you one."

"Bruno," she murmurs, lightly grazing her head and wincing. "He made me put his on, just in case. The last thing I remember is someone coming in here and shooting at us."

"You must have hit your head after you got shot. I guess they figured you were already dead with the number of bullets lodged in this thing," Dante says.

"What about Bruno?" she whispers. "And Nate?"

Dante gets up and walks toward the altar, dropping to the carpeted floor. "Christ," he mutters. "Bruno's hit."

My heart damn-near stops as I wait for him to drop the bomb. "Is he—?"

"I can feel a pulse!"

I let out the breath. "Fuck, but we have to find Matteo. What if Becerra sent us here to—?"

Dammit! That's exactly what he did!

I help Jaelyn onto the pew. "Dante, stay here. I'm going after Becerra. Give me your gun!"

"Dude, you can't hit shit with those bum hands. Let me go!"

"No, this is my problem to fix." My words to Matteo come rushing back. I did this to our family. I brought him in, brought all of the shit in.

It's up to me to blast it all the fuck out.

I backtrack toward Nate's room, the sound of sirens getting louder and louder with each second that passes. I don't understand how they haven't made it here yet, but there's no way Becerra walks outta here in cuffs.

He's gonna be dragged out in a fucking body bag!

My legs pick up speed as I round corners in the direction of the emergency surgery room. At least they still work the way I need them to. I skid to a halt outside of the closed door and kick it open, to find Matteo standing right inside, next to Nate's gurney.

Becerra is standing right behind my brother, guarded by Matteo's massive chest.

"Glad to see you could make it to *this* meeting," I say, holding the gun in my outstretched hand. "Looks like we have business to handle after all."

"Not much, actually. Just one decision. You've seen what I can do, what my men can do. Bring me into your syndicate and Matteo walks out of here without a single bullet wound. I may cut off his hand though. You know, an eye for an eye and all of that shit." Becerra smirks from his position behind Matteo.

Matteo's jaw twitches as Becerra shoves his gun into his back, making it arch. "I don't give a shit what you cut off, but you're not getting near our organization, you cocksucker!"

"We'll see about that," Becerra says with a shit-eating grin on his face. "I have other tricks up my sleeve if the other families need any more convincing. I've come a long way to make this arrangement work. Killing the rest of the Torres family was just icing on the cake. I knew I'd need to hit it big to be considered by your syndicate." He snickers. "Pun intended."

So taking out Jaelyn and Nate wasn't his real play?

This guy is a twisted motherfucker.

Becerra nods at me. "Make the call and your brother lives. You've already lost plenty." He looks at Nate lying on the operating table, the sound of bleeping machines piercing my brain as I search for an out.

Any out.

Becerra reaches over and pulls the plug on the machine helping Nate breathe.

I pull out my phone and hold it up.

"Nice," Becerra says. "Now make the fucking call or I kill you *and* Matteo!"

I dial a number and a second later, Becerra's phone rings. He pulls it out of his pocket and clicks to accept the call.

"Hey, it's Sergio. You want a piece of me? You can suck my fat cock!" I fire a single shot at Matteo's left shoulder and he crumbles to the ground just in time for me to fire off a round of shots into Becerra's chest.

And one between the eyes.

Just because.

I rush around the gurney and dive over Becerra's body to plug Nate's machine back into the wall, letting out a breath as the bleeping picks up speed.

"Goddammit!" Matteo thunders, clutching his shoulder.

I kneel down next to him. "You know, I always wanted to do that."

"You're a real prick."

'And a damn good shot, if I say so myself."

"So this is how you fix shit, huh? You shoot your boss? Don't ever put that on a resume. Nobody will hire you." He rolls his eyes and falls back onto the floor.

"Eh. I'm not going anywhere. I'm after *your* job, bro. And in the meantime, just call me Mr. Fucking Fix It."

Chapter Twenty-One
JAELYN

I put my hand on top of Bruno's, smiling as his brown eyes flutter open. They meet mine and his lips slowly curl upward as if it even hurts to smile.

"I had to be here when you woke up, to say thank you," I whisper, giving his hand a little squeeze. "You saved my life with that vest, Bruno."

He coughs a little and shifts on the bed. "Yeah, well, Serge said to do anything I needed to protect you." He lifts his hand, pointing at my swollen head. "That looks painful."

"At least I'm alive to feel it." My eyes pool with tears, the memory of all of those gunshots exploding into the air and then plugging the Kevlar shirt I had on underneath my own. I was sure in those moments that the shirt wouldn't be able to withstand the impact and that the bullets would ravage my body.

I'd have resembled Swiss cheese if not for Bruno.

"I will be forever grateful," I whisper, giving him a kiss on the cheek just as the door creaks open.

"Ahem," Sergio says, clearing his throat. "So this is how it's gonna be, huh? What do they call this? Some Florence Nightingale shit?"

I straighten up, grinning at Sergio. "Jealous?"

He walks over to the bed. "Of this guy? Never. How many lives you got left, Bruno? I can count 'em on one hand, bro. And if you get any ideas about taking off with my woman, I can promise that number will go down to zero."

I let out a snort of laughter. "Oh yeah?" I say, nodding to his arms, both in matching slings. "How exactly are you going to manage that?"

"I've got three legs, or don't you remember?" Sergio says with a wicked glimmer in his ice-blue eyes.

"Oh, right," I say, walking around the bed. "How very fortunate for you."

"And *you*," he murmurs, dropping a kiss on the tip of my nose.

The door opens again and a nurse rushes in. "Bruno, is everything okay? We heard the alarm go off."

Bruno looks at us with a wicked smile. "Yeah, I did that. Now get the fuck out of here so I can rest, okay? And if you resist, my friend Nurse Sandy will kick your asses out."

Sandy flashes a stern look at us and I blow Bruno a kiss before leaving the room with Sergio. "Thank you," I mouth to him once more.

He gives me a thumbs-up with a half-smile before his hand drops back down to the bed.

We walk out of the room and meander through the corridors to get to the waiting room.

Matteo is huddled in the corner with two police officers, I guess giving them a statement, and Dante jumps up from his chair when he spots us. "Hey, how are they?"

"Nate is still sleeping," I say. "They said they'd come to get me as soon as he wakes up. And Bruno is good. Thank God." I shake my head. "If he hadn't given me that Kevlar, I'd be lying on a slab in the morgue right now. He saved my life."

"How's the head?" Dante asks.

"Sore, but hey, I'll take it. Beats death."

"Yeah, that's like my mantra," Sergio quips, nudging me closer the best way he can since he doesn't have full use of either arm.

I look around the hospital. There's crime scene tape everywhere. Turns out the cops had been detained on their way over here earlier. A car bombing a few miles away took them off-course, giving Becerra enough time to take over the hospital without any outside interference.

Of course, he didn't anticipate that Sergio would turn out to be more detrimental to his cause than the authorities.

I look around at the people sitting in tight groups, fear etched into their faces.

I don't blame them.

It's the same type of fear I'd lived with since fleeing Miami.

But it's a fear I can finally bury with all of the other useless emotions that came along with it.

We've officially closed the book on Becerra and the Bowman family.

And we can finally breathe again.

Matteo walks over to us, running a hand through his hair with his good hand since his other one is hanging in a sling that matches Sergio's.

"Did you finish with the cops?" Sergio asks. "Feed 'em some bullshit to chew on?"

He nods. "Yeah, I gave them my story about how we ended up on Becerra's radar, that they didn't like the fact that Nate picked us over Becerra as a partner for the Sapphire Lounge. It's why they shot him at the hotel and why they came here to finish the job. We just did our civic duty by defending our new partner with our legally obtained firearms." He winks at me. "Don't worry, I conveniently forgot all about the Miami connection."

I grin. "Thanks."

"Crazy shit," Sergio mutters. "Can you believe Becerra actually thought he was gonna use us to get into the syndicate? That was his fucking play, not revenge. It was always about the money."

"Not for the other Bowman brother," I mutter.

"Hey," Sergio says, nuzzling my ear with his lips. "You don't have to worry about him or the rest of them ever again. It's over, babe. Really and truly over."

My shoulders sag. "I know. I just can't believe it. We've lived this for so long, it's hard to imagine that it's all finally in the past."

"If you live this life, you'll find out very quickly that there's always a new enemy hanging around in the shadows, just waiting to pop out with a machete," Matteo says with a snicker.

"Ugh, no machetes," I groan, burying my head in Sergio's chest. "But I can handle the rest." I sneak a look up at Sergio and smile.

"Oh yeah, you're definitely ready," he murmurs.

"Miss Torres?" A pretty brunette rushes over, a smile on her freckled face. "Your brother is awake and asking for you."

I gasp, flashing a smile at the guys. "I'll be back!"

I follow her into the recovery area for the emergency surgery wing and run right up to my brother's bed. "Nate! Oh thank God, you're awake!" I grip his hands, pressing them to my lips.

"Your head…you're hurt?" He makes a funny noise as he shifts slightly on the bed. "What the fuck happened?" he mutters. "I heard the nurses and doctors talking about some attack?"

"Oh, wow, that's a loaded question." I let out a sigh before giving him the rundown of what happened while he was under anesthesia.

"Fuuuuck," he breathes once I get to the end. "Jae, you could have been killed."

"You, too," I say, a gaggle of tears clogging my throat. "But thank God, we're both okay. The doctors were able to finish your surgery and Bruno saved my life. They were looking down on us, Nate. Mom and Dad. I am a thousand percent sure of it. They protected us, just like they always tried to do when they were alive." One tear slips down the side of my cheek. "They made sure we would still have each other. I love you so much, Nate. I don't know what I'd ever do without you." My head falls onto his arm and his fingers ruffle the top of my hair.

"Stop crying," he croaks. "I'm never leaving you, Jae. I will always be here to watch over you and keep you safe." He clears his throat. "But I won't be the only one with that job, will I?"

I raise my head, a small smile tugging at my lips. "Well, first of all, I am very capable of taking care of myself."

"As evidenced by the grapefruit-sized lump on your head," he grumbles.

I roll my eyes. "Okay, that aside, I'm pretty damn tough in case you haven't noticed."

"So tough that you got yourself kidnapped by a fucking mafia goon who probably can't even add two plus two."

"He's a little jagged around the edges," I muse. "But I like it rough."

Nate groans, holding his side. "Don't ever say that again."

I giggle. "Oops, sorry. I didn't mean it like that. I mean, it's true, but—"

"No more!" Nate growls.

I smooth back his hair. "He's an acquired taste for sure."

"Great, that's what people say about sushi. Why the fuck would I keep trying something I hate?"

"Because I..." I pause. I what? Lust him? Like him? More than like him?

All of the above?

There is one thing I know for sure. Sergio Villani came into my life for a reason. And whatever the reason may be, I'm not letting him go.

EPILOGUE

Sergio

FOUR MONTHS LATER

I stretch my arms overhead as the late-afternoon California sunshine beats down on my flushed skin. Damn, it feels good to be mobile again. It also helps in the bedroom. Hands-free sex is all fine and good, but I need full use of all limbs to perform at my best, especially when taming a vixen by the name of Jaelyn Torres.

I close my eyes, listening to the crashing waves as they break at the shoreline. The salty scent of the Pacific consumes me, and for this tiny sliver of time that we're here in Palm Springs on a much-needed vacation, I actually feel somewhat relaxed.

It's been a long four months since the fallout with Becerra and his crew. I finally got my seat at the table, my efforts earning the respect I'd been after. But it turns out, I didn't need their approval after all. That wasn't gonna fix my splintered relationship with Matteo. But saving his life definitely helped it.

And that's a good thing since he and Heaven decided to stay out here in Vegas for a while longer. Turns out, my sister-in-law prefers the dry desert weather than the four seasons in Manhattan, and since she's about five months pregnant, she's the one calling the shots right now.

We closed down our nightclub Verve. It wasn't worth the cash injection to keep it operational. Instead, I turned all of my attention to my new nightlife venture. Even with two bum arms, I jumped right into my new role as co-owner of the Sapphire Lounge and all of its sister clubs. And while Nate took a few weeks to recover, I had Jaelyn by my side, running her show, her way.

As always.

Even now, I can hear her grousing a few feet away, barking orders to her assistant Ashleigh into her phone.

Although, I have to say, for as much of a control freak as she is, I've thoroughly enjoyed taking little impromptu meeting breaks throughout the nights. That's when the rest of her freaky sides come out to play.

"Leave her alone and get down here!" I call out to her, licking my lips as I eye her in that slick red bikini. Fuck, I can't wait to tear it off of her with my teeth once we get back to the hotel suite.

"Okay, I'll be right there!" she says, doing a little hip swing as she runs over to our chairs and tosses her phone onto one of the towels. She runs toward me, her full tits bouncing in that barely there top. Her bronze skin glows against the fiery red fabric as she dances toward the shore. A growl escapes my lips as she flings her tight body into my arms.

"Have I told you that I love you today?"

"Yeah," I say with a grin. "But I never get tired of hearing it."

"I love you," she murmurs.

"And I fucking love *you*," I say.

"God, it feels so good for you to hold me like this," she says with a contented sigh as she leans against me. "I know it's been a while since your arms healed, but having them wrapped tight around me never gets old." She drops a kiss onto my lips. "And I'll never take them for granted. Ever."

I run my fingertips down her spine and her head falls back, a loud moan slipping from her lips. "Mm, that's making me want to take you back to the hotel, Jae."

"Why wait?" she whispers, snaking a leg around me.

I flash a wicked smile and slide my fingers into her bikini bottom. She lets out a gasp as they plunge into her soft folds, toying with her clit as I drag them out. My cock thickens under the water, and she pulls my board shorts down far enough so that it springs to life outside of the fabric. I slide the head of my cock against her opening, sinking into her as I gather her in my arms. Her pussy is warm and wet, clenched tight around me as I roll my hips, the friction making my balls ache with the need for release. She clings to me, her tits rubbing against my chest as tiny moans escape her mouth. Her nails lance my flesh, scraping and dragging down my sunburned back. I clench my teeth, pressing my hands into the small of her back as I thrust deeper into her pussy. Her legs lock around me, pulling me farther into her until we're so connected, I don't know where she starts and I end.

And that's exactly the way I like it.

I drop my head back, staring up at the horizon, pinks, oranges, and purples exploding against the sky as the orgasm tears through me, filling her with everything I have…and everything I want.

She falls against me, her legs still wrapped tight around my waist as her breathing calms. "My God, you're incredible."

I trail soft kisses along the back of her neck. "This wasn't exactly what I planned when I asked you to join me out here."

"Was it better than what you had planned?" she asks with a mischievous smile on her face.

"No." My smile fades, my face now serious.

Her eyes widen and she loosens her legs, dropping to the submerged sand in front of me. "Oh…well, I can't imagine anything could possibly trump what we just did, but okay." She lifts an eyebrow when I don't immediately respond.

She doesn't know why.

She's gonna have to be patient, especially since board short pockets aren't the easiest thing to unzip.

Especially when you're under water and working with one hand.

Jaelyn tilts her head to the side, an expectant look on her face. "So…are you going to share your plan now or wait until my whole body prunes up?"

My fingers finally fish out the ring box from my pocket. Yeah, I could have done this back at the hotel, or even at dinner tonight.

But I can't wait another second. As it is, I've waited about four months too long.

I snicker. "God, you're so fucking controlling. I love it. And even if you were shriveled up like a prune, I'd still hammer you like a jackrabbit."

"So romantic," she groans sarcastically, giving me a little punch in the chest.

"Maybe I can redeem myself," I say with a knowing smirk, pulling the ring out of the water and holding it up in front of her. Her eyes widen and she gasps, reaching for the sparkling gem that I'm holding just out of her reach.

"Easy. You haven't said yes yet."

"Then ask me!" She giggles, still trying to grab for it.

I grab her arm and hold it to my heart as I bring the ring directly into her line of sight. "Jae, you make me completely crazy…er, I mean, I'm completely crazy about you."

She laughs, her tear-filled eyes glimmering like emeralds. "And?"

"And what? You want me to keep talking about how nuts you make me?"

"So long as you're talking about what I do to you in the bedroom." She winks.

I squeeze her tight. "You are tough and loud and powerful and strong. So full of passion and life. Just being around you makes me feel more alive than I'd ever imagined. Your

energy, your spirit…" I shake my head. "My God, you're just incredible. And not to mention, sexy as fuck."

"Can't forget that," she quips.

I shake my head, the ring still on my finger as I cup her face in my hands. "I want you by my side forever. I want you to be my wife."

She smirks at me. "That's not a question."

I furrow my brow.

"I can't say yes unless you ask me the question!"

"Will you marry me?"

"Yes." She lets out a loud whoop as I slide the large diamond onto her finger. "Oh my God, Sergio, it's *huge!*"

I give her a wink. "Not the first time I've heard *that.*"

She tilts her head up at me. "Yeah, I am a *very* lucky girl."

THE END

SNEAK PEEK OF SAVAGE BEAST

CHAPTER ONE: ROMAN

"I swear I didn't touch her!"

My fist tightens around the collar of the guy whose head I currently have held over an open flame. His name is Salvatore Giaconne, a guy my brother Matteo fired before he took off for Vegas with his wife, Heaven, a few months ago. I don't know how the hell Salvatore even got in here tonight, but it looks like I need to have a chat with the door guys after I dispose of this piece of garbage.

Without warning, I shove his face closer to the burning wick as he yelps like a little bitch. I grit my teeth and pull him away from the lit candle, throwing him against the wall. It shakes from the impact, the framed photos hanging next to him fall to the floor, glass shattering around his feet.

"Don't lie to me," I creep toward him, my shoulders squared and my lips twisted into a sneer. "Do you understand the rules, fucko? Or do I need to translate them into another language for you?"

The guy shudders against the wall, all six feet and two hundred and fifty pounds of him.

He could crush me with that mass.

But he doesn't, because he knows I don't need mass in order to do the same...or worse...to him.

"N-no," he whimpers. "Please, Mr. Villani. I didn't mean to—"

I roll my eyes. Fucking pussy. He got caught with his hands in the cookie jar and now he thinks he can cry and beg and walk out of here with his cock still intact?

With a quirk of my brow, I fold my arms over my chest. "So now you're admitting that you did something."

The whimpering stops. Idiot. If you're gonna be a pussy, at least own it. Don't play a game that you know is gonna get you maimed. That's just fucking stupidity right there.

Salvatore blinks fast, obviously realizing a little too late that he is a complete fucking moron for contradicting himself like that. "It was an accident," he says gruffly.

"Oh, so you didn't mean to tear off Zoe's G-string with your teeth while you held her down with your knee? It just got caught in your teeth and when you pulled away, you took it with you?"

And that's when I see it.

The flicker of annoyance in his deep-set eyes and he grimaces. Now he reverts to his tough guy routine. "She had it coming," he hisses.

I narrow my eyes. "Oh yeah? And what exactly did she do to deserve your face between her thighs?"

"I don't answer to you anymore," he says coldly.

"When you're in my club and you've just been caught harassing my employee, then yeah. You fucking answer to me!"

Adrenaline floods my veins as I launch myself at him, grabbing the sides of his jacket and slamming him against the wall as hard as I can. Christ, it's so hard, I think I scrambled my own brain for a second.

He makes a loud woof! sound when his body collides with the sheetrock and a loud crash next to us makes my back stiffen. The glass jar candle I'd almost plunged Salvatore's face into tumbles onto the floor and cracks against the marble floor tiles. The flame shoots out, dangerously close to igniting the woven area rug in the center of the room. I stomp it out just as it catches the edge of the carpet, gritting my teeth at the damage I've almost certainly done to the soles of my Ferragamo loafers.

Salvatore lets out a loud grunt as he lunges for me. I sidestep the still-lit candle as he charges, swinging one of his fists at my temple. I'm just about his height but since I don't weight the same as a baby elephant, I dance around him, narrowly avoiding his next punch.

A loud pounding at the door reminds me that one of my security guys, Ray, is waiting outside, ready to jump in if I need him.

But that's not how I operate. I put up with security but I prefer to handle things on my own.

My way.

That's what happens when you're the youngest in a family of gangsters driven by bloodlust. Everyone already has their own calling card, and they've established their own reputations. Nobody has anything left to prove to the rest of the underworld.

Except me.

Matteo left me in charge here in Manhattan to run shit while he's in Vegas. He gave me his trusted security team as backup, but I can't delegate this kind of thing to anyone.

Security, my ass.

If I can't handle scumbags like Salvatore on my own, nobody will take me seriously, including my own brothers. They won't regard me as a leader. And they sure as hell won't give me my own territory when the time comes.

People who delegate the hard shit don't command respect. And if you're trying to claw your way to the top of the food chain, delegating equates to weakness.

Weakness will get you eaten alive.

So I ignore Ray's furious knocking and duck down and around Salvatore's next punch. His fist pummels the sheetrock wall, leaving my nose and jaw still intact. He lets out a sharp groan, clutching his bloody fist. Spittle flies out of the corners his mouth, his breaths morphing into angry pants.

I could kill him.

But I don't.

I know there's only one reason why he's here tonight.

Revenge.

He figured I'd be an easy target since Matteo is away.

That I wouldn't have enough backup to take him and his thug crew on.

He didn't count on the fact that I am my own muscle and that my sole priority right now is making sure the kingdom we've built is strong enough to withstand assholes like Sallyboy and his gang of fuck nuts.

I thought about putting a bullet between his eyes but then I'd never find out why he's really here.

It's not because of Zoe's pussy.

Matteo has his fair share of enemies and they're always lurking, angling to find a crack in the foundation of our empire.

They will search tirelessly, but they'll never find one.

And just to make sure Salvatore's guys get the message too, I think I need to show them that their searches will come up empty, that while this empire is in my hands, it won't ever fucking crumble.

Salvatore fists his hand, wincing as he clenches his scratched knuckles.

"Looks like it hurts," I say in a mocking voice. "Maybe you shoulda sent someone else in here, someone who can actually make contact with something other than the wall."

That pisses him off and he launches a fist out at me again.

But when that big body of his loses balance, I yank the back of his collar, pulling him back toward me. I want to make sure he hears this next part before his ears go up in flames.

Literally.

I grab the jagged piece of the candle holder and fist his hair, singing the bottom of his ear with the flickering wick. "You cross me again and I'll make sure you're incinerated, not just a little seared, do you understand me?"

He roars as he leaps toward me, shoving me into an end table. It falls against a wall with me on top of it. A lamp crashes against the floor along with a tube of lube, a pair of handcuffs, and a flogger.

I smirk as I regain my footing, jumping off the table and inching toward him. I drop the candle, stepping on the wick with the heel of my shoe. "Haven't had enough yet, have ya? You still want more, Sallyboy? Come and fucking get it!"

Another guttural yell pierces the air and this time when he swings his fist out, I grab it, twisting it backward. Now he's really crying like the bitch I always knew he was. "You feel that?" I hiss at him. "That's how your wrist feels when it's about to break." I twist harder, my grip tight on his hand. "So unless you want me to take the next step and break the goddamn thing, why don't you tell me why you're here?"

"Fuck you!" he yells.

"Oh, yeah?" I scream back.

Good God, I want to break it so badly. I want to prove to him that he can't screw me over, that I'm just as strong, if not stronger, as the rest of my family and if he doesn't give me what I want, that I'll cut off his tongue, too.

"You owe me!" He screams. "And you're gonna pay!"

"You didn't deliver," I seethe against his ear. "So, no, I'm not paying you a fucking cent!" I press his wrist farther back against his forearm so that the top of his fingers are practically kissing it.

"Then Zoe ain't the only one who's gonna be violated tonight," he growls.

My eyes widen, my teeth clenched tight as I snap his wrist, shoving him face-first at the cold tiles before I open the door to the room in the bottom floor of Risk.

The screaming isn't a big deal.

There are plenty of other, way more disturbing sounds floating into the hallway from other closed doors in the vicinity. I'm sure nobody gave Salvatore's screeches a second thought.

Ray comes into the room and glares at Salvatore writhing on the floor. He then looks up at me, his forehead pinched. He lets out a deep breath, shaking his head. "You should have let me in sooner."

"I had to handle things with Salvatore," I say, sweeping a hand through my hair.

"That's the thing. Salvatore isn't the problem. He's the distraction."

"What the hell are you talking about, Ray?"

"You know the shipment of blow that was delivered this afternoon and locked up in the storage room below the club?" Ray's lips press together into a tight line. "I just got confirmation from Johnny. The lock was sliced off. The blow is gone." His eyes narrow as they fall upon Salvatore. "And so is Zoe."

CHAPTER TWO: MARCHELLA

"Why are you so fidgety?" I ask my brother Frankie as I smooth my hair back into a ponytail. "You're going to wear out the rug from all of your pacing. And since I just vacuumed, it would have been nice for you to take off your damn shoes first!"

"Sorry," he grumbles, raking a hand through his hair. With a nod toward the rug, he shrugs his shoulders. "Not like the vacuuming helps, anyway."

I purse my lips. "That's hardly my fault. And so we're clear, I'm working endless hours to make sure there's still carpet beneath our feet." With a raised eyebrow, I glower at Frankie. "What about you, hmm? Did you collect any money this week?"

Frankie's nostrils flare. "You know, Chella, I'm doing the best I can!"

"Really?" I fold my arms over my chest. "Because I haven't seen a freaking penny from you in the past two weeks! You do know that rent is due at the end of the month, right? Or are you just counting on me to save us. Again!" Anger bubbles deep in my chest, threatening to boil over for about the tenth time today.

"Stop being such a fucking nag!" he thunders. "Do you realize how much stress I'm under right now? No! You don't! And you want to know why? Because you're too busy being a goddamn martyr!"

I gasp, my eyes widening. "Did you seriously just…call me…holy shit, Frankie," I mutter, shaking my head. "Do you realize if it wasn't for me that we'd be on the street? Hungry? Homeless? Possibly dead?" I clench my fists, my voice rising. "I had plans, too! Did you know that? Did you even care? Do you think I wanted to give up my dreams to move into this shit-ass apartment in one of the worst areas in the city? Do you think I have any desire to live in this fucking hell?" I stomp toward him, stopping directly in front of him. "No!" I scream at the top of my lungs. "I didn't! But here I am!"

He flashes me a sheepish look then averts his gaze. "I'm sorry."

"Sorry for what, exactly?"

"Being an insensitive ass."

"And?" I say in a sharp voice.

"And for taking advantage of your good nature," he mumbles, sneaking a look at me. His lips curl into a grin.

"And?"

"And for wearing my shoes on the shitty rug."

I flop onto the worn sofa that we were lucky enough to score from a nearby Salvation Army store. Its more apropos to say we were probably more lucky that it wasn't infested with anything that could eat us alive. "What the hell are you going to do?" I murmur, dropping my head into my hands.

Frankie sinks down next to me. "Chell, we're gonna be okay. I promise."

I roll my eyes, collapsing against the back of the couch. "Oh yeah?"

"Yeah. I've, ah, got some things in motion." He scrubs a hand down the front of his face and I see his spine stiffen.

I jerk upward. "Frankie," I say slowly. "What the hell is that supposed to mean?"

He shrugs, still not meeting my suddenly panicked gaze. I love my brother to pieces, but he's not at all the hard-working type. He's more the avoid-working type. And by avoiding work, I mean doing shady things that can get him hurt, arrested, or killed.

It's how we got into this mess in the first place.

"Why aren't you answering me?" I say. "Do you want to end up like Dad? Rotting in some minimum security jail cell because he chose the life over his family? Because he was always after the money and never cared about consequences? He lives in that hell just waiting for someone to pop him, which you know is going to happen!"

His eyes blaze as he stares me down. "Don't say that shit about Dad," Frankie grunts darkly.

"How can I not?" I yell. "I mean, look at us! Mom is gone and we have collection agents camped outside our door, breathing down our necks for hundreds of thousands of dollars we owe in medical care and an assortment of other bills that got pushed aside when we were trying to make ends meet?"

"Dad did the best he could," he retorts.

"Well, I don't really see things the way you do," I mutter. "He could have gotten out. He made a choice!"

"He did what he felt was right for our family!"

I let out a disbelieving laugh, waving my hands around me at the small, cluttered space we now call home. It's a far cry from the penthouse apartment where we lived in Central Park East. Now we have an Inwood address, so far uptown, we're practically in the Bronx. It's clean-ish, and that's probably the best it'll ever be, regardless of how much I scrub and sanitize and disinfect. But it's still in the city, the only home we've ever known. And even though it takes me almost an hour to get to one of my jobs downtown, I can feel that connection to Mom just by being here. She always loved living in Manhattan and I inherited that same love. So we scrimp and pinch to get by until things get better. But good God, I hope they get better soon. "Yes, well, that's exactly what I'm trying to do right now and why I need to go to work at an actual job, to make real, legitimate money to pay our painfully real, legitimate bills." I give my head a quick shake. "What the hell are you doing, Frankie?"

We've had this argument so many times in the past six months. It gets super-heated when it comes time to sign away all of the hard-earned cash I've made for the monthly payments we're now responsible for handling.

Mom's long-battle with cancer came to a devastating end, but the bills keep coming. I didn't realize how much financial trouble Dad was having when she was sick. But he's not the kind of guy to ever admit defeat, so he stole from Peter to pay Paul and it finally caught up with him. I rub the back of my neck.

Christ, did it ever.

I keep waiting for the call from the prison that someone iced him in his sleep the night before. Whenever my phone rings with an unknown number, my chest tightens and I can't squeeze out a breath until I hear that it isn't the warden bearing horrible news.

"Fucking A, Chella!" Frankie jumps off the couch. "You think you know everything, but you don't! You have no idea—" He stops, mid-shout, and I furrow my brow.

"I have no idea about what?" I ask, my eyes narrowed. "About how our father committed a murder to collect a quick buck? About how he had zero regard for his son and daughter's well-being after their mother died and took a risk that would crush their lives, too? About how he could have gotten out of the organization but chose to stay and then lost his livelihood because of a stupid fucking decision?"

"He isn't some deadbeat, Chell. He saved…" Frankie's voice trails off and once again, his gaze drops.

"He saved what, Frankie? Who?" I say softly. "Because as far as I can see, there isn't one single person in this family who isn't struggling to put the pieces of their life back together right now."

Frankie stomps into the kitchen, which is about five steps away, and pulls open the refrigerator door. He peers inside and grabs a can of Miller Lite, popping off the top and guzzling the beer before answering.

I let out a deep sigh. I really didn't want to get into this with him tonight but the pile of bills on the kitchen counter got my mind and mood in a serious twist. I walk over to him and place a hand on his tensed shoulder. "Look," I say in a quiet voice. "I don't want to fight. We're all we have, and I love you, okay?"

He slams the empty can on the counter and turns to look at me. "I love you, too, sis."

"We'll figure things out," I say. "Hey, maybe we can go for a run in the park tomorrow if you're around? Get some fresh air, maybe scrounge some money together for a dirty water dog or five." I grin, nudging his shoulder. "It would be fun."

He pauses then gives a stiff nod. "Yeah, it would be."

I force a smile. There's a look in his dark eyes that I don't like, but I don't press him on it. I have a long night ahead of me and I can't be worried about what glimmers in the depths of my brother's gaze right now. "I'll see you in the morning," I say, squeezing his arm. "Please be careful."

"You say that to me every time you leave," he grumbles.

"It's because I worry."

He rolls his eyes. "I'll be fine."

"I'm going to hold you to that," I say, picking up my handbag and jacket. "'Night."

"Night," he replies and there it is again. That damn look.

It makes my stomach twist because it always means trouble.

And we really can't afford any more of that.

Literally.

We can't afford anything.

I carefully pull the apartment door closed since the landlord who goes by the name Mr. Raynor lives on our floor and I don't want to alert him since I won't be able to cover the rent for this month and last month for another week. Yes, I'm behind. Yes, I want to choke my brother for putting me in this position because he insists that working for the Villani family will pay off for him.

A chill slithers through me as I take the stairs as lightly as possible so as not to make any unnecessary sounds. Mr. Raynor has ears like an elephant and the only way I know to keep him off our backs is to flash him a glimpse of boob every now and again when he confronts me.

I really don't feel like watching the lecherous look on his face tonight as his eyes drop down the front of my shirt.

Blech.

But hey, it is what it is.

Who knew that six months ago our entire world would come crumbling down around us the way it has?

Regardless of the reason, Dad killed someone. I'm not naïve enough to believe he's never done that before, but at least he hadn't been caught red-handed. I could have convinced myself that he was innocent if it wasn't for the fact that he quite literally had the man's blood on his hands.

Second-degree murder. That verdict just about blew my whole life out of the water.

He claimed it was self-defense, but if you saw my dad and the guy he popped, it doesn't really add up. Luckily for my father, the jury bought it and that's the only reason he wasn't sentenced to death.

Unluckily for me and Frankie, all of the money we had that wasn't already seized by collections for my mother's medical bills was sucked up by exorbitant court fees and defense lawyers who couldn't seem to get out of their own way enough to win a 'not guilty' verdict.

The bank took our house and our cars, and we had to sell any possessions with value just to cover necessary expenses.

Talk about seeing your future get swallowed up by a black hole.

And at twenty-three, I'd just barely began my career in elementary education before my job was yanked away from me halfway through the year. Seems as though New York state wasn't a fan of hiring teachers whose parents are convicted murderers.

Some people can be so prickly.

Insert eye roll.

I was fortunate enough to have kept a good relationship with the owner of the bar I'd worked at through my years at New York University and even more fortunate that he re-hired me after being dishonorably discharged by the New York State Board of Education.

The pay is shit, but hey, it's still pay.

I tell myself that someday, we're not going to have to live paycheck to paycheck anymore.

Someday, we'll catch a break.

That is, if nobody breaks Frankie first.

I really don't think my reputation can handle another mob crime black mark.

Those will sink you faster than an anchor chained to your ankle.

I walk outside of the building, hoisting my bag over my shoulder as I head toward the subway station. By the time I get down to the platform, a crowd of people has gathered. Tiny beads of sweat slide down my back as the minutes pass. It's always so oppressively hot down here, even in the winter, and I say a silent prayer that the next train flashing its lights is the A train.

I check my phone for the time.

Ugh! Forget the heat. If it's not the F train, I'm going to be late.

And my boss Jimmy is only so forgiving.

I let out a sigh of relief when I see the train screech to a stop at the platform. The doors slide open with a loud double ding and I practically leap into the car. I lean against the pole since I refuse to ever touch it. If I can't get a seat, I find a place to rest my ass or my arm, preferably not on a fellow passenger, although it has happened in the past.

Regrettably.

That guy still gives me the creeps when I think about him.

As if I meant to rub myself against his crotch. For Pete's sake, the train was crowded! And touching the pole – good God, the germs! Just thinking about it makes bile rise in the back of my throat.

Twenty minutes later, the train arrives at my stop. West 4th Street in Washington Square Park. The Grammercy Tap Room is only a few blocks away and the weather is unseasonably warm for March, so the walk is actually refreshing.

I try not to focus on Frankie and whatever scheme he's running because he definitely is doing something. That glimmer in his eye is unmistakable. I just hope that whomever is the target doesn't find him out otherwise who the hell knows how I'll find him in the morning?

Or, if I'll find him.

People that Frankie associates with are magician-types and their best trick is making others disappear.

He thought he got a break when he got a job working for Roman Villani a few months back. From what Frankie told me, Dad had some business with Roman's older brother, Matteo, awhile back so they threw Frankie a bone. I guess the underworld doesn't discriminate. But Frankie still hasn't made the windfall he thought he would. Personally, I think they hired him knowing he's a liability and they wanted to do a test run before giving him anything big.

Big meaning dangerous.

I don't know much else. Dad always kept me away from that part of his life, so any names are just that. I don't know faces, and I'd like to keep it that way.

I just hope Frankie doesn't do something stupid to prove himself to those thugs.

I know from experience what they'll do in retaliation.

I let out a deep sigh as I walk past my old dorm. NYU doesn't have a traditional campus, so the buildings are spread out in Greenwich Village. I remember long, raucous nights of bar crawls with friends, treks to Bleecker Street Pizza at two in the morning when pulling all-nighters, and parties with cute fraternity guys. I loved those times. I had no cares in the world other than getting good grades and having a freaking amazing time.

Graduation came much too fast.

And then Mom got sick.

I trudge the remaining block to the bar, the heaviness in my gut weighing me down like there is a pile of bricks sitting on my shoulders.

It's hard to accept that she's really gone.

Walking these streets brings back such bittersweet memories of us embracing the little time we had left and basking in the sunshine of Washington Square Park. She always loved the village and would often come down here when I was living here to take me shopping or to dinner.

A pang assaults my chest.

God, I miss her so much.

I'd give anything to hold her hand again and to traipse through the foliage and brick pathways in the iconic landmark of lower Manhattan.

Tears sting my eyes and I blink them away before they have a chance to fall.

She wouldn't want me to cry. Lord knows, I've done enough of that over the past year. She'd want me to be strong, to find some sliver of light in the murky existence that's become my life. And dammit, I've been searching for a while, coming up empty every time.

There has to be a way out of this ominous maze that's become my dismal life. There has to be a way to finally regain control over my future.

I pull open the door to the bar and flash a smile at Michael, the big, broad bouncer. He gives me a wink and steps aside so I can pass. I run my eyes over the tables in the main dining room as I scurry into the back room. I give Jimmy, the owner, a little wave as I hurry past the bar, stopping only to scoop up the wrap of a woman sitting on one of the stools.

"Thank you so much," she gushes when I hand it to her.

I grin. "No problem." I'm about to turn around when a hard force collides with my back. A cold drizzle slips down the back of my black shirt, soaking the fabric, and I gasp, jumping at the unwelcome wet and sticky sensation now assaulting my skin.

When I turn around, I find myself staring into the bluest eyes I've ever seen. So deep, so penetrating…oh, crap. Why did I have to think of that word? Penetrating. It's been a long time since that word had any applicability to my life.

Chiseled jaw, rich olive skin, full lips curling into a sinfully seductive grin. A fringe of thick, dark hair falls over his one quirked eyebrow. And when this man-god speaks, holy shit. The vibrations ripple through me like I'm a lake and he's a smooth stone skipping over the surface.

"Consider yourself lucky I didn't order a double," he murmurs. "I think you owe me one now, though."

CLICK HERE TO PRE-ORDER SAVAGE BEAST- FREE IN KINDLE UNLIMITED

KU MEMBER? GET RELEASE UPDATES:
CLICK HERE TO JOIN MY VIP NEWSLETTER

She owes me a debt, and it's time to collect.

With a gorgeous face, porn-star body, and a criminal streak, Lindy thinks she owns Sin City. But my new obsession made a fatal choice when she walked into my Las Vegas casino.

She trusted the wrong people, put greed before common sense, and lost everything.

Now, there's a debt to be paid.

To me.

But I don't care about money.

I want her as my payment.

READ MERCILESS ON AMAZON - FREE KINDLE UNLIMITED

She may be a mafia princess, but I'm no knight in shining armor.
I craved her from the second I saw her.
Pure and untouched, with a sinful body made just for my hands.
Serena Vitale is the heir to her family's empire, an innocent dove who captivated me with her beauty and her heart.
In another lifetime, I'd make her mine, give her the happily ever after she deserves.
But women like her and men like me don't mix in my world.
She's too good, too perfect.
And I'm too dark, too broken.
I can only bring her pain.
But when a twist of fate puts me in front of a bullet meant for her, I find out she's not as perfect as she seems.
Maybe we're more alike than I thought.

READ WANTED ON AMAZON - FREE KINDLE UNLIMITED

MEET KRISTEN

Kristen Luciani is a *USA Today* bestselling romance author and coach with a penchant for stilettos, kickboxing, and grapefruit martinis. As a deep-rooted romantic who loves steamy, sexy, and suspense-filled stories, she tried her hand at creating a world of enchantment, sensuality, and intrigue, finally uncovering her true passion. Pun intended...

Follow for Giveaways
Facebook Kristen Luciani

Private Reader Group
The Stiletto Click

Complete Works On Amazon
Follow My Amazon Author Page

VIP Newsletter

Click Here To Join My VIP Newsletter

Feedback Or Suggestions For New Books?

Email Me! kristen@kristenluciani.com

Want To Join My ARC Team?

Join My Amazing ARC Team!

Want A FREE Book?

Click Here To Download!

Instagram

@kristen_luciani

BookBub

Follow Me on BookBub

facebook.com/kristenlucianiauthor
twitter.com/kristen_luciani
instagram.com/kristen_luciani

Printed in Great Britain
by Amazon